Love burn

ASHLEY ANTOINETTE

Ashley Antoinette Inc.
P.O. Box 181048
Utica, MI 48318

LOVE BURN Copyright © Ashley Antoinette

All rights reserved. No part of this book may be reproduced in any form or by any means without prior consent of the Publisher, except brief quotes used in reviews.

ISBN: 9781980760245

Trade Paperback Printing April 2018
Printed in the United States of America

This is a work of fiction. Any references or similarities to actual events, real people, living or dead, or to real locales are intended to give the novel a sense of realism. Any similarity in other names, characters, places, and incidents is entirely coincidental.

Distributed by Ashley Antoinette Inc.
Submit Wholesale Orders To:
owl.aac@gmail.com

Chapter 1

NONI

Whoever said it was better to have loved and lost, than not to have loved at all was full of shit. The papers she held in her hands proved it to be false. As Noni looked at the divorce settlement her eyes burned with tears. She could not believe that it had all come down to this. The feeling of despair that filled her was so potent that she couldn't stomach it. She pushed back in her chair abruptly, rushing to relieve the sick feeling that corroded her stomach before she threw up all over her Yves Saint Laurent. She grabbed the trashcan that sat underneath her desk and hugged it tightly to her chest as the contents of her stomach erupted. The depths of her cringed as she felt her chest grow heavy. *Breathe, just breathe,* she thought, trying to calm her weary soul. Panic attacks had plagued her life ever since the first time she had allowed her husband to break her heart. She was fragile and the repeated infidelities in her marriage had her spirits at an all time low. She had never understood how a woman could let a man break her, until it became her reality. Now she felt nothing but despair and it was a paralyzing pain that kept her life at a standstill while the rest of the world seemed to be passing her by.

What the hell was she supposed to do now? Who was she without him? Why did it feel like she was dying without him by her side? Noni hated herself for being so weak. She was accomplished, ambitious, and even when she wasn't the prettiest girl in the room, she was always the one who shined most. She shouldn't need a man, especially not the one she had been putting up with. They had met by chance and fallen in love overnight, but now she felt trapped by her emotions…deceived into a lifetime commitment by his empty promises. He had cheated, lied, over and over again, he had betrayed her. *Why the fuck am I afraid to live without him?* She thought as she sobbed. Noni hated the fact that she wasn't strong enough to realize that she was worth more, but truth was…she felt worthless. She placed the trashcan down and buried her face in the palms of her hands. She had never felt anything like this. This love was excruciating, it burned through her. It seared her heart as coal sized lumps formed in her dry throat. It made every part of her hurt. Abandonment. That is what it was. Her husband…the man that was supposed to be hers for life had abandoned her. A part of her felt stupid because it was Noni who had initiated the divorce. His bullshit had gotten old and she was tired of the broken promises and repetitive lies. She had been hurt so many times that no other option seemed viable. There was no working it out and at the time that she had filed, her anger had fueled her, but now as she sat in the house that they had once shared, surrounded by their memories and what had once been a flawless love… regret filled her. She mourned over those divorce papers as if it was her husband's corpse that was lying before her. A myriad of emotions pulsed through her, but the one she felt the most was grief. She picked up the pen to place her signature on the page, but her hand didn't move. She could not let the ink spill onto the dotted line…not yet…not ever… not now, after all that she had endured.

She placed the pen atop of her desk and grabbed her cell phone instead. She dialed his number, knowing that hearing his voice would be the perfect bandage to cover this emotional wound. Despite the fact that he was the one whom had caused her the most pain, he was still the only person in the world that could soothe her. It was irony at its finest and Noni was convinced that love was God's cruelest joke. When her heart and her head conflicted, she was always left feeling stupid in the end. She had known long ago what she should have done…what needed to be done. The infidelity was no longer a surprise. In fact, she somewhat blamed herself for staying. It only continued because she allowed it too. A blind eye couldn't see, but after the first discovery of her husband's transgressions her vision had been crystal clear. Each time her intuition had tried to warn her of foul play, she silenced it, allowing her heart to lead her further into darkness. Now she was completely lost.

When he answered the phone her heart skipped a beat. Even after all of the hurt, he still made her swoon. She was hopelessly in love with a hopeless cheater and she hated herself for it.

"'Hello," he answered.

"'Hey," she replied.

'She sat silently on the phone because a greeting was all she had been prepared to deliver. She didn't know what to say next. Every other aspect of their union was perfect. They were best friends, lovers, he could practically read her thoughts. They were so in tune with one another that often times she would start singing lyrics to a song as he thought of them in his head. They were perfect for one another, but he had a problem with his dick. The feeling of one woman wasn't enough for him. He was a man who enjoyed variety, which made for a shitty husband.

"'Noni, what's wrong baby?" he asked. Her silence was usually a sign of her pain. He could hear her heavy breathing on the phone.

It was like all of the heartbreak he had put on her had weighed her down. She didn't even breathe the same. It was like she was drowning in sorrow.

"'I got the papers from your lawyer today," she said. Her voice came out in a whisper, but she couldn't hide the agony. She sniffed as she wiped a tear away.

"'I thought this was what *you* wanted Noni," he replied.

"'This was never what I wanted. It's what you forced me to do," she sobbed. "What else am I supposed to do?"

"'I'll be over there, stop crying, ma. I'm on my way."

'CLICK.

Chapter 2

DOM

Dominick Meyer was successful at many things. He wore many hats. The businessman, the hustler, the friend, the son, the philanthropist…he exceled at life on so many levels. The one role, perhaps the most important of them all, he was miserable at. Husband. He had to be the world's worst and as he hung up his cell he sighed heavily, knowing that he had singlehandedly ruined a good woman. He wasn't heartless. He loved Noni more than she would ever know, but he was selfish. He had come up with nothing and now that he had climbed his way to the top he wanted everything. He didn't like rules or limitations and marriage came with so many of those things. Don't do this. Do that. Come in the house at a certain time. Look, but don't touch. Take out the trash. Call if you're late. The fuck? Being married made him feel like a little ass boy sometimes, as if his wife made all the rules and he was simply there to obey. He was 36 years old and at the top of his career, he wanted to enjoy the fruits of his labor. He was just trying to live without limits. It didn't mean that he didn't value what he had at home with Noni. He adored her. She was the only person on earth who truly understood him, but over the years he had taken her for granted. One woman had become two and two things on the side had become four. He had become a womanizer without even realizing it.

"'I *know* you aren't leaving?"

'The sweet voice called out over his shoulder and Dom grimaced. Too much of a sweet thing always hurt in the end and this affair was one of those things. Like sugar to teeth, the sweetness of this woman had rotted him. Sliding in was always so easy, but making his exit was a struggle every time. "I have to Tat," he replied with a sigh. He knew that she wouldn't like it. It was always the same routine with her. Whenever it was time for him to go back home she bitched the world's biggest fit. She knew the deal from the very beginning. He was married. He couldn't and wouldn't stay the night, but still she pushed. He had conquered many women and been unfaithful countless times, but Tat was his biggest regret. Things with her had gotten out of hand, he was just in too deep to let her go. Before her, he had been able to manage his infidelities quite well. Noni hadn't been completely oblivious to his ways, but she didn't reach her breaking point until Tat came into the picture. Noni knew nothing of their involvement, but she knew his actions all too well. Trapped in a lustful game with Tat, Dom had almost been forced to neglect his home, causing Noni's intuition to go haywire.

"'I bet you I can think of a few ways to make you stay," Tat said seductively as she dropped her robe, revealing her svelte yet curvaceous body beneath. His manhood reacted instantly as it jumped in excitement as she crossed the room. She was so used to walking in heels that she walked on her tiptoes. Her sex appeal had been what had lured him in. She was the forbidden. She was off limits. The fact that he wasn't supposed to touch her made him want her even more. He watched her as he sat on the edge of the bed.

"She doesn't sound good. I have to get home," he said. He knew that his words would cause static. The thought of his wife always enraged Tat.

"So the fuck what, Dom! When are you going to tell her about us? Your marriage is practically over so why the hell do you care about her finding out now? She already hit you with the divorce papers," Tat argued. "That bitch can't force you to stay. Just sign them already."

"Watch your mouth," Dom warned sternly as his jaw clenched in anger. "You don't talk about her. We both knew what we were getting into when it started. Now that you caught feelings and you want more I'm supposed to just pull the trigger on a divorce?"

"Yes!" Tat shouted as she put her hands on her hips. It was rare that she let her anger get the best of her. She was a mistress...his something on the side. She knew the rules, but lately she had been breaking them all in an attempt to pressure Dom for more. "And don't sit your ass in my house and defend your wife."

"I bought this house," he snapped.

"Because you love me not her," she reminded him.

"Because I got tired of fucking you on different sheets in shitty hotel rooms," he corrected.

"You bastard!" she shouted. He could see the fire in her eyes as they began to water. "You're not leaving here tonight."

"You hear yourself? Get yourself together. She's my wife! That's my home!" he shouted in frustration. He wished that he could turn back the hands of time and do things the right way. He didn't even want to be with Tat, but the secrets she held over his head were too big for him to walk away from. He didn't want to lose Noni. Despite his neglect, he loved her more than anyone. She had shown him a love and loyalty that he didn't think existed. He was just a young man when they had met. He wanted her as his own, but wanted the option to share himself with everyone else. Yes, he had received her terms of the divorce, but he knew Noni. Her anger made her impulsive. She wouldn't throw their union away, and neither would he, at least not officially. They would both hold on until it killed them. She had no idea how much he wanted to change. If he could be the man she imagined in her head, he would be…things were just beyond reproach. The other flings with random women she could probably forgive but the mess that he had gotten wrapped up in with Tat was unforgiveable. He knew it. So did Tat. That's why she constantly threatened to reveal their affair. He couldn't allow that. He would lose Noni forever if she ever discovered all of the details.

"Dom," Tat whispered as her features saddened. "I just want you here, just for the night."

'Tat kneeled in front of Dom and placed her hands on him as she began to stroke not only his ego, but his length as well. Dom looked at the time on his phone. *I can get in this and still make it home within the hour,* he thought as the hardness of his manhood began to cloud his judgment. As he watched Tat's head lower, he closed his eyes and enjoyed the skills she had mastered. Like most men he was weak when it came to resisting. Tat was easy and available to him whenever he called. She was sexy, she never said no, and she was easy to conquer. Those things. Those basic things. Her lack of strength and the tricks she did in the bedroom were what had gotten him caught up. He had a queen at home. He hadn't been looking for another woman to build him up. He had needed one that he could tear down, one who didn't have standards, one who didn't expect anything of him. A spontaneous handbag here and there was all that Tat required. He wanted easy and that's exactly what Tat offered. As she put her head game down on him, he remembered how he had become so entangled in this web of lust and lies. He knew he wasn't shit. His actions were nothing but wrong, yet still he continued. He was going to have sex with Tat and then drive home to comfort Noni. How foul could he be? He pushed Noni to the back of his mind momentarily as his head fell back in pleasure. He fisted her hair and controlled her rhythm, making her do it exactly the way he liked. It was always about what pleased him. In sex, in life; even in his marriage and that was his biggest problem. Selfishness was his disease and he feared that there was no cure.

Chapter 3

NONI

Noni hadn't seen him in weeks. Their latest blowout had left them at odds and had kept him away. She couldn't help but feel excited that he was coming home. *If he would just do right, we could make this work,* Noni thought. She stood to her feet and grabbed the small trashcan, making her way to the kitchen. She tossed it in the larger bin and ran her fingers through her hair as she thought, *I can't let my marriage crash and burn. If I can just get him to be the man I need him to be, things will get better.* She rushed up the stairs to her bathroom and ran herself a bath. She needed to remind him where home was. It wasn't in the streets, or in the beds of random women. He couldn't make a home with his side chick. It was here with her and as she prepared for his arrival, she was determined to remind him. The lotion she rubbed between her petite hands melted over her silky, brown, legs like butter. She sprayed the light scent of Chanel and stepped into La Perla, topping it off with her highest pair of heels. As she stood in front of her full-length mirror she had to give herself a bit of credit. She was beautiful. She was more woman than any of the little girls that her husband used as his playthings. From time to time he caused her to become insecure. She often wondered if it was

LOVE BURN

something that she lacked that caused him to cheat, but no one could deny that she had kept her shit together nicely. Her weight had gone up and down right along with the hills of the emotional rollercoaster that she had been forced onto, but through it all she still maintained her curves. Her waist was slimmer than her hips and her gut was smaller than her round behind. No love handles, maybe a bra roll, but most men just called it thick. She was the epitome of a black woman and as she stood admiring herself for the first time she realized that her husband's foul ways had nothing to do with her. She wasn't lacking anything, he was... his ass lacked commitment. She poured herself a glass of wine, started a blaze in the living room fireplace and sat by the window as she waited for him to arrive. The snow fell in flurries out of her window as she sipped her merlot. Her impatience caused her to peek out of the blinds ever so often. She had played this waiting game many times before and as the minutes turned into half an hour and that into an hour, it began to feel too familiar. *He isn't coming,* she thought. Her mood went from optimistic to dreary as a knot of resentment formed deep in her belly. Her cell phone buzzed on the table and she anxiously retrieved it. *Please let this be him. He better be on his way,* Noni thought. She was already ready to curse him out. Her attitude was on ten.

'When she saw his name pop up on her screen she realized he had sent her a text message. Disappointment filled her before she even looked at it. Being a man's wife made a woman an expert on behavioral patterns. Noni knew when her husband was hiding something just by observing his mannerisms. She could tell when he was lying by the tone and inflection in his voice. She knew when he was sleeping with another woman because suddenly his stinking drawers would go from Hanes to Ralph Lauren. Nothing went unnoticed when you were a wife, especially a wife scorned. Married women were the world's greatest detectives, only difference was that wives normally ignored the evidence; even when it stared them right in their faces. Noni knew that a text message was a cop out. Her husband wasn't coming...he just didn't have the balls to call and tell her. She picked up the phone and slid the bar across the touch screen. Tears immediately filled her eyes when she saw the picture she had been sent. Her heart thundered in her chest as uncontrollable anger pierced her soul. She was staring at a picture of her naked, sleeping husband, in another bitch's bed. His trifling ass hadn't even wiped the cum off his dick before falling contently asleep.

'No need for him to come home. He's good and comfy right where he is. Lol.

'When she read the message she immediately pressed call. In that moment she was glad that she had no idea where her husband spent his time. Had she known where he laid his head when he tricked on uncouth whores she would not have been able to stop herself from riding through the spot. In the mood she was in, it would have taken an entire army to stop her from killing the petty bitch that had sent her this picture. Her grandmother had warned her about side bitches. On the day that she had said 'I do', she had told her that the women who couldn't get their own men would come for hers.

'"The problem with a mistress is that she lacks true self-worth. They have no problem being number 2 because they know that no man will ever make them their priority. They'll never be number 1, so they are fine with taking the crumbs that you sweep off your dinner table. They're disgusting and they find pride in destroying families. You have to guard your marriage from those types of women, because the dirty hussies will use every trick in the book to make you miserable and to

put distance between you and yours. You hear me? You don't let them run you away from your man. You got papers on him. He's your property. You don't give up your dog because it shits in another yard, do you? That's your dog. You train it. You train it and retrain it until the dog gets it right. Such is life with your husband. You train him. He's yours now. Once you say I do, you own him. No matter how much pussy he's getting on the side, those whores will never amount to anything. His name and his heart are yours…he would never even make it down the aisle if he didn't want you to have them."

The words of her mother played through her mind as she listened to the voicemail sound off in her ear. "Fuck this," she whispered as she snapped a screen shot of the text. "Fuck this motherfucking bullshit ass man…this marriage…fuck this house…fuck it all!" she shouted, enraged. She stormed upstairs and opened the safe. Inside lay a small fortune and as she reached her hand inside she found the plane tickets they had purchased months ago.

St. Tropez, she thought sadly. He had promised to take her there. They had planned out every detail of their trip. It was supposed to be a chance for them to bond, a chance for him to make things right, an opportunity for him to make up for all the pain he had caused. She scoffed as she looked at the boarding passes in her hand. Dom had made her so many promises, but it was her fault for believing them. She had allowed him to sell her a dream that she knew would never come true. She grabbed her luggage, pocketed the tickets, and swept the money from the safe into her bag. There had to be at least a half million dollars inside. *Fuck it,* she thought as her emotions overwhelmed her. *I'm done.* She felt no remorse because she was only taking what she was owed. They had another million in a joint account. She quickly logged onto the bank's website and transferred it into her individual checking account. Then her eyes bulged in shock as she saw another account listed. "Ten-fucking-million-dollars," she whispered. She didn't even know that they had that type of money, at least not in a lump sitting in the bank. "Looks like your side bitches weren't the only secrets you were keeping from me." She planned to be at the bank first thing in the morning to empty that account. "Consider it severance," she snapped. The house and the contents in the safe weren't sufficient enough, and truth be told neither was the riches she had just discovered. No amount of money could compensate for the years of her life that he had taken. She couldn't get that back so this was her settlement. He was lucky she hadn't killed him. Considering that his life insurance was worth five million alone, he was blessed to leave with his life. A lesser woman would go for it, but she simply wanted out. The money was just payback because she knew it was what he valued most. Honestly, she just wanted out of this marriage, out of this house...she wanted Dominick Meyer out of her fucking life. She packed a bag full of belongings and grabbed her passport. Maybe they weren't going to renew their love on a beach in St. Tropez, but she was going...even if she had to go solo and she knew that she wouldn't soon return. It was time for a change. She had always played the role of predictable wife. Maybe that's why he had grown so bored. She had fallen into a mundane way of living. Their life was so comfortable that she didn't have any desire to switch things up. She was faithful, loyal, and lived her life to the routine that they had planned together. It was he who had detoured from their plan. Now she was no longer willing to stick to the script. It was time for him to do the guesswork. When he was ready to come home, she wouldn't be there and her absence would undoubtedly drive him insane. Noni had some soul searching to do and there was no better place to do it than half way across the world.

'She walked out of the house and loaded her bags into the G-series Mercedes truck. The six figure vehicle had been another 'I'm sorry' gift from one of her husband's many fuck ups. He had always lavished her with jewels, trips, clothes, cash, and cars... but the material things never fixed anything. They were merely emotional Band-Aids but her wounds were more than superficial. The damage that he had done always bled through and she could feel herself slowly dying. She was exhausted. The one thing she wanted, he refused to give her...himself. She was tired of waiting....done hoping...through praying...she was finally... leaving. This move had been a long time coming. *He is leaving me no choice,* she reasoned. It was crazy that she had to talk herself into this. Even after all of his betrayal, she felt disloyal for giving up. She got into her car and pressed the ignition as the German beauty came alive. The purr of the engine filled her heart with false courage as she put the car in reverse. She looked down in her passenger seat and noticed a book that she had purchased. The cover read, *Single Ladies.* The model on the cover looked radiant as happiness oozed off of the page as if she had it all under control.

'*Single...I don't even know how to be single,* she thought. Noni had been apart of a pair for so long that she didn't know how to be alone.

She wiped a tear from her cheek as a heavy sob escaped her lips. She was doing the best she could to keep her composure, but she knew that there was many more trying times to come. It would take a million tears to mourn over her lost love. St. Tropez was as good as place as any to start anew. She pulled off into the night with a heavy heart and an empty soul, regretting the day that she had ever even uttered the words, "I do."

Chapter 4

Dreaming of the past
(5 years ago)

"Hmm, bitch do you see that beautiful creation of Gawd?!" Harper said a bit too loud as she gawked at the different men in the room.

'Noni pinched her best friend's arm so hard that Harper howled in pain. "Ouch! Did you just pinch me?" she cried in protest.

"'Harp, chill. I need to make a good impression on these people. I need a job. That Master's degree is literally burning a hole in my pocket. Now that I'm done with school, I can't even keep up with my student loans! I'm even behind on rent. I need this. Everything is riding on tonight so behave," Noni said as she ran her hand over her Prada dress. She was trying her hardest to keep it in impeccable condition, because she was so broke that she couldn't even afford the clothes on her back. Tomorrow morning it would be going right back to the store.

"'As fine as you are, you better throw the landlord some pussy to buy yourself some time," Harper said, completely serious as she grabbed a glass of complimentary champagne off of a silver tray that the penguin suited waiters carried around the room. "Pretty girls don't have rent problems," Harper concluded. Noni shook her head in disbelief because she knew that Harper wasn't above bartering herself in order to make ends meet. It wasn't Noni's game however. She wasn't a saint, but she didn't sin in that way that's for damn sure. It took a lot more than a dollar to get in her panties. While she had done her fair share of conning older men in her teenage years, she wasn't a young girl anymore. Her days of chasing men with money were over. She would leave that to the fresh faces on the scene. She was focused on becoming a woman with assets of her own. She had been through the ups and downs of being kept. She had been gifted cars and clothes only to go from riches to rags when the nigga who gave them to her decided it was time to leave. Nah, that game was old and at the end of the day women became worthless. She knew that if she played the game long enough she would be like a used car…depreciated. Once she realized her own worth, playing wifey to a man with heavy pockets took a backseat to acquiring heavy pockets of her own. While her best friend Harper had accumulated tramp stamps on her passport, Noni had accumulated not only two bachelor's degrees, but a Master's as well. Her primary goal had been to better herself, but that resulted in a severe drought. It had been so long since she had felt the hands of a man that she had forgotten how good it could be. Her drawer of special toys was all the action she had seen for almost two years. Sure she had dated, but almost every man she had met didn't meet the standards she had set for herself. It took more than a nice whip and swag to impress her. She couldn't cash a swag check. She had outgrown the allure of a street guy long ago. Noni wanted a man who was loyal, educated, accomplished…but who also wore his pants around his waist, not hanging below his behind. She wanted someone with vision. *Apparently, that is too much to ask for,* she thought. She centered herself as she made her way around the room. The Annual Michigan Business Gala was a black tie affair and invitation only. Every person in attendance was apart of the millionaire club and the amount of black faces in the room was slim. Membership was exclusive and she stood out like a diamond amongst stones as she made her way through the crowd of elegantly dressed guests. She had hustled herself onto the list now all she had to do was network her ass off. Only a person with no ambition could be in a room full of money and walk out empty handed. Although Harper wasn't the ideal companion, Noni was grateful for her presence. At least she wasn't flying solo. In this room full of gold, Noni was sure that Harper was far from bored. She would find some unsuspecting gentleman and dig her way to the lavish life.

"Let's find our seats," Noni said. "We're at table 7."

'The ballroom inside the GM building was beautifully decorated in silver and ivory. The grand chandelier sparkled as the important guests danced and conversed beneath it. The flower arrangements alone must have cost a fortune. Each table was heavily decorated in white roses and Swarovski crystals while gold-rimmed china sat atop of each place setting. It was truly spectacular. Noni was mingling amongst the movers and shakers of the entire state. From politicians, to ball players, even automotive executives...everyone in attendance was heavy with clout. There was something about being in a room with that many powerful people. It made Noni feel small, insecure, unimportant. Even her highest accomplishment paled in comparison to the big shots in this room. She was the belle of the ball, but in a circle this prestigious it took more than looks to command respect. In the world of big business 'pretty' was underappreciated.

'She led the way through the thick crowd, nodding and smiling at the friendly faces that she passed until finally, she located her place setting. "Excuse me," she said as she pulled out her chair.

'When she saw him, her heart skipped a beat. He was a beautiful creation of a black man. Dark like imported chocolate, he looked edible and he had eyes that Noni could get lost in for days. Brown with specks of hazel, they appeared ablaze as he stood from his seat and towered over her.

'"Let me help you beautiful," he said as he pulled out her chair and motioned for her to sit.

'"Thank you," Noni said with a smile as she watched him move to pull out Harper's chair for her as well. His broad shoulders hung the Ferragamo suit he wore quite nicely. He was handsome as ever and he smelled like new money. She could tell he wasn't a trust fund brat or a pretentious heir. The diamond earring that sparkled in his ear revealed the fact that he had a little bit of hood in him, despite the fact that he hid it well.

'"You're welcome," he replied. He unbuttoned his jacket before reclaiming his seat.

'The live band played a soft melody of jazz but no one danced. As Noni shifted in her seat the stuffiness in the room almost choked her. She was swimming in a pool full of sharks and she was more than intimidated. She inhaled sharply and then exhaled deeply, trying to calm her nerves. Noni was definitely out of her element and her gum popping best friend wasn't making it any better. Despite the fact that she was dressed impeccably, in fact, she was more ravishing than any other woman in the room, but her resume was still the shortest. She felt see through as if everyone at her table knew that she had snuck into the party. Noni was venturing into a world that was much bigger than her. This was the business realm and up until this point she hadn't been anything more than a pretty girl with a big brain and even grander ambitions. She fidgeted in her seat and then placed the white linen napkin in her lap.

Just calm down. These people are no better than you. Everyone starts somewhere, she thought to herself as she sat with the poise of a Japanese Geisha. She wanted to attribute her posture to good manners, but the truth was she was uptight. Her nerves were getting the best of her. The rest of the guests at the table conversed with one another as Noni sat awkwardly. She tried to find her place. She wanted to jump in and contribute something witty to the moment…make her mark in the memories of these prestigious men and women, but she was at a loss for words. She had always imagined herself wowing the crowd and being a woman of action if she ever got the chance, but here she was, in a room full of power and she was choking. She cleared her throat and motioned for the waiter that was passing by. "Can I get a glass of wine?" she asked. *Patron would be better,* she thought in exasperation.

"What kind of wine miss?" the waiter asked.

'Suddenly Harper chimed in. "I'll take a pink Moscato."

'Noni cringed inwardly as her face flushed in embarrassment. Sure, Moscato was the drink of choice when she was kicking it at a girls night out or sitting back in the comfort of her home watching *Love Jones*, but she knew that it wasn't what the uppity crowd had their glasses filled with tonight. Harper may as well have hollered that she wanted malt liquor. It was like a DJ scratched a record as the table fell silent. The date of the handsome gentleman beside her chuckled snidely under her breath as the waiter gave Harper a sympathetic look. "I'm sorry we don't have Moscato. There is a list of the premium wine selections that we are serving tonight next to your place setting," the waiter responded. "I'll come back around once you decide?"

'"Not necessary," the guy to her left said. "You can bring two bottles of Methusela for the table."

'The waiter hesitated as he leaned down between Noni and the handsome stranger. "Sir, that's a $17,000 bottle of Champagne," he informed.

"'I'm aware," the guy responded as he pulled a black card out of his inner breast pocket and handed it to the waiter. "Start a tab. The entire table's drinks are on me. No more of this house Champagne. This isn't much better than Moscato," he said to the table, eliciting laughter from the bourgeois bunch.

'The waiter made his escape, leaving 8 sets of eyes on them as everyone at the table suddenly realized that the Noni and Harper didn't belong. They had been infiltrated by the lower class and it was apparent.

"'Guess its true. You can take the girl out the hood but you can't take the hood out the girl huh?"

"'Excuse me?" Noni responded as she cut her eyes, her brow dipping low.

"'Don't get offended honey unless the shoe fits," the girl replied with a condescending laugh. "You are in the room with the upper echelon. You didn't think that we would be able to sniff out the fake?" the girl snapped as she took a sip from her glass. "No offense," she added, before turning her attention back to her man.

"'None taken," Noni answered. "But from the looks of that knock off Zac Posen clutch you're carrying, I'd say you have a hard time distinguishing real from fake yourself. Now if you'll excuse us," she said as she arose from her seat with Harper following her lead.

'Noni stalked over to the bathroom with pure rage pulsing through her body. "I could have snatched that bitch right out of her seat," Noni seethed as she retreated to the powder room with Harper right on her heels. She was so livid she was seeing red. The girl had pulled her out of character before Noni had even had a chance to impress anyone.

"'I don't know about you but its too uptight in here for me. I don't have time for this Noni. It is boring as hell and uppity bitches talking slick. I'm going to get out of here and check for you later, okay?" Harper said.

'Noni nodded in defeat and responded, "Okay. I'll call you later."

'The two girls emerged from their temporary retreat and went their separate ways as Noni bee-lined for the bar. She wasn't ready to head back to the table just yet. She desperately needed to take the edge off.

"'What can I get you pretty lady?" the bartender asked.

'Before she could respond, the guy from her table invaded her space as he leaned into the bar, facing her.

"'She's good," he said. "I have the best bottle of champagne in the entire house." He held up the expensive bottle that he had ordered and two flutes before placing them on the countertop. She stared at him curiously as he filled them both.

"'I thought that was for the table?" she questioned.

"'It was for you," he replied. "Have a drink with me?"

'She glanced over her shoulder to find the seat where his date had been was now empty. "You sure your little girlfriend won't have a problem with that?" she said with a smirk.

"'Not my girlfriend, ma," he corrected. "And she's in a cab on her way back to the East side right now."

"'Cheers to that," she commented snidely as she picked up her flute and tapped it against his before her lips spread into a reluctant smile. "Bitch," she said under her breath.

'He smiled, amused at her candor. He heard her and she knew it. He was impressed that she was unapologetic about it. "Where's your friend?" he asked.

'She laughed before replying, "In a cab on her way back to the East side." He smiled at her wit and shared in her laughter.

'She felt his eyes all over her as he admired her. "I'm Dom," he said.

'"Noni," she replied. She quickly remembered that she was at a business function. This handsome man had disarmed her and made her forget that she was on a mission. "Antonia Welch," she corrected.

'"I think I prefer Noni," he replied as he licked his lips.

'Noni looked at him skeptically. She immediately recognized the look of lust in his eyes. Most men she encountered were drawn to her. She had an appeal that most men found hard to resist. She wasn't sure what it was. Yes, she thought she was beautiful, but nowhere near sexy, and certainly not anything to write home about. She found herself to be a bit above average, but everyone around her treated her as if she were a rare gem. "I have to say I'm grateful for your presence," he said.

'She rolled her eyes as she asked, "And why is that?"

'"You're beautiful. I'm often invited to these types of gigs and its always uneventful. The same stuffy niggas in suits doing the same ol' two step. Your presence is..." he paused as he took her in with his eyes, making her shift in her stance uncomfortably. He was commanding, assertive, powerful, and the way he looked at her made butterflies form in her stomach. "Refreshing," he finished. He had the charm of a dope boy, but was obviously so far above the street life. He was established and powerful with a hint of danger that shone in his eyes, despite the fact that he tried to keep it concealed. Who the hell was this man that had her heart beating out of her chest? The subtle flirting was just right, enough to make her blush, but not too much to offend. She hated when niggas pushed up on her with too much interest. She immediately became disinterested, but Dom, he had the laws of attraction down to a science.

'Noni cleared her throat as she placed her flute on the bar. "I'm umm..." she was flustered as she tried to think of a way to bring the line of professionalism into focus. "These circles may be boring and uneventful for you, but I'm very grateful to be in this room and I came to wow some exec into giving me a job. So as much as I would love to listen to you tell me the same sweet nothings that I'm sure a hundred women before me have heard, I have to remember why I'm here," she said.

"A job?" he asked. "What do you do?"

"I do nothing at the moment. I'm a college graduate with a Master's in International business and a bachelor's in accounting," she revealed.

He nodded in approval. "I'm impressed."

"Yeah, well those fancy degrees came with a shitload of debt. Tonight is important and I can't keep wasting all of my time with a man who is just trying to take me home at the end of the night," she said honestly. She smiled then added, "Which was never going to happen by the way."

"I didn't think so," he said with charm. "Well you aren't going to meet anyone by hugging the bar all night either." He extended his elbow to her. "Let me introduce you to a few people."

"Why would you do that? You barely know me," she responded.

"The more you tell them, the more I get to learn about you," he answered as she looped her arm around his bicep, leaning into him.

"I bet this little irresistible, mysterious, gentleman, act you got going is popular with the ladies," she smirked.

"I seem to be striking out with you so apparently not," he answered with a wink.

"Robert," he greeted as they walked up on an elderly white couple. Noni gripped his arm a bit tighter as she smiled graciously. "Good to see you."

"Dom, my friend. Its great to see you," the man replied. "You remember Ann."

"Of course," Dom responded as he took the woman's hand and kissed it gently. "Good to see you again. This is Antonia Welch," Dom said, pulling Noni into the conversation.

"Nice to meet you Antonia. You two make a stunning couple," Ann complimented.

"Oh we're umm…we," Noni stammered over her words until Dom interjected.

"I think Antonia would increase the value of any man that she stood next too," he replied.

Ann hit her husband playfully and pointed to Dom. "You hear that Robert? That's how you deliver a compliment honey," she teased. She winked to Noni and said. "When you get my age they get used to you. Have to keep this old man on his toes."

Noni smiled as Dom extended himself to Ann. "Well why don't we switch. I can fill your ear with compliments while Noni makes Robert here look good for awhile. May I have this dance?" he asked.

Robert chuckled as Dom whisked his wife off to dance to the smooth sounds of jazz. "That woman, that woman," he chuckled. He turned to Noni. "How about it young lady?"

Noni graciously accepted his hand as he led her onto the dance floor. The couples danced side by side as Robert began to pick her brain.

"Tell me pretty lady, what is it that you do?" he asked.

Here it is. The interview… sell yourself with tact, she reminded herself before she began to speak. "I just finished school actually. I have a Master's in international business and a BS in accounting," she answered.

"Beauty and brains," he exclaimed. "Very rare, but let me tell you young lady a degree from one of these small schools with no integrity won't get you very far."

"Then I guess its good that I graduated summa cum laude from

Michigan than," she said as she pulled back to look at the shocked expression on his face. She smiled.

"Very well than," he said as he spun her around before the song came to an end. He removed a card from his trouser pocket and said, "Give my office a call on Monday."

She read the card and her mouth fell in an O of surprise when she realized she was in the presence of Robert Ginwald, president of General Motors. "Wow. Mr. Ginwald," she gasped.

"Lets not start with the formalities now, Antonia. I just stepped all over your toes with my two left feet. Call me Robert," he said with a wink.

She flicked the card in her hands before placing it in her clutch. "Thank you Robert," she said. Ann and Dom walked back over to them laughing jovially.

"Thank you Dom. You're much more graceful than this one," Ann joked as she comfortably leaned under her husband's arm.

"The pleasure was all mine," Dom responded. "Now if you don't mind. I believe Antonia owes me this one?" He nodded out onto the floor and she blushed before taking his hand. He led her across the dance floor, leading her away from the crowd. "Where are you taking me? I thought you wanted to dance?" she asked as she followed him out onto the wrap around terrace. The winter air nipped at her bare arms instantly as he pulled her outside. "Its freezing out here," she protested.

He pulled her closely as the two began to sway to the music that was wafting out through the open French doors. Her body pressed against his and she gasped at how good it felt to be this close to such a gorgeous man. Sparks flew between them as Dom placed his hand on the small of her back and pulled her to him while holding her right hand in his. To her surprise he was good on his feet as they danced, intimacy creeping into their embrace. The heat from their chemistry made her forget about the brisk wind that whipped through her hair. His body pressed against hers, protectively, gently, almost lovingly. He had her hot. In that moment they felt like lovers who had done this dance before, despite the fact that they were merely strangers. "You really are beautiful Noni," he whispered, his lips touching her ears, causing a familiar jolt of desire to electrocute her.

She pulled back, hesitantly, but he refused to let her go. He pulled her back into him as they continued to dance. "I'm not going home with you tonight Dom," she said, being straight forward. She cleared her throat before continuing. "I have rules and sex with a strange man, no matter how handsome, is definitely breaking one of them," she whispered, only half believing herself.

"I'd never try to take a woman like you home on the first night," he replied. He brushed a stray hair out of her face. "A part of me wants to offer you a job just to guarantee that I get to see you everyday. Running across a woman like you is rare."

"'A woman like me?" she questioned. "I'm sure you've had your share of pretty girls."

"'Your type of pretty shines through from the inside, ma. Much different from what I'm used too," he replied seriously. She stepped back as the song ended, leaving the warmth of his embrace.

'She shivered and he took notice, immediately offering her his jacket as he wrapped it around her shoulders. What he didn't know was that it wasn't the cold that had her shaking, but the electricity between the connection that she felt with him. She was walking in the danger zone and she knew it. As they stood on the balcony, under the blackest sky, they admired the stars of the country setting. Noni knew that this man had money. His ego was too grand to have anything less than 7 figures in his bank account, but there was so many other things that she had yet to determine about him. He was street. She knew this simply by the way he controlled his environment. The way he led her with his hand assertively placed on the small of her back. The way his shoulders squared confidently as if he had a few shooters positioned throughout the party, ensuring his wellbeing. The way he locked eyes with her while clenching his jaw tightly to stop himself from gaming her too much. The way he answered her questions vaguely, without divulging too much too soon. He was cautious, he moved in silence. She had met men like him before, but they usually came from the underworld, not the corporate one. He had all the makings of a boss, but here he was at the most prestigious social event of the season. Who was this man? And why was Noni so smitten? Why did her body tingle in every place that he touched? Despite the poker face she wore, he made her pulse race and her panties soak.

"'I better get going," she said.

'He placed a hand over his chest as if her sudden departure had broken his heart. "Can I call you?" he asked.

"'I don't think that's the best idea," she answered. She knew that he was the type of man that would have her wrapped around his finger. "I'm just not focused on dating right now."

"'See…you're different. I haven't heard the word no in a very long time," he admitted, clearly amused by her lack of interest in him. Little did he know that her thighs quaked at the thought of him. His charm was undeniable and if she stayed in his presence much longer they would be fucking tonight.

"'Well now you have," she replied. She held out her hand. "Thank you for making this night a lot more comfortable for me. I appreciate that." He shook her hand, his affections for her shining brightly in his stare as he pulled her into him unexpectedly.

"'I know you have your rules, ma. You won't go home with a nigga on the first night. I respect it. What does your rulebook say about me taking you to breakfast tomorrow?" he asked.

'She hesitated. "What about your little rude girlfriend?" she asked.

"'You say the word and I can make her a memory," he assured.

"'Just like that, huh?" she countered.

'He nodded. "For you...just like that."

"'You're full of game," she said with a bashful smile as she shook her head.

"'You're full of promise," he replied, admiring her without shame.

She studied his handsome features. His full lips, head full of lazy waves, and those bedroom eyes. "Fine. You did introduce me to the president of GM. The least I can do is join you for breakfast. My treat though," she replied.

'He smirked as a smile spread across his lips. "Okay ma. You got it. Your treat, but I get to choose the place. Deal?" he asked.

She smiled. "Deal."

"We better get going than," he said as he walked over to her and grabbed her hand.

'She frowned. "Get going? Where?"

"'Mexico," he answered casually. "I'm on the red eye to L.A. tonight and I'll catch a connector to Cabo. My flight leaves in two hours. By tomorrow morning we'll be having breakfast on the beach," he said.

"'What? Wait. You didn't say anything about Mexico," she protested. "How do you even know I have a passport?"

"'International business major. You've got a passport," he said.

"'But wait, I don't even know you. You could be a serial killer or something," she protested, only half joking.

'Dom ignored her as he led her out of the building and handed his ticket to the valet. "Where's your car?" he asked.

'She pulled out her valet ticket and handed it to him with an exasperated sigh. He in turn handed it to the next kid who was waiting at the valet station.

"'Dom, listen...I can't go to Cabo with you," she said.

"'Is that against your rules too?" he asked.

"'Kind of," she admitted. "Yeah. This is a little crazy considering I just met you not even two hours ago."

'A pearl white, Escalade pulled up and Dom nodded. "This is me. I'd really like you to join me. My assistant will book you a seat on the next flight out tomorrow morning. Sleep on it. If you decide to come, I'll make sure you don't regret it. If not, it was nice meeting you gorgeous," he said. He leaned in and kissed her cheek before walking toward his car.

"Hey! Your jacket," she called after him as she began to remove it from her shoulders.

He held up his hand and responded, "Keep it, ma. It's cold. As a matter of fact, give it back to me when I see you tomorrow." He winked, leaving her smiling as he pulled away from the building. She shook her head in disbelief.

"'There is no way that I'm going," she said to herself. As she waited in the cold night air for the valet to bring her car around she put her arms through the sleeves of his jacket. As she stuffed her hands in the pockets she felt something inside. Curiously she pulled it out and shook her head incredulously. Dom Meyers' passport was in her hand and she couldn't help but think that he had known that all along.

Chapter 5

Noni raced into the airport with her luggage in her hand. She hadn't had time to pack much. Her passport, a few swimsuits, and a sundress or two was all she had been able to find in such a short period of time. Flustered and a little winded, she approached the counter. Noni couldn't believe that she was going through with this and as she peered through the crowd of travelers searching for Dom she almost changed her mind. *This is insane,* she thought. She turned around to make her exit only to bump directly into him. His 6-foot frame towered over her and almost instantly those sparks of electricity pulsed through her. Her attraction to him was uncanny. She had been approached by many men before, but there was something about the way that Dom looked at her that lowered her defenses. He had her at hello.

"'Glad you could make it," he said with a slick grin.

"'Well I didn't have much of a choice now did I?" she asked as she went into his suit jacket and held up his passport. "I didn't have time to change. I would have missed the flight."

"'You're good, ma. I just appreciate your presence," he replied honestly.

"'Yeah well I have a few stipulations," she said.

"'More rules?" he chuckled as he rubbed his hand over his neat waves and raised his eyebrows in curiosity.

"'I want my own room. Mexico is a hell of a first date, but it doesn't mean that you just purchased yourself some pussy. So if this is just a way to pay for it, I can go back home. I'm not for sale," she said.

"'Everything is for sale," he replied. She frowned, growing defensive as she prepared to G-check the shit out of him. He had her confused, but before she could even part her pretty lips he continued. "But don't worry. I've never had to pay to play. Women usually give it up for free and much more willingly than you, might I add. Nothing will happen that you don't want to happen. I'm a gentleman if nothing else," He smirked before grabbing her luggage out of her hand. She was stern, guarded, as if she had been sold many dreams before...dreams that had never become reality. He could tell that she was going to be a challenge, but he was more than up for it. He wasn't the type to make promises he couldn't keep or the type to make them to just any girl. In a world where pussy came too easy for him, he enjoyed her resistance. He was up for the chase. It had been so long since a female had made him work for it, he looked forward to putting in the effort to gain access to her heart or her panties... which ever came first was fine by him, although he preferred them both. "You'll have your own room," he assured. He placed his arm around her shoulders and pulled her into him as they headed towards the check-in counter...headed to paradise.

'As soon as Noni felt the warm sun kiss her skin she erased any negative thoughts that could ruin the trip. Yes, she felt crazy for leaving the country with a man she had just met and yes she was a bit intimidated of what may happen, but fuck it. She was throwing caution to the wind. This is how all the great love stories began right? Unexpectedly? At least that is what she kept telling herself to prevent her thoughts from running amuck. She knew that if she thought too hard about it, she would turn around and hop on the first flight back to Detroit and ruin this free vacation. Lord knows she deserved it…hell she had earned it. The countless hours of studying and working low paying jobs to put herself through school had left little time to jet set. *Just think of it as your pay off,* she thought to ease her nagging conscience. The smell of salt lined the air, letting her know that the ocean wasn't too far away. The warmth settled into her chilled bones. There was nothing like an impromptu escape from the infamous hawk of Michigan's winter and a smile graced her face.

"'So, she smiles?" Dom commented as he looked at her out of the side of his eye.

"'Only when there is something worth smiling about," she replied. She grabbed her small bag and walked beside him as they headed to the awaiting, blacked out SUV that sat curbside.

'Nervous energy danced through Noni's body as she kept her eyes off Dom. She looked at everything except him. The beautiful scenery outside her window passed her by in a flash as she tried to think of what to say to this man who had just whisked her away. She had some questions for him. Was he single? Did he fly every girl around the world so easily? Did he have children?

'

"'Get out of your head Noni," he whispered as they rode in silence.

'Her lips melted into a smile. "I can't help it. This is crazy. Tell me something about you that nobody knows," she said.

"'There isn't much to tell, ma. I'm just a cool breeze ass nigga," Dom responded with a coy grin.

"'I find that very hard to believe. You're a complex man Dom," she replied.

"'Which is why I need a complex woman," Dom answered. "You have your secrets I'm sure, I have mine. Your past is deep. Mine, you would drown in. The only thing to help weed through that confusion is time. We only have a weekend. Let's just enjoy it."

'She nodded and replied, "Okay." His logic was pure poetry to her ears. He wanted to live in the now with her. Fuck the past, disregard the future…none of it mattered. He was a man interested in a woman. She was curious to see where it may lead.

'They settled into a comfortable silence as they pulled up to a private ocean side villa. "This is where we're staying?" she asked. "I thought we would be at a resort?"

"'I value my privacy," he replied. The driver opened the back door and Dom slid out and then turned to hold out his hand to her. She scooted across the seat and allowed him to help her out of the car. "Welcome to paradise, Noni."

'She looked around at the huge waves that crashed into the shoreline and the stunning home that sat in solitude on the vacant beach. "Is this your place?" she asked.

"'One day," he replied. Dom was 26 years young and heavy in the game, but unlike most he only wanted it for the meantime. He flipped bricks and he did it well, but the thing that allowed him to rub elbows with the elite was the string of funeral homes he owned. Born and raised in Flint, MI he had come up around nothing but death and destruction. He knew that his hometown had a crazy body count and he couldn't think of a more lucrative endeavor. Niggas got busy in Flint and murder was a common phenomenon. He figured somebody had to profit off it. Why not a young black kid from the same neighborhood? But Dom was smart. Instead of opening one mortuary in one city, he chose the four most crime ridden cities in Michigan and opened four.

Pontiac, Saginaw, Detroit, Flint. It had taken him 8 years to hustle up the $500,000 that it took to start the first business. From the time he was 16 he hit the block, fisting sales, risking his freedom. At that age he hadn't known what he was saving up for, but he trapped every dollar. He piled up his earnings in a safe under the wooden floorboards in his room. He didn't spend on flashy stuff. In fact, the other d-boys on the block would clown him for his humble appearance. What they didn't know was that they were hustling backwards. He was hustling with mental precision. When he was 24, he purchased his first building, everyone called him crazy, but within two years his business took off. He hit the jackpot and entered the million-dollar club. He hadn't shined as a youngster, but he was shining now and his pockets were heavy while the same niggas he came up with was hustling on the same blocks. Stuck in the trap of it all. Still his plan hadn't quite come together because he hadn't fully separated from the streets. In fact, he was in it heavier than ever. His connect wouldn't let him go. He moved too much work and even worse the legit guys came to him to clean up their messes. He did more dirt for corporate guys in suits than he ever did for the real bad guys. Everyone had dirt on their hands. From politicians to mobsters. Someone was always in need of his services. He disposed of their bad deeds and even better, Dom had selective memory. As long as the payment was right he could make any transgression disappear, whether it be tax documents, evidence that needed burying, or a body that needed to disappear.

"'I'm not into international real estate yet. I own a few houses in Michigan though...the inner cities. Investment properties," he explained. "Nothing like this."

"'Where do you live?" she asked.

"'I'm around," he answered vaguely.

'She blushed. "I don't mean to pry," she said. "You probably think I'm nosy as shit." She laughed away her nervousness as he took her hand.

"'Don't worry about it. Hopefully one day I can take you to my place. Maybe one day you'll be waking up every morning at my place. We got to get there first, though. I got a trust problem. I don't extend it easily," he admitted, looking slightly uncomfortable as he divulged something so personal to her. He wasn't the talking type. He rarely opened up to anyone, which is why his circle was so small.

"'So basically you want to get to know me but it's going to be hard for me to get anything out of you," she said.

"'All this don't count?" he asked with a grin as he led her inside.

"'This is nice but I have a feeling that you've given all of this to chick after chick. Clothes, trips, jewelry…maybe even a nice little c-class Benz," she paused as she placed her bag down and turned to him. His silence was a dead giveaway. "Am I right? You're in the upgrading business?"

"'Dead on actually," he replied honestly.

'She scoffed and then added, "Than nah, this definitely doesn't count. I want authenticity, not plush gifts to keep me content. I'mma have to put you onto that new."

"'That new, huh?" he asked, intrigued at the way she spoke to him. She spoke as if she was schooling him, reading him like a text book that she had studied many times. She spoke like she knew him. She nodded. "That's real," he said with a smirk. He didn't fully smile. She was noticing that. He had more of a mischievous grin, but every time he did it she felt butterflies in her stomach. "There isn't much that I haven't experienced before."

"'I have a feeling that you've never been in love before," she said. "When I put you up on that, you won't be thinking about flying any other chick anywhere. That's the 'new' I'm talking about," she responded, rather arrogantly. "Now where's the master bedroom?" she asked.

'He smirked. She was interesting. Noni handled him in a way that no other woman ever had before. She wasn't taking any shorts. *I can dig that*, he thought. He nodded toward the glass stairs. "Top floor. Last door on the left," he replied.

'She sashayed up the stairs and he enjoyed the view from behind as he swiped a hand over his goatee. She stopped halfway up and turned to him. "I like French toast by the way."

'"Huh?" he replied, temporarily dazed by her aura.

'"Breakfast...that's what we here for right?" she answered, her stunning smile blinding him.

'There was something about her that was so genuine. He appreciated that quality in her.

'"Breakfast," he confirmed.

'Noni stepped into the long, color block, pleated, sundress and stood in front of the full-length mirror as she admired her figure. She was trying so hard to make it look like she wasn't trying so hard. Make-up on a sunny beach was extra. Curls on a hot day would sweat out. Dom had met her at her best...all glammed up. She sparkled with the best diamonds in the bunch when she had too, but this setting was so intimate. It was just the two of them. There weren't any pretenses to hide behind. She pulled her hair up into a large bun, leaving a few baby hairs to rest against her hairline. Large hoop earrings, oversized shades, and a dab of lip gloss completed her simplistic look. She stepped out of the room and immediately the breeze that blew through the open floor to ceiling windows refreshed her. She wandered out onto the terrace and down the stairs that led to the golden sand. It was so hot that she had to hustle across it as she approached the table. The scenery was breathtaking. Turquoise water served as the backdrop while a white canopy covered a table that was decorated with fresh flowers. To her surprise Dom was in the water, swimming his heart out. She smiled as she grabbed a towel off of the table and walked to the water's edge. She waved her hand, motioning for his attention.

"'You swim?" she asked as he came out of the water. His defined abs were quite the distraction as she tried to keep her eyes on his and off his well-maintained body.

"'Light work," he replied as he breathed heavily. She held out the towel and he accepted it. "You want to go in?" he asked.

'She frowned and shook her head. "I'm good. I agreed to breakfast only…"

'He nodded his head non-chalantly. "Yeah, yeah, I hear you… you took all that time to get gorgeous for me. Dope dress, hair all pinned up…" he turned to head back toward the table then suddenly pivoted toward her, scooping her off her feet. He threw her across his shoulder as she squealed at the top of her lungs as she hit his back playfully.

"'No, Dom don't! My hair!...I swear if you…!" her protests were drowned as he tossed her into the water. She bounced up, blowing the water out of her mouth. Hair ruined, dress ruined, but she couldn't help but laugh. "Boy, I'm going to kill you!" she shouted as she lunged at him, her legs moving in slow motion as the water resisted her strides. He chuckled as she splashed him, but he quickly came up on her and wrapped his arms around her waist. She wrapped her legs around him and her arms around his neck as he walked deeper into the ocean. "I can't swim…wait Dom, don't go to far out," she whispered, a slight panic settling into her voice.

'He paused briefly and pulled his head back to stare at her. "Trust me Noni," his words were so sincere that even he was surprised at how much he meant them. She nodded and he eased further into the water. Her body tensed at the threat of her own vulnerability.

"'Relax,' he whispered. They were cheek to cheek as he held her but he looked out toward the open ocean while she stared back at the shore. "You're so tense. What you scared of?"

'As she held onto him, her fingertips clasped around his neck and her shoulders hunched in mounds of tension. Looking in his eyes she realized, she hadn't ever trusted anyone. It was hard for her to hand over control of things, especially her heart. As his stare burned into her, his forehead creased in inquisition, she realized yes, she was afraid...she was in too deep. These waters were nothing compared to the emotions that were threatening to engulf her.

"'Drowning," she replied, knowing that his type of affection was one that made it hard to breathe.

'He brought his face close to hers and she closed her eyes, anticipating his lips on hers, but when he kissed her cheek instead her eyes fluttered open, slightly embarrassed that she had expected more. Wanted more...his strong embrace, her pelvis pushed against his, her wetness mixing with the fluidity of the ocean water. She wanted him. He had her here, now she wanted him to take advantage of her presence.

'She looked up and the sight of a man, standing, in the middle of the hot beach, fully clothed in a black suit caused her to frown.

"'Do you know him?" she asked.

'Dom turned toward the shore, never releasing his hold on her. He squinted, his expression turning serious as he made his way back toward the beach. When they were in shallow water he set her on her feet. His mood had gone cold and despite the heat, a shiver traveled down her spine.

"'Is everything okay?" she asked as she came out of the water.

"'Lupe," Dom greeted. "I thought our meeting wasn't until this evening. I wasn't expecting you."

"'I tried to reach you. I see now why you were unavailable," the man replied. He held out his hand to Noni. She stood, soaking wet as her ruined dress clung to her curves. She reluctantly reached out her hand. "You are a beautiful distraction."

'At a loss for words she stumbled over an awkward, "Thank you," as he kissed the top of her hand. He was older...established... maybe in his early 50's. His slick hair was brushed back neatly and although it was hot as hell outside, he didn't break a sweat. He was collected, in control, and suave as he stared so long that she was forced to look away.

"'Listen Noni, I need to handle a few things. I don't mean to leave you alone but you think you can entertain yourself for a little while. My driver. He'll take you wherever you want to go. There's a black card, in my wallet. It's on the living room table. You think you can do something with that?"

'She was distracted by Lupe, looking back and forth between the two men before nodding. "Sure, that's fine," she said.

'Dom stepped closer to her and placed a finger under her chin as he stared her in the eyes. "You sure?"

"'Yeah, I'm a big girl. I can find something interesting to get into," she replied with a smile.

'Her eyes twinkled as her beautiful smile melted him and a twinge of guilt burned through him...not because he was leaving her, but because his intentions with her were not as pure as he wished they could be. He had an agenda. Problem was, he liked her...

'Dom had never let a woman get in the way of his money. He had a plan. He had come to Mexico to re-up. It was a monthly trip and each time he made it, he brought a different accessory...a girl. He sweet talked chicks into coming away with him and then planted a kilo of cocaine in their bag on the way home. Customs would receive an anonymous tip about a girl attempting to traffic drugs and she would be arrested as soon as they searched her bags. It was all a tactic of distraction. While customs was preoccupied with the little fish, the big fish, got off the hook. Dom always had a second mule on a private flight. He moved 25 kilos twice a month. He never thought twice about the innocent girls who got caught up because they were all the same...sack chasers, gold diggers, strippers, who saw him as a come up. So far, luck had been on his side and he was getting rich in the process. *This is the same as every other time. No different,* he thought to himself as he watched Noni walk toward the beach house.

His heart ached slightly however. The mere sight of her was hypnotizing. He had never felt so much intrigue over one woman. He didn't know what it was about her. It was more than a physical thing. Her mind was right and in a world where women had become a flock of birdbrains, her intelligence and drive was like a magnet. This time his conscience was fucking with him. He had chosen a different type of girl...one that he didn't want to sabotage. Noni had pulled him in, but he knew he had to remain focused...there was money on the line.

'"What is she doing here?" Lupe asked. "You never bring them to my place. What happened to her staying at a hotel? That's how you've always done it? Now she's seen my face. She is lovely, but this is serious business Dom. You use her for her intended purpose. There is no room for things to get complicated. She's just pussy. Pretty pussy, but still pussy."

'Dom swiped the water from his face. "There's no complication. I know what she's here for and when the time comes, she'll do what I need her too, just like all the others. I've got it under control."

"'I hope so my friend," Lupe replied sternly. "You've only been in Mexico for a few hours and already she has you moving differently. The meeting with Josiah has been moved up. Get dressed. We'll be in the car."

'Dom paused. "We?"

"'Gia is in the car. I could barely stop her from coming in here to get you herself. Make it quick," Lupe stated.

'Dom nodded before retreating inside.

Chapter 6

Dom stepped into his expensive slacks and stood before the full-length mirror as he slipped into his designer oxford shirt. He buttoned it slowly, covering his tattooed torso. There were no nervous jitters. He had pulled this routine off before without a hitch. It was business as usual, the only thing was the way he was feeling…this attraction he had for Noni was completely unusual. He wasn't on a pussy chase. He was about the paper, but he couldn't help but picture Noni's smile in his mind every time he closed his eyes. "Get a grip," he whispered to himself as he walked over to the closet. He bent down and lifted one of the floorboards, revealing the handgun he had hidden inside. He had never had to use it while making his transactions in Mexico, but should the need ever arise he wanted to be ready. He would rather be caught with it then be caught without it. He couldn't wait until the day that he could step away from the game for good. He wanted to go completely legit, but he couldn't step away without Josiah's blessing. If he did, he would spark a war that he would lose so instead he played his position, hoping to one day earn his way out. He put on his suit jacket, concealing the weapon, before heading out of the door. He stopped by Noni's room and paused when he noticed the door was cracked. She was wrapped in nothing but a towel. Her toned leg was propped up on the bed as she spread lotion onto her skin. He knocked, feeling voyeuristic as he admired her through the small slit in the door. Each time she moved out of his vision his heart dropped.

'She turned toward the door and tightened the towel around her body before she said, "Come in."

"'I'm just stopping in to make sure you're good before I head out," Dom stated.

"'You don't have to keep asking me," she said as she cocked her head to the side and smiled. "I'm good." He didn't move, but his eyes scanned her body. From the top of her head to her pretty feet she had him mesmerized.

"'You're staring," she said as she blushed.

"'You make it hard not to," he replied.

"'You're too smooth for your own good," she said. "I'm not in the market for dreams Dom, so I hope you're not selling them."

'He didn't want to lie to her so instead he said nothing. Instead, he pulled out a band of Ben Franklin's and sat it on the edge of the bed. "Whatever you need."

'He left the room.

'Dom walked out and stepped into the car that was waiting curbside for him.

"'It's about time. What the fuck took you so long and why is that bitch here with you? And why aren't you answering my calls?"

'The woman that sat inside the chauffeured vehicle, was the same woman that had accompanied him to the gala. Gia, his girlfriend, and partner in crime, sat fuming as she stared at him in irritation.

"'Kill all the questions G. I'm here now," Dom said as he slid into the car.

"'I'm just saying, you're slipping. You're so far up that girl's ass that you didn't even know that Josiah wanted to see us early.

You're lucky I didn't come in there and snatch that little bitch up," Gia stated, displeased as she crossed her arms across her chest.

"'Relax. It just business...like always," he responded coolly as the car eased away from the home.

"'Yeah well they've never stayed with you before. It's usually me sitting pretty in that villa..."

'Dom turned to her and gripped her wrist firmly. "Look Gia. Ain't no room for that jealousy shit. You know what she's here for. Play your role and let me play mine," he stated, eyes menacing. "She's not some dancer, some broke chick trying to snag a new bag. I can't just tell her anything. If I want this to go off right than she has to trust me. It has to feel real to her. So shut the fuck up about it," he stated. Gia pouted but didn't press the issue further. He knew she was green with envy. He smirked as he pulled her across the seat and planted a kiss on her lips. "Stay focused."

"'Tell yourself that," she grumbled.

'Lupe was silent in the front passenger seat as his driver drove them through the city. Dom was on edge. "Why are we meeting tonight?" he asked. Dom had met Lupe years ago when he was 16. Lupe had come through the hood, wearing his expensive Versace shirts, and driving a pearly white whip. He had gold and diamond dripping from his neck. At the time, Dom was working blocks working hand over fist, and although he was young he was known for his gunplay. When he first noticed Lupe, he knew that it wouldn't be long before someone either robbed the Hispanic man or killed him. Niggas in Flint were starving and Lupe came around looking like a meal ticket. He would pull up with a different chick in his passenger seat almost every day. Needless to say, Lupe was making unseen enemies. He was shining too hard and before he knew it, the young wolves on the block had snatched his chain and stolen his car. Dom knew the deal however. Lupe's Hispanic roots ran deep...straight to the border where his uncle reigned supreme in the underworld. Dom didn't want that type of heat on his blocks. He didn't even want to be associated with the cats whom had robbed Lupe, so he told them to return Lupe's belongings. In exchange he would put them on.

'Lupe had been so grateful that he began to supply Dom with quarter kilos of cocaine, but he was moving through them so quickly that eventually his uncle wanted an introduction. The rest was history. Although his ties ran deep and he had been in business with Josiah for many years, he didn't trust him. There was no loyalty, no love…just business and as long as he had been connected the routine had always been the same…until now. The air inside the car was thick with tension as he awaited an answer.

'"Josiah didn't say," Lupe said, revealing nothing.

'Gia raised her eyebrows and Dom bit his cheek as the unknown caused paranoia to creep into his heart. They pulled off onto a dirt road, leaving the main highway. Dom looked around trying to gather his bearings. He was uncomfortable, but he said nothing. It was too late to be weary now. Josiah already had him in the middle of nowhere. Whatever was about to go down couldn't be stopped. He finally spotted Josiah and his men in the distance. They stood in front of two Mac trucks. They were uncharacteristically cool in black suits despite the scorching heat outside. A black Mercedes was parked off to the side, windows tinted.

'The driver rolled to a stop and Lupe turned around and eyed him.

'"You want to give me a heads up on what this is about?" Dom asked, tone serious, almost threatening.

'"You will find out in due time my friend," Lupe said.

'Gia reached over and gave his hand a reassuring squeeze, but it did little to calm him. He took a deep breath and slid the pistol across the seat to her. "Take her back," he said to the driver. The man didn't respond to Dom, but instead looked at Lupe.

"'I don't think that is necessary Dom. There is no malice here. Just relax," Lupe assured. His response was vague.

"'I'm okay," Gia said.

"'Just stay in the car," he whispered. He glanced out of the window and grit his teeth. He popped open the back door and stepped outside, adjusting his suit jacket as he approached.

'Before he could get close to Josiah he was halted. Used to the routine he lifted his arms and allowed Josiah's henchmen to search him. When they were done he lowered his arms and placed his hands in the pockets of his slacks as he walked toward Josiah.

'Josiah's presence was powerful. He was short in stature, unusually so in fact. He only stood at 4'9" but what he lacked in height he made up for in heart. Josiah was a vicious cartel lord. His glass eye and missing pinky finger were only two indications of the many attempts that had been made on Josiah's life. Still, he stood, a legend in the flesh. He moved more cocaine than all of the other Mexican organizations combined. Once you were in bed with Josiah, it was hard to get out of it. Business usually only ended one way…in death.

' "I have to admit, I'm not comfortable with the change of plans," Dom said.

"'Sometimes change is necessary," Josiah said. "We've done good business for quite a few years Dom. In that time you've never been caught, never come short, never done bad business."

"'I haven't," Dom responded.

"'I have made you a lot of money, yes?" Josiah asked.

"'We've made each other a lot of money," he answered.

"'So why do I get the feeling that you are trying to pull out of our arrangement. Instead of your orders growing, they are declining. 25 kilos? You went from buying 75 to 25? That is chump change to you."

"'I'm moving in a different direction," Dom said. "I'm willing to buy my way out."

"'Out?" Josiah asked with a laugh. "I didn't know there was a way out."

"'I have no interest in continuing to take these risks," Dom said.

"'I have no interest in your interests," Josiah shot back bluntly.

'Dom had to hold his tongue. The men in black suits with heavy artillery around him kept his wit on a leash. Josiah nodded toward the Mack trucks. "Take a look Dom."

'The henchmen lifted the gates to the backs of both trucks and Dom walked toward them. His heartbeat sped up and the hairs on the back of his neck stood straight up when he looked inside.

'Bodies wrapped in clear plastic were lined up in the bed of one truck. Duck tape was around the heads and the feet. A neat package of murder had been presented to him. Inside the other truck was bricks of cocaine, neatly stacked and wrapped in plastic as well.

"'This is your choice," Josiah said. "If I could offer another option to you, I would. This is not personal. You are simply too valuable to my business."

'Dom had a temper problem but he knew better than to be quick to anger in this circumstance. He was in bed with one of the most notorious men in the world. He chose his next words very carefully. "How much to buy my freedom?" he asked.

"'Not how much," Josiah said. "How long." He paused and steepled his fingers under the tip of his nose. "Five years Dom. You give me five more years of good business and at the end of it all I will let you buy your way out of this game."

'Knowing that this deal wasn't negotiable he nodded and began to retreat to the car.

"'And Dom?" Josiah called.

'Dom turned and looked Josiah square in the eye. Josiah snapped his fingers and one of his men handed Dom a small duffel bag. Dom already knew what it was. 25 kilos of pure cocaine lay inside.

"'25 a month won't cut it. Starting next month you need to prepare yourself for more…much more, at the least ten times that amount," Josiah instructed. Dom nodded knowing that he had just promised the next five years of his life to the devil.

"'What did he say? What did he say?" Gia asked as soon as he lowered himself inside the car.

'Dom didn't answer. He simply looked out the window as the driver pulled away.

'He was silent as they rode back….thoughts of money and death filled his mind. "Dom, you coming up?" Gia asked as they arrived at her hotel.

'Dominick shook his head. "You know I can't."

'Gia had never been jealous of one of their marks, but he could see it in her eyes that she wasn't fond of Noni.

"'I know you're just using her. I know we've done this a million times, but if you fuck her Dom…" her voice trailed off because she knew that Lupe was ear hustling from the passenger seat. She pleaded with him with her eyes. Dom could see it. He felt her begging him for reassurance. "She's just like all the others, right?"

"'Good night Gia," he said sternly. "Keep your head in the game."

Chapter 7

Twenty-five kilos. The white bricks sparkled in front of him as he loosened his tie and unbuttoned his shirt. He had done this song and dance so many times that the thrill of it was gone. Or maybe it was Noni's presence that was throwing him off. He knew what had to be done, but a part of him really didn't want to do it. This woman, he wanted to know. A knock at the bedroom door interrupted him as he coolly pulled the bed spread over the drugs before replying with a cool, "It's open."

'It was past midnight and he was surprised that she was awake. When she peeked inside his door he said, "I'm sorry for dipping off earlier. I hope you spent every dime of that bread I left you with," he replied. "I've learned that shopping is the best way for a woman to pass the time."

'She shook her head as she leaned her back against the wall. "No, actually I didn't spend any of it. I went into town. They have these markets where the locals come to sell crafts. It's amazing. I found a café and I read a book…came back here to lay out in the sun a bit…"

"'Damn, now I feel really bad. Leaving you here to do nothing all day," he answered.

"'I've been in school for the past 6 years busting my ass every day. Nothing is exactly what I wanted to do. It was cool," she replied sincerely with a small smile.

'It was that. That humility. Her simplicity drew him in. She was dope. The dopest female he had ever encountered. "I'll make it up to you tomorrow," he promised.

"Not necessary. The trip in itself is enough," she said. "I was going to go for a walk on the beach, but I noticed your light was on."

"You want some company?" he asked.

'She smiled. "I've been solo dolo all day. It's about time," she teased, giving him a wink.

'The beach was dark and stretched for miles as the sound of waves crashing against the shore provided a tranquil sound. A slight breeze blew humid air as stars illuminated the night sky. Noni inhaled and then exhaled deeply. "It's so peaceful out here. Its like I never noticed how bright the stars are until now."

"Or maybe you just never took the time out to look up," Dom said.

"So are you going to tell me where you went earlier? Or is that too personal?" Noni asked.

She noticed him shut down instantly as thick tension filled the air. With one question she had reminded him that this wasn't a date. They weren't on a real vacation. He had no intentions of getting to know her but she had a personality so appealing that it was easy to forget. This was a play...a hustle...and she was his mark. *Damn*, he thought. He had never been so remorseful. He was about to ruin her entire life. This damsel, this beautiful woman...this simple, independent woman...with her degree and her rules and her morals. He was about to strip her life away. He felt guilty for making her smile, for making her trust him. He wished he had chosen a different chick, but he hadn't. Noni was here and whether he liked it or not, the job had to be done.

"Hey, it's not a big deal, you don't have to answer," Noni said. "I know you have layers. It'll take some time for me to get to the deepest parts of you."

She walked to the waters edge and sat down allowing the coolness of the foamy ocean to soak her legs. "I kind of already know your type anyway," she said.

He raised a brow as he took a seat beside her.

"What do you know, Noni?" he asked.

"Well I know that you're used to getting what you want. I know that you don't mind ruining a pair of Gucci slacks," she said with a chuckle as she motioned to the expensive pant he was wearing. "You're private…almost secretive…which means that you aren't so proud of every move that you make. I don't even know if you would call yourself a good guy, but I can see the good in you. Its just buried deep, beneath the arrogance and the money and the power."

She didn't look at him as she spoke. Instead her eyes were trained on the moon that illuminated the black waters in front of her. He on the other hand couldn't stop staring at her. He studied her profile.

"Sounds to me like I could be the bad guy," he said.

"Bad guys are usually made from bad women," she replied. "Whether it be an ex girlfriend that made you bitter, a girl you couldn't attain, or a mother who didn't love you. Bad men are always created by bad women." She shook her head in disgrace. "All it takes is the love of the right kind of woman to turn all that around."

Dom cleared his throat and shifted his gaze towards the stars. Her conversation was deep, meaningful and she was reading him like a book. Describing him as if she had known him her entire life…as if she had witnessed his mother walking out on him, or as if she could hear that his heart was off beat from years of not knowing real love.

"I have too much karma coming back my way to ever find a woman that will love me that much," he replied honestly as he thought of all the girls he had brought on this very trip. All the women that he had lured into the game unknowingly. He had used them as pawns. Disposed of them without thinking twice. It was the nature of the business. Not once had he felt badly about it, because he had never chosen a girl like Noni before. He had stumbled across her and now he wished that he hadn't. '

"'You must have broken many hearts to have karma like that," Noni said jokingly.

'He smirked and lowered his head, deep in thought, but remained silent.

"'Just don't break mine?" she asked.

'He looked up at her. Their eyes connecting in a way that sent an invisible energy pulsing between them.

"'Never," he replied.

'He felt like a scumbag as he sat making promises to her that he knew he couldn't keep. This time tomorrow she would be sitting in a Mexican jail because of him. The knot in his stomach told him this wasn't right and yet still it was inevitable.

'The rising tide caused the water to rush them suddenly, wetting their entire body.

"'Agh!" Noni screamed as she scrambled to her feet and ran back onto dry land.

'He grimaced as he joined her, the wetness of his clothes was clearly uncomfortable. He began to unbutton his shirt and slid out of it, revealing the work of art that was his chest and arms. It wasn't the definition of his body that made her swoon, although his physique was on point. It was the ink that covered him that appealed to her. This man that she had met at a business gala had a bad side to him. He was far from what she had assumed him to be. He moved in rich circles, but had a gutter demeanor. He was from the bottom. He just happened to be sitting on top.

'They began walking down the beach, back toward the villa and as natural as the imprints their feet left in the sand, their hands intertwined. She leaned into him, resting her head on his shoulder as they walked under the stars.

'Lights and the sound of a mariachi band could be heard and seen in the distance. "Looks like a wedding," she said as she noticed guests celebrating seaside. "How perfect is that? A beach celebration in the middle of the night. That's exactly how I would do it. Small, simple, and under a sky like this." She looked up, smiling genuinely and in that moment he broke all of the rules. His hand graced her face and eventually tilted her chin down, forcing her eyes to meet his. She said nothing, but the spark between them turned into a blaze of passion as he inched closer to her. When their lips met she let out a sigh as if she had been waiting for him to kiss her all day. As if she had been love parched and he was quenching that thirst.

'*He feels so good,* she moaned in her mind as he cuffed her behind with a strong hand, pulling her into him. He handled her like she was his…like she had given him permission many times before and she loved it. In all of her years of kissing toads she had never felt like this. Her heart raced and her body ached so good. She could feel his wanting as their bodies smashed together. She had told herself that she hadn't come her to get fucked and dumped, but she was past the point of stipulations and rules. In that moment, she wanted him. The silkiness building in her panties confirmed it, but still she didn't know Dom well enough for this. They were rushing it…moving to fast. Whenever she let things go at this pace they crashed and burned. She pulled back, her shoulders tensing slightly.

"'Can we slow this down a little?" she asked, breathless.

'He smiled as he wiped her lip gloss from his lips. "Yeah I think maybe we should." He held out his hand and she took it as he began to walk up the beach, passing their villa.

"'Where are we going?" she asked.

"'We're going to crash a wedding," he said.

'She smiled and replied, "but we're soaked."

"'It's a beach party. No one will even notice," he replied.

'They walked toward the celebration hand in hand. "Looks like we're too late. The party is coming to an end," she said as they watched the guests begin to filter back into the villa and cars began to depart on the main road.

'Dom walked over to the band and pulled out a wad of money. It was semi-wet but it served the same purpose. He tossed it to one of the men. "Keep playing," he said.

'The music came back alive and Dom pulled her onto the dance floor. The look of humor and disbelief on her face pleased him as they danced. Soon the only people on the beach were the two of them and their personal band. Their laughter filled the air as the two danced the night away.

"'I have two left feet," Noni laughed as she danced around him.

'She beamed as he suddenly spun her around, pulling her into his chest. Her brilliant smile and infectious energy was restoring his dark soul. "You're the type of man I could love," she whispered as they swayed slowly despite the fact that the music was high paced. They were drowning out the world as they looked into each other's eyes.

"'I wish you could, ma," he whispered.

"'What's stopping me?" she answered .

"'Me," he replied. He pulled her closer so that she was looking over his shoulder and they continued to dance in silence. A part of him wanted to put her in a cab and just send her home. She was too good for this…too good for him and he knew it, but he was selfish. He couldn't back out of this deal no matter how much he wanted to. Once the bricks were in his hands they were his responsibility.

'They stayed on the beach for hours. Even after the band called it quits they sat, talking, and enjoying each other's company. Before he knew it shades of amber and orange appeared in the sky and Noni's head rested in his lap. She had fallen asleep mid-sentence. He picked her up and carried her back to the villa as she rested peacefully in his arms. Without waking her he laid her down in her bed and then retreated to his own room. As soon as he was inside he picked up his cell and called Gia. She answered on the first ring.

'"Change of plans G. We're flying out today so be ready. I'm on my way over," he said. There was no way he could spend another night with Noni. Being around her too long would have his mind all messed up. The sooner they could get this over with the better because she was chipping away at the ice around his heart, whether he liked it or not.

Chapter 8

Guilt burdened Dom as he pulled up to the airport. "Safe travels Noni," he said as he stroked her hair gently and massaged the nape of her neck. He couldn't help but pull her into him. He planted a single kiss on her forehead. "I have a few more things to handle here. I'll call you when I get back in town."

' "Thank you for breakfast," she replied with a wink. He eyed her bag as she stepped out of the car and made her way into the airport. His belly churned with indecisiveness. He wanted to call off the entire thing…to say fuck it, but he couldn't. Somebody had to be the distraction. He just hated that it had to go down like this.

'Gia spotted Noni as soon as she stepped foot inside of the airport. *Bitch ain't all that*, she thought as she placed her oversized Chloe shades over her eyes and adjusted the large sunhat on her head. She was dressed to precision. Business attire. Six inch Kates on her feet and an expensive pencil skirt two-piece suit to match, she didn't look the part of a drug trafficker. She carried two medium size suitcases. One was filled with clothes and had her name on it. The other was filled with cocaine and had the name, *Mary Smith*, written on the luggage tag. She would check both and when she arrived back in Detroit she would pick them up from the luggage carousel without incident. If things went badly she could just pick up her luggage with clothing and leave the drugs unclaimed. While the police waited for *Mary Smith*, she would be in the wind. It was foul proof and she had done the routine with Dom so many times that she didn't even get butterflies in her stomach anymore. Noni simply served as a diversion. As long as customs thought Noni was the one trying to move weight, they wouldn't be focused on Gia. Usually Gia felt badly for the girls they set up...but she couldn't wait to see Noni get caught. *Nigga tripping over her like she's somebody*, Gia thought. Gia watched Noni carefully as she checked in for the flight and then she slyly followed her to airport security. She gripped her ticket in her hand as she got in line, making sure to let at least five people go between her and Noni.

'Her cell rang and she looked down, frowning at the words RESTRICTED NUMBER.

'"Hello?" she picked up, but kept her eyes focused on Noni.

'"Has she made it to the security line yet?"

'It was Dom's voice. "Why are you calling restricted?" Gia asked.

'"Is she in line?" he repeated this time more sternly.

'Gia frowned in confusion as she watched Noni place her bag on the conveyor belt.

'"Yeah she's going now but they're..." Gia paused and watched in shock. "They're letting her through."

'CLICK.

'"Hello?" Gia said. Her chest fell as if it had caved in as she saw Mexican police filter into the airport. She quickly opened her bag. Dom had been the last one with it. He had called her...last minute, changing the plan, asking to see her that morning. She unzipped the bag and her life seemed to play in slow motion. In her heart she already knew what she would find. Panic filled her as she looked up. The police were bee lining directly for her and when she looked down in the depths of her hand bag there it sat. A half brick of cocaine.

"'Bitch!" she mumbled as tears filled his eyes. She looked toward Noni as she walked without a care in the world through the security checkpoint.

He traded me for her, she thought as tears filled her eyes.

'Two men in suits approached her. "Miss you need to come with us," one of them said.

'She wanted to run, but it was too late. She knew what was next and she bowed her head as they escorted her out of the airport and into an awaiting police car.

' "Hello?" Noni answered. She looked at her cell phone screen to make sure she had service because all she heard was silence on the other end. Placing it back to her ear she said, "Dom, can you hear me?"

"Yeah I hear you ma," he replied. "Are you on the plane?"

She stood and gathered her belongings before getting in line.

"I'm boarding now," she answered.

"'You remember that wedding on the beach?" he asked.

"'Of course, that just happened last night," she replied with a laugh.

"'Why don't we have one of our own?" Dom shot back. He didn't know what he was thinking. He wasn't the marrying type, but he knew how she made him feel. He knew what he had just given up for her. The thought of her at risk made his temperature rise. All he wanted to do was be around her, get to know her, exclusively. He wanted her for himself.

'Noni's mouth fell open, but no sound came out. "I...I don't know...what am I supposed to say to that?" she finally managed.

"Don't say anything...just walk out. I'm waiting out front," Dom said.

'Noni's mind told her to get her ass on that plane, but her feet were already headed for the exit. She emerged from the airport to find him, leaning against the chauffeured car with his arms folded across his chest. Versace shades covered his eyes so she couldn't see if he was joking or not.

"Are you playing with me right now?" she asked as she walked toward him slowly. She was so uncertain.

"I know the shit is crazy. It makes no sense. I just met you. You don't know me, but here's the thing, ma. I've been with a lot of women and none of them are like you."

"And you know this from one night with me?" Noni asked, squinting in confusion.

"I knew that after five minutes with you," Dom replied. "So how about it? You gone marry me on a beach in Mexico? Or are you gone walk back in there and catch your flight?" he asked.

'She shifted in her heels as she adjusted the bag on her shoulder. "Can I ask you something first?"

"Anything..." he replied.

"What do you do? I mean really do?" she asked.

'He stepped away from the car and walked into her space. "I'm a businessman, Noni. Like all businessmen I have some underhanded dealings, but know that none of that will ever fall on you and if you say yes I will always take care of you. Just give me a chance, ma. I'll buy you the world and if you ever want out I'll make sure you're taken care of. Just take this leap with me. I've done a lot of bullshit in my life. I've done a lot of wrong, but this is something that feels right. Show me how to be right, Noni."

'She hesitated. Her internal alarms were sounding off, but were dulled by the intense beating of her heart. Dom made her heart ache…she yearned for him. All it had taken was 24 hours for them to fall in love. She had felt it at the gala and again when they went swimming, and yet again on the beach the night before. If being with him was a mistake, she would enjoy it while it lasted.

"'Okay," she responded finally, nodding her head. "This is crazy, but okay."

"'Okay is a yes?" he asked as he did that half smirk half smile that she adored.

"'Yes," she replied.

"'Whooo hoo!!!" he shouted, embarrassing her as he picked her up and spun her around. She blushed as he kissed her, passion oozing into her, giving her life as she cupped his face in her hands.

"'I'm going to love the shit out of you ma," he said. She could see the happiness on his face. It was like a weight had been lifted. He had been so serious, so guarded before and now it was like he was giving her the key to him.

"'You'd better," she replied.

Present Day

'Noni awoke as the impact of the plane's wheels hitting the tarmac rattled her into consciousness. Her dreams had been so emotional that a tear escaped her eye as soon as she opened them. She wished that she could go back to the day she had met him. *I would walk right by him,* she thought. *I would erase his ass like he never existed.*

She knew that it was her anger speaking and even still it was unconvincing. She couldn't help but love Dom, despite his shortcomings. But love didn't erase the bitterness she felt. It didn't take away the shame she endured and it definitely wasn't enough to make her stay…not anymore. She feared what he would do when he found out she was gone. Would she even get a reaction? Or would he move onto the next chick and replace her as if she had never meant that much to him anyway. She didn't know and only time would tell. As she got off the plane in the South of France she had never felt more lost, but she was in search of herself and she had a feeling that this was the place she needed to be in order to become reacquainted with the woman she was before…the woman she could be without him. She had no idea that the money she had taken wasn't Dom's to steal. It was Josiah's. Five years had passed and it was time for Dom to pay up.

Chapter 9

DOM

"Good morning daddy."

Dom cringed every time he heard his son call him that. Daddy. Father. He had a kid. He had a kid that Noni knew nothing about. He loved his son, dearly. In fact, he was the only good thing in his life at the moment, but the hurt that the child represented made Dom feel sick to his stomach.

"Good morning champ," Dom replied as he picked up the two year old and pulled him into the bed. Thomas would have been the perfect blessing if Noni was his mother. Instead, he symbolized betrayal in the flesh. He was the one reason why Dom couldn't just leave Tat alone. She had him by the balls. If he even thought about breaking things off with Tat, she would expose their child to Noni. Dom had gotten Noni to forgive many things, but an illegitimate child would break her. He knew that one fact would be the straw to break the camel's back. Tat stirred beside him. "Hey baby boy," she crooned as the toddler climbed between them. "You see your daddy stayed the night? You want him to stay the night every night? Don't you big boy?" Tat said.

Dom climbed out the bed. "Don't," he stated sharply. "Don't bring him in the middle of our shit."

Tat rolled her eyes as she bounced baby Thomas on her lap. "You just want your daddy here with you," she cooed in a baby voice. "Instead of running back home to that bitch of his."

Dom shook his head. He had weaved himself a deadly web that he just couldn't get out of.

"Watch your mouth," Dom stated. "And she isn't a bitch when you're borrowing money from her. When she's watching Thomas for you. Or when she's helping you with job applications."

"Nope she's still a bitch then too. Just a dumb bitch," Tat snapped.

"She's your best friend!" Dom shouted. "We crossed a line Tatiana! Don't you get that? She thinks that little boy is our godson. We sold her a sob story about how your baby daddy left you to raise Thomas on your own. I cheated on my wife and had a baby with her best friend. My blood runs through his veins and she held your hand while you gave birth to him. She treats him like he is her own. How fucked up are we for this?" Dom asked, his eyes red from stress.

"You should have told her before it got this far!" Tat shot back.

"She's the only innocent mu'fucka in this situation. I'm not going to be the one to turn her bad. I can't," Dom whispered.

Tatiana blinked away tears, not because of the things that she had done wrong, but because of Dom's passionate defense of Noni. She and Noni had known each other since childhood. Their mothers had been friends, which inevitably made them closer than close.

"I feel bad, okay, but it doesn't change things," Tat said. "You need to tell her. This baby isn't the only secret we're keeping from her." Tat stood and placed the baby on her hip as she walked toward him. "If you don't tell her, I will and I'm going to give her every little detail."

Dom grit his teeth, flexing his temple as he tried to control his anger. He shook his head before storming out, headed home.

His mind was clouded as he got into his 6-series and pulled out of the driveway. He hadn't been able to think clearly for three years. Since the day Tat told him she was pregnant his guilt had burdened him. He had tried to get her to have an abortion. He had practically begged her to, but Tat could recognize a come-up when it fell into her lap. He had foolishly sexed her raw. He had gotten cocky, arrogant, and careless with his sidepiece and now the repercussions were severe.

He knew that he was about to walk into World War III as soon as he stepped foot inside his home. *She probably waited up all night,* he thought. Dom was half of a man and his shortcomings was something he was fully aware of. He had turned into the type of man that he never thought he would be. His lies had twisted upon themselves. He had to tell lies to cover lies and more lies to cover those. He hadn't told the truth in so long that he wasn't even sure how to anymore. At first it was about conquering women. He was in the business of cocaine and power. He had wanted to enjoy the spoils of the game, but when he met Noni, he just couldn't let her become another man's queen. He wanted her in his castle. He wanted her on the throne next to his, but once he crowned her, he forgot to nurture her. He had forgotten just how much he had wanted her when she wasn't his. *I took her for granted,* he thought. Now he was afraid to lose her.

Dom pulled up to their home. He had built it for her. Seven bedrooms, four baths, with a finished basement and a chef's kitchen. At 6,000 square feet it was a mini-mansion. He never spared any expense on her. In fact, he overly lavished her to make up for the fact that he couldn't be faithful. The one thing that she had asked him to give her he had failed to. His loyalty was more valuable to her than gold, but some men just couldn't grasp that fact. He was one of them. He held down his colleagues, his connect, his friends, hell even Tat got more loyalty and respect than he gave to Noni. With her, he played on her love for him, manipulating her heart. He made her crazy, denying things that they both knew were true and running her in mental circles trying to catch him up in infidelity. He had dogged out a good woman. He knew it so did she and still her loyalty kept her by his side. He climbed out of the car and walked into the house. Usually she would meet him at the door. The argument would have begun as soon as he stepped foot inside. This time, he was met with silence. An eerie, cold, empty silence.

"Noni!" he called. He frowned when she didn't respond. "Baby where are you?" He went from room to room searching for her until he finally made it to their bedroom. He gripped the frame of the door when he noticed that her drawers were emptied. He rushed to the closet. Her things were gone. "Where the fuck--" He pulled out his cell and immediately dialed her number.

His heart sank when he got a busy signal. She had blocked him. He noticed the painting on the wall was slightly askew and he rushed over, pulling it off the brackets and tossing it to the floor. The safe that sat behind it had been opened. He could tell. He always left it resting on the number seven and today it was positioned differently. He already knew what to expect, but he prayed that he was wrong. *She wouldn't take from me,* he thought as he put in the combination. Finding it empty his temper flared as he immediately dialed his accountant.

"Dominick, what can I do for you this morning?"

"You can tell me my money is still in the fucking bank. That's what you can do," Dom snapped, his tone malicious. He placed a balled fist on the wall in front of him and then leaned his forehead against it.

"It was transferred to another account. I got the alert on my email when it happened...is there a problem I should be aware of?" the man asked.

Dom closed his eyes. "Fuck!" he shouted.

"Dominick, who transferred the money? I assumed it was you and you were just moving some things around," his accountant said.

"My wife," Dominick revealed. "I put her on the account just in case something happened to me. I didn't know she knew about it. I hadn't told her. Is there a way to get the funds transferred back?" Dom asked.

"Unfortunately not. You aren't on her accounts so you can't transfer them back. She would have to do that," the man stated.

Dom hung up the phone and immediately dialed Noni, but his response was the same. He couldn't get through. He tossed his phone across the room in frustration as he sank against the wall. She had taken every dime. He had never been angry with her. Not one day in their marriage had he felt anything bad for her, but in this moment rage burned inside of him. Half of the ten million was supposed to be paid to Josiah. In seven days he was supposed to buy his way out of the game. It was what he had worked for, what he had hustled for all these years. In the blink of an eye it had all been put in jeopardy. The stakes had been raised and his life would be the ultimate cost to pay if he didn't find Noni and get the money back. She knew what business he was in. She knew that he dealt with dangerous men. She hadn't known at first, but she had quickly discovered it. As he leaned his head back against the wall he closed his eyes, thinking back to when they were good... back to the days when she would never take his money and dash. Back to the days when they held each other down...

The Past

"Wow," Noni gasped as she walked into his home. "You made it seem like you were living modest. You renovated an entire building and turned it into one spot. She walked inside as her chin hit her chest in awe. "You have the bridge to Canada and the Detroit River as your view." She laughed in amazement as she placed her hands on the floor-to-ceiling windows. .

'"Our view," Dom corrected. "This is your place now too."

'She smiled and ran over to him as she jumped up, wrapping her legs around his waist. He kissed her. Their passion was one that only new couples could display.

'"Looks like I'm the only one doing any work."

'Noni pulled away from Dom in embarrassment as she blushed. "Sorry Merci," she said as she watched Dom's best friend walk inside with a large box of her things. They had been back for a week and Merci was the only person who knew about their marriage. He was Dom's right hand. They had met in the streets years ago when they were hustling the same block. Two young men coming up in the heart of the Detroit's west side, they could have easily ended up enemies but instead the two became quick friends. Instead of warring over corners, they watched each other's backs and made money together. Once Dom got his connect, they expanded and Merci moved to Ohio to take over a new market. Dom's ultimate goal was to go legit, but Merci never planned to leave the game alone. He was a king and he planned on running his kingdom until the death of him. They were old friends with new money and trusted no one but themselves.

"It's all good Noni. I'm just fucking with you. There are a few more in the truck," he said with a wink. "I'll grab those and then I'mma hit the highway."

'Noni placed her hands on her hips. "You're not staying for dinner?" she asked.

'Merci's forehead creased in confusion as he shot Dom a look.

"He didn't tell you about the dinner?" Noni asked. She looked at Dom.

"I thought I was just helping with the move while I was in town," Merci said with a chuckle as Noni playfully hit Dom on the arm.

"Merci don't do shit like that…he's low key. He not with meeting the family and getting approvals and all that," Dom stated.

'Noni pouted. "But we just met. I want to get to know you. I want to hear all the embarrassing stories about you and Dom coming up. You're the only family he's got. It's only right that you entertain his new wife," she said. She put her hands together in a pleading motion as she gave him the saddest face she could muster.

"Please?"

"You're going to be in trouble fam if you ever have to tell her no," Merci stated with a chuckle.

"You might as well say yes now," Dom said. "Don't feed me to the wolves dolo bro," Dom stated.

"They're not wolves," Noni said. "It's just my two best friends and my Gram." She kissed Dom's cheek. She turned to Merci and continued. "My girls are pretty cool. It should be a good time. There will probably be a lot of drinks flowing so you can just crash here and leave out in the morning."

'Merci smiled. He was charming and he had light eyes that most women got lost in. His honey colored skin and Marley type dreads made him a beauty of a man, but there was an edge to him. He was a bad boy hidden behind a nice smile. He had a street swagger that oozed off of him. He was rugged…dangerous…and usually unbendable, but for Noni he complied.

"'What time is this dinner supposed to start?" he asked as he looked around at the boxes sprawled about.

"'In like an hour," she said as she frowned pessimistically.

"Yeah okay, I'll stay," Merci agreed.

Noni beamed as she walked over to her handbag and retrieved a piece of paper. "This is a list of things I need to make dinner. I take it the two of you can handle that," she said.

Dom took the list off her hands and rubbed the top of his head. "This is what that wife life is like huh? You just point and I fetch," he teased.

She winked. "Pretty much," she said with a laugh.

"You're in trouble," Merci added as he shook his head. He gave Dom a pat on the back. "We've got it, ma. You do what you do and we'll grab whatever you need to make this thing happen."

"Thank you," she said graciously as they made their exit.

Only a few minutes passed before she heard knocking at the door. She placed down the box that was in her hand as she frowned, rushing to answer. "You forgot something?" she asked, pulling open the door curiously.

She was greeted by the barrel of a .45 millimeter pistol.

"You scream and I'm blowing your head off. You do what I say, when I say it and you'll live to see another day," the man said. His gruff voice caused goosebumps to rise on her arms. She was frozen…her fear had paralyzed her as she looked at the two men in black masks. She never had a gun pointed at her in her life. Terror seized her.

Her world seemed to move in slow motion as they pushed her backwards inside the home. "P...p...please," she stammered. Tears clouded her vision and fell swiftly down her cheeks as she put her hands up.

"Ain't no point in begging. You know what we here for. Where's the stash?" the other guy said.

"I...I...don't know what you're talking about? What stash?" she replied. She was trembling so badly that she could barely speak.

"Bitch you playing games with me?" he asked as he rushed her, putting his hand around her neck and pushing her against the wall. Her head hit the plaster so hard that it cracked, leaving her dazed. She grimaced as her mouth fell open in pain and her hands shot up to the back of her head. She pulled them away to find blood on her fingertips.

One of the intruders chambered the gun and then pressed it point blank against her skull.

"Please! I don't know what you're talking about!" she screamed.

The other attacker intervened, pulling the trigger happy goon away from her.

"Fuck is you doing?! Are you stupid? I ain't come here for no murder. Let's just get what we came for and go!" he said. "Watch the window, I'll handle her." They had quickly assumed the role of good goon, bad goon but it really didn't matter...both of them terrified her.

She shriveled up against the wall, wishing she could disappear but good goon pulled her off the wall and shoved her toward the bedrooms.

"Holler if you see anybody pull up," he said to his partner before disappearing down the hall with Noni. "If I lived in this big motherfucka where would I hide a hundred kilos of cocaine?" he asked as he urged her forward with the gun.

She hesitated but didn't turn around. "Cocaine? What are you talking about? There are no drugs here. You have the wrong house or something. My husband is a businessman. He owns funeral homes," she said, desperately trying to convince him.

"I know exactly who your nigga is," he sneered. "Now we can do this the easy way or the hard way."

Noni's mind was numb. It was like she couldn't think as she led him down the hallway. She had no idea what these men were after. Dom was legit. He was straight laced. *Isn't he?* She thought. Doubts about the man she had committed her life to surfaced as she began to second guess him. What did she really know about Dom? He was young and successful, but with a gun to the back of her head she began to wonder. *Successful at what?*

She didn't know where she was leading him. She really had no idea what these men were in search of, but she remembered seeing a gun in the closet when she was putting up some of her things. She didn't even know if it was loaded. She had never shot a gun a day in her life, but she knew that it was the only thing that gave her a chance to make it out of this situation alive.

"The...the key to the safe is in here," she said as she clenched her hands, balling them into fists and releasing them over and over again to calm her nerves.

She entered their bedroom and walked over to the dresser. She reached inside and curled her hand around the gun. "It's...it's in here somewhere," she stammered, buying herself time to work up the nerve to actually shoot him. In a brief moment of distraction, good goon turned to look at the door giving her time to react. She pulled the gun out and pointed it at the man. "Get out of my house," she said in a stern, low tone as she shifted from foot to foot nervously.

"You gone shoot me?" he asked, chuckling. He didn't respect her gangster, her shaky aim revealed the fact that she was scared. If she was going to shoot him she would have pulled the trigger by now. He walked up on her, arrogantly.

"Don't come near me!" Noni threatened through clenched teeth as she backpedaled slowly. She was trapped against a wall and a madman. She was terrified as her heart thundered in her chest. The gun in her hands was her only defense and she wasn't sure if she had the courage to use it.

The man ignored her. "Word of advice shorty. When you pull a gun on a nigga, make sure you're ready to use it," he said.

He advanced on her and she closed her eyes, squeezing the trigger.

CLICK!

When it didn't go off fear seized her, as her eyes grew as large as golf balls.

"Safety's on," he said before lunging at her. "Bitch give me that fucking gun," he growled as he grabbed the barrel of the gun. She struggled to keep ahold of it, but he flung her around like a rag doll. Her finger felt like it would break as he tried to rip it from her hands.

Finally, he pointed his own gun point blank range against her head. "What now, bitch? Let the shit go," he barked, out of breath from their scuffle. She cowered as she eyed the gun, spotting the safety. She flipped the switch with her thumb and...

BOOM!

The gun went off in her hands and she dropped it instantly, afraid of the aftermath. Good goon slumped and she scrambled toward the door, but was blocked as bad goon appeared.

"Sit your ass down," he yelled as he hit her with the butt of the gun. Blood leaked as he split her head wide open from the force of the blow. It was so much that it blinded her as blood leaked into her eyes. The guy rushed over to his partner and kicked his booted foot. "Yo' get up…get up nigga," he said, panicked. When his friend didn't move he fisted both sides of his head in angst. "Fuck!" he shouted in frustration as he paced back and forth. In his distraction, she bolted for the hallway but she didn't get far before he was on her heels. He pulled her down by her hair and threw her violently against the wall. "Bitch you show me where the safe at or I'mma twist your fucking cap back," he seethed.

"I don't know!" she screamed in terror as she sat, curled up with her hands over her ears. She closed her eyes because she knew that he would kill her. He had come here searching for something and he wasn't leaving until he found it. She heard him pull the hammer back on his gun and she began to pray.

"Please God, please…please."

BOOM!

She heard the weight of his body hit the floor and when she opened her eyes his eyes were peering at her through the mask as blood pooled beneath him. She trembled uncontrollably as she looked up to see Merci reaching down to help her up.

She clung to him for dear life, in shock, as she stared at the body on the floor.

"Don't look at him," Merci said as he pulled her head into his chest and led her towards the living room. Tears just fell and fell, so effortlessly that she didn't even realize that she was crying. She thought it was the blood leaking from her forehead that she felt. She reached up to feel her wound. Her hands shook so badly that he had to grab her wrist. "It's okay Noni. It's okay," he whispered.

"Noni!" Dom shouted as he rushed through the door.

"Dom!" she cried as she ran into his arms.

"I heard the shot..." he said as he looked down the hall where Merci was snatching the mask off of the goon he had laid out.

"It's another one in the bedroom," Merci said. "Get her out of here. She don't need to see this," Merci said.

"I shot one of them. I...I found your gun and I just shot him," she whispered, frantic. She was so distraught over what had happened that she couldn't think straight. "Call the police. We have to call the police."

Dom pulled her close. "We can't. The police can't come here Noni," he said.

"But...I...they're dead. I killed..."

"Shhh, shhh, it's okay ma. Just let me take care of it," Dom said.

Merci walked up and whispered, "You need to take her somewhere fam. Clean her up and then meet me at the funeral home."

"No," Noni said, crying, completely hysterical. "Please you can't leave me by myself. I just want to be with you."

"Okay ma, okay. I'm not going anywhere," Dom assured.

DING! DONG!

They all froze.

"Who the fuck is that?" Merci whispered.

"It's...it's probably my Gram and....and...my friends," she panicked.

"Get rid of them," Merci said.

"No, get rid of them why?" Noni asked, completely confused. "Why aren't we calling the police Dom? This isn't my fault. We're innocent. They came here with guns trying to rob us..."

Dom looked at her. "I promise I'll explain everything to you Noni, but your people can't be here right now and we cannot call the police," he said as he rushed to the kitchen and grabbed a towel. "Just get rid of them. Don't even open the door. They can't see you like this."

Her eyes reflected her confusion as she stood there, speechless...afraid.

"Just trust your man, baby," Dom said.

And just like that she did. She went to the door. "Who is it?" she called, voice trembling.

"It's us, let us in!" Her friend Tatiana said.

"The dinner is off Tat. I'm not feeling well," Noni lied as Dom rubbed her back in support.

"What?" It was Maya who replied this time. "We just drove all the way across town Noni! Are you okay? Maybe we can help you feel better?" she called through the door.

"Noni baby, it's Gram. Open up, let me get a look at you."

"Tat, take my Gram home. I don't want to get y'all sick. I'll call y'all tomorrow when I'm feeling better," Noni said.

There was a long silence and Noni leaned against the door, feeling woozy, wishing that they would just go already.

"Noni? Are you sure you're good? Just open the door so I can see your face," Maya said. "Tat is walking your Gram back to the car. It's just me."

Noni reached for the door but Dom stopped her, shaking his head no.

"She isn't going to leave here until she sees me," Noni whispered.

"Noni, don't play with me. I will break this door down," Maya threatened. "I know you. I can tell you've been crying."

"Maya just go. I'm fine. I'll call you tomorrow," Noni stressed. After a brief moment of silence Maya finally gave in and Noni turned to Dom.

"Let me clean you up," he whispered. "I'm so sorry baby. I should have never brought you here. With you I have to move different."

He bent down and scooped her in his arms, carrying her to the kitchen. He set her on the countertop and then wet a towel before attempting to clean her wound.

"This is bleeding bad ma," he said, kicking himself. He should have known better than to bring her into his world. Before her he had no attachments, no weaknesses but she was his wife now and that alone made him vulnerable. "You're going to need stitches for that. I'm going to take you to the hospital but you can't tell anyone what happened here tonight."

"The bodies?" she whispered.

"Merci will handle it," Dom said. "Just keep pressure on that."

Dom grabbed his keys and tossed them to Merci, knowing that he would need them to get into the funeral home. Merci tossed his own back to Dom. "I'll call you when it's done."

Dom nodded then scooped Noni in his arms and carried her to the car. Already his lifestyle had affected her...already he had failed to protect her and as Dom jumped in the driver's seat and sped away from the curb, he couldn't help but wonder if bringing her into his life had been one big mistake. He had gotten her to marry him under false pretenses. She didn't know exactly who he was and now he feared that once she found out she would wash her hands of him. Deep down in his heart he knew that she deserved so much better than this.

"How did you get this again?" the doctor asked as he stitched up her forehead.

Noni was quiet as Dom stood against the wall, his arms folded as he looked to be in deep thought. She swallowed hard and then confidently responded. "I fell. We were moving into a new place and I tripped coming up the stairs. Hit my head right on the railing," she said.

"Well lucky for you the wound is right at the hairline. You'll have a scar but it shouldn't show much," the doctor said. He finished her sutures and then placed a bandage over the wound. "Keep it clean and let it heal. The stitches will dissolve themselves in about three weeks."

"Is she good to go?" Dom asked.

"She's good to go. Here is a prescription for the pain," the doctor said as he handed her a piece of paper.

Dom held out his hand and shook the doctor's firmly. "Thanks doc."

"No problem, no more stumbles," the doctor said before making his exit.

When they were alone Noni looked at Dom. "They were looking for drugs," she said.

"Not here, Noni," Dom said as he started toward her. She held up her hand and shook her head.

"Yes here Dom, because depending on what you tell me, I may not be leaving here with you," she replied, seriously. "Why were they in our house? Why would they be looking for bricks? If you're a businessman, if you own funeral homes and real estate, why would those goons rush into our house?"

Dom sighed as he sat down on the rolling stool that the doctor had used.

"Can we just go home? I'll tell you everything you need to know," Dom said.

"That's the problem. You can't be the one deciding what I need to know," she replied. "I want to know everything because I get the feeling you're leaving a bunch of shit out."

"I sell drugs Noni," Dom admitted. "A lot of them and I'm not talking about no corner boy shit. I move weight. When I went to Mexico," he paused and cleared his throat. He was about to be brutally honest with her. Fear seized him because he knew that she may leave him once he told her the truth, but she deserved it. He didn't want her to be married to him because of the illusion he had created. He wanted her to stay because she felt the same way he did. He wanted her to love him and he knew that by starting off on a foundation of lies that their marriage would crumble. "When I took you to Mexico I was down there to re-up. It was the reason I asked you to come. I was supposed to plant cocaine on you and send you into the airport to be caught at customs. You would be the distraction that allowed the real mule to get through."

"What?" she gasped as tears came to her eyes. "So it was fake?" she asked.

"Everything that happened between us was some game to you? You were going to set me up? I could be in jail right now!" she said.

"I couldn't. I started loving you the moment you told me your name, Antonia," he whispered.

"Get out," she whispered.

"Noni, please baby just let me..."

"Get out!" she screamed loudly, putting him on blast.

Dom didn't want to leave. He wanted to make her understand. He wanted her to know that he was in this for real, but she was bringing too much attention to them. She was angry and getting loud. He could see her trying to control her emotions, but every time she looked at him her disdain was revealed. She was hurt, but most of all she wasn't buying it.

LOVE BURN

Dom pulled out his wallet and placed a credit card on the counter next to him. "I'll call the credit card company and make you an authorized user. You get whatever you need. Get a room, clear your mind. If you want out, I'll give you that. I promised you that you would be taken care of whether we rocked or not. If you want an annulment I'll have my lawyer draw up the papers and deposit a hundred grand in your bank accounts. You can walk away free and clear Noni. But let me be clear. Everything I felt and said to you in Mexico was real. I want you in my life Noni. I'll fall back. You can reach out when you're ready. Call me if you need anything," he said. He walked out, leaving her sitting there, blinking away her tears.

Chapter 10

"Noni, it's been three days why don't you just call him?" Tat asked.

"I don't know him," Noni said.

"You act like you found out he was cheating on you," Maya said. "Wait, did he cheat on you? I mean you haven't said much about what happened at all?"

"I just want to sleep," she said. "Ya'll can leave now."

"You're not eating Noni. Don't make me call your Gram bitch," Tat threatened.

"Too late," Maya said. "She's on her way."

Noni sat up and threw a pillow at Maya's head. "What is wrong with you?" Noni asked. "Call her back right now and convince her not to come."

"Too late now. I'm already here."

Noni sat up and saw her 70-year old grandmother walking into the room. Her silver hair and fair skin was beautiful. Her kind eyes filled with worry. She walked right over to the hotel room bed and climbed in with her. Noni lifted her head into her grandmother's lap.

"Now tell me what's wrong," Gram said.

Tat and Maya eased out of the room, knowing that their friend was now in good hands.

"Did he hit you?" Gram asked.

"No, he didn't. He wouldn't. He's just a liar Gram. I just thought he was prince charming. He seemed so perfect. He was successful, he was saying all the right things, doing all the right things…but it was a lie," Noni said.

Her tears spilled out of her eyes effortlessly as her grandmother stroked her hair. "Don't talk in circles Noni, just tell me what happened. Not your version of the story either child. I want the truth."

"He's a drug dealer," Noni said. Her Gram was the only person she would ever tell that secret.

A silence filled the room and Noni closed her eyes, waiting for her Gram to judge.

"How did you hurt your head?" Gram asked, gathering all the facts.

"Two men ran into his house while I was there. They tried to rob him," Noni said.

"No man is perfect baby. Not one walking this earth. Do you love this man?" Gram asked.

"I don't want to," Noni whispered.

"That wasn't the question," Gram responded.

"It's crazy because before I met him I never knew I wanted him, but now that he's mine, I never want to be without him. I love him Gram, but he's a bad guy," she said.

"They all are baby. Some are drinkers, some liars, some cheaters, some schemers…all men are bad men, we just have to love the good in em'. When you find the man that's yours you take the bad with the good, because when it's good baby…it's the best thing in the world," Gram said. There was a nostalgia in her voice that made Noni wonder if she was speaking from experience.

"So you think I should go back?" Noni asked, unsure. Her heart and her head were in direct conflict. She had never been a stupid girl. She didn't let her emotions cloud her judgment and she definitely wasn't in the dream buying business. But Dom made her feel so giddy, so irrational, so stupid. She loved him, even still knowing what he had intended for her, she still had him on the brain.

"I think that the vows of marriage are serious. For better or worse, sickness and in health, til' death. That's what you said. That's the promise you made to God. You see the flesh is weak. We're human. We are all imperfect so mistakes are inevitable baby, but God. He is strong. You make the vows to him so that when your husband is weak you still have a reason to hold onto the promise you made. This is an imperfect love held together by a perfect God, Noni. So if you want to go back. Go! Don't let your pride stop you. Everything will work itself out. You made a stupid choice by marrying this man that you don't know, that don't nobody know. Didn't even give me the decency to meet him first, but it's done now. You've got to stick by your decision because those vows ain't nothing to play around with. You should have never said em' if you didn't mean em'."

"Neither should he!" Noni shot back.

"Let me ask you this. Did he lie to you before or after he put that ring on your finger?" Gram asked.

"Before," she whispered.

"And once you got back...once you were his wife he came clean?" Gram continued.

Noni nodded.

Gram shrugged. "Seems like he's trying to me. He could have kept lying to you. He could have started off on the wrong foot. Give him credit for that. Some of these niggas will look you in the eye and lie right to your face. There's some value in a man that can tell the truth."

Noni laid in her grandmother's lap until she fell asleep. It was all just too much to think about. Should she leave? Stay? Run? In her heart, she knew that she was going to forgive him eventually. She just needed time to clear her mind before going back.

When Noni walked into his office Dom's heart dropped. She was gorgeous…casual in a grey crop sweater and high waist jeans. Her eyes were red and swollen from all the sleepless nights she had suffered.

He put down his pen and looked up at her, but remained silent as she stepped inside, slowly as if she wanted to run back out the door.

"I watched the news for a week straight. I didn't see anything about the men who broke into your house," she said.

"You won't," Dom replied. "And it's our house."

"What happened to their bodies?" she asked, unsure if she really wanted to hear his response.

"They were cremated. Me and Merci got rid of the ashes and the car they drove," Dom revealed. "That's the type of shit I do. My hands are dirty, Noni. I run a business, but I run the streets too. Women like you don't love men like me."

"I didn't know I was loving a man like you," she whispered as she twiddled her fingers nervously.

Dom went into his desk drawer and pulled out a document and placed it on the oak top. "It's the annulment papers. All you got to do is sign and we can pretend this didn't happen. There's an account with a hundred grand in it waiting for you. You can just walk away."

Noni picked up the paper and held it in her hands as she looked at Dom with tears in her eyes. She ripped it in half. "I just want to be with you."

The Present

Dom remembered it like it was yesterday and he had to sniff the emotion away just to keep his composure. He was a broken soul. He had known it the day he had married Noni and he knew it today as he sat underneath his empty safe. He had chased her away with his lies. He was the reason why she had felt like a slave to her loyalty. He had made her flee. Now he had to find her and his money before it was too late.

Chapter 11

NONI

St. Tropez was like unlike any place she had ever seen. It was where the wealthy vacationed and its historic architecture mixed with its seaside appeal made Noni feel as if she was worlds away from home. Her resort sat on the edge of Port Grimaud. The ocean was so close that the smell of the water invaded every inch of the luxury hotel. She could hear the waves and she closed her eyes, exhaling deeply because it all put her in such a tranquil state. She stepped into the line, eager to check into her room. After the long trip she just wanted to shower. This trip was supposed to be a celebration. He had promised her that after five years he would get out of the streets. This year marked five. They were going to renew their vows in a small, private, ceremony on the beach and toast to the good life that Dom had built for them. He had promised her he would leave the women alone, he would leave the drugs alone… he would be the husband that she deserved. She scoffed; laughing at herself for ever thinking any of these promises would become reality. *He's the same as every other nigga, doing the same nigga shit. There's no changing Dom,* she thought.

"Welcome to St. Tropez, Miss. Can I have your confirmation?" Noni was shaken from her thoughts as she stepped up to the check-in counter and handed the clerk her passport.

"Welcome Mrs. Meyer, we have been preparing for you and Mr. Meyer's arrival for quite some time," the friendly man said. "Your other guests have arrived and I've put both parties on the top floor in adjacent penthouse suites," he informed.

Noni frowned, confused. "Other guests?" she asked. "What other guests?"

The clerk nodded behind her and she turned to find Merci standing in the lobby. He was clad in an expensive Gucci suit and loafers. His shoulder length locks were pulled back in a ponytail. On his arm was one of his revolving girlfriends because his ideology was a beautiful woman was a man's best accessory. Her mouth fell open in surprise as she turned back to the clerk.

"Here is your room key, we hope you enjoy your stay. You can leave your bags. The bellhop will deliver them to your room shortly."

Noni took a deep breath and approached Merci. She couldn't dodge him. He had already seen her. *What the hell is he doing here?* She thought.

"Surprise beautiful," he greeted as he opened his arms to embrace her. "This is Jen," he introduced. Noni reluctantly held out her hand for the girl.

"Nice to meet you," she said. "Noni." She cocked her head to the side and frowned as she turned to Merci. "Can I talk to you for a second?" she asked.

Merci stepped off to the side with her, hands in his pocket, poised as he towered over her. He looked into her face and when he saw the look in her eyes he immediately recognized something was wrong. "Where is Dom?"

Even the mention of his name caused her to tear up. "I'm

leaving him," she whispered as she looked at her feet and then back up at him. "I came here without him. I need some space. Imagine my surprise running into you."

Merci sighed as he squared his shoulders. "I haven't spoken to Dom in a few months. Right after he asked me about coming out here for this trip. We've both been busy, working and making sure this last run went smoothly. He never mentioned y'all were having problems. This was supposed to be a good time. We're getting out of the game. He said y'all was renewing y'all vows and shit. He wanted me here as a surprise. I had no idea shit between you two had gone left. I'm sorry Noni," he said sincerely.

"We've been having problems for a while now. It's nothing new. I don't want him coming here to bring me home so do me a favor and don't tell him I'm here," she said. She knew that she was asking a lot. Merci wasn't her friend. He was Dom's. His loyalty wasn't to her. "Please?"

"Yeah, okay," Merci stated.

Noni looked tired...broken and his heart went out to her. He reached down to hug her. "You good out here by yourself? You want to eat? We're headed to the bistro. You don't have to be out here alone, ma," Merci said.

"I'm fine. I'm just going to head up. No point in my drama ruining your trip too. You two have fun," she said as she turned toward the elevator bank. "It was nice meeting you," she called to his date.

Noni pressed the call button for the elevator. She could feel his eyes on her as she stepped inside. She was grateful when the doors closed. She didn't want him to see the sadness that was eating her alive. She didn't want to face anyone. At this moment all she needed was a bottle of wine and a plush bed so she could drink her worries away.

LOVE BURN

'It took two bottles of Merlot to get Noni to sign her name on the dotted line. Dom had already signed them. Her scribe made it official. They were divorced. Once his attorney got the paperwork, it would be public record and the past five years of her life would all be for nothing. She sealed the papers up in the envelope and leaned it against the empty wine bottle. She planted her face in her hands as tears escaped her. She had thought the money would take the sting of it all away, but it didn't. Instead of being a broke, divorced bitch. She was just a rich, divorced bitch. The size of the pill she had to swallow was still the same. What would she do? Who would she be? After marrying Dom, she had given up her dreams to play Susie Homemaker. He wanted a baby, a family, a home. He wanted dinner waiting for him when he arrived, a clean house, and an eager wife. She had given him these things…well she had tried. The one thing she hadn't been able to produce was a child. They had tried, every night for two years before giving up. The problem hadn't been getting pregnant, but staying pregnant. She had miscarried four times and every time she sat over the toilet with life bleeding out of her, their marriage suffered a little more. It was then that her self-esteem had taken a hit. What kind of woman couldn't give her husband offspring? She became bitter and he became distant, soon other women filled his time and she was left preparing dinner for one. She was drowning in grief and red wine. Her head spun and nausea threatened her. "Room service," she whispered, remembering she hadn't eaten in over 24 hours.

'KNOCK! KNOCK!

'Noni tightened the white waffle robe and then rushed to the door.

"Oh!" she exclaimed in surprise. "Merci, what are you…I wasn't expecting…" she was visibly flustered as she finally managed. "What do you want?"

"I thought you would need some food," he said as he held up a takeout box and a bottle of wine. "Apparently you already discovered the mini-bar," he said with a sympathetic smile.

'She turned and walked into the suite as he followed her inside. "Thank you," she said as she sat down on the couch, folding her feet beneath her.

'Merci looked at her disheveled appearance and at the empty bottles of wine strewn about.

"Where's your friend?" Noni asked as she uncorked bottle number three.

"I sent her home," Merci replied as he walked up on her and took the bottle from her hands. "Looks like you've had enough Noni," he said. He walked over to the mini bar and pulled a bottled water out. He handed it to her along with her food. "Eat, you'll thank me later."

"I thank you now," she said with a smirk. "I was just about to call room service before you came." She dug into the food and savored it as she closed her eyes and leaned her head back in appreciation. "Hmm, this is amazing."

"Came from the most expensive restaurant in town," he said. "I figured you've been cooped up in here all day. You going to spend your entire vacation in this room?" he asked.

"Sometimes when there's nothing left to do, all you can do is cry it out your system," she said.

"Let me ask you this. You think he's crying right now?" Merci asked.

'Noni stopped eating and thought long and hard before she

LOVE BURN

replied, "I think he's doing exactly what he's been doing...him."

'Merci's brow raised as he said, "So don't you think you should be doing you?"

'Noni continued eating. "Why are you here? You're his friend. I thought for sure you would have called him by now," she said.

"'I respect your wishes and yeah that's my man, but when a nigga can't see what's right in front of him it's not my job to point it out. I've known Dom for a long time and I know that he won't miss you until you're no longer his," Merci said. He headed for the door. "I've always thought you were out of his league, ma. Dom and I, we're street dudes. Yeah we clean up nice and we're transitioning to the legit life, but at heart we'll always be from the bottom. We're new money, ma."

"'I'm from where you're from," she said, confused. "I didn't come up with a silver spoon in my mouth. I worked hard to..."

"'To be what? A wife?" Merci asked. "You let Dom downgrade you. He killed your dreams. He made you his trophy wife, but women like you are meant to do more than look good on somebody's arm. I thought you would change Dom, but sadly, you let him change you."

"'I just wanted to be what he liked," she said with the hint of tears in her eyes. She followed him to the door.

"'Look at you Noni...when I first met you your eyes were full of life. They sparkled when you smiled. Being around you was like taking a deep breath of fresh air, ma. Now all I see are your insecurities," Merci said.

'He stepped out into hallway. "Why did you send your friend home?" she asked as she rested her head against the doorframe.

"'Once you told me what was up, our presence didn't seem appropriate. I'm flying out in the morning. I only stayed behind to make sure you were straight before I left," Merci explained.

"'Thanks Merci," she said.

"Anytime," he replied. "I hope you find the old you over here, Noni."

"Me too," she whispered as she stepped back inside. "Goodnight."

'He nodded and she closed the door.

'She put her back against the door as his words swirled in her head. He was right. She had lost so many pieces of herself during her marriage. Now that it was time to rebuild she had no clue where to start. Merci had always been so easy to talk to. He was genuine and kind. He had the humility of a pauper and he had always shown her so much love. He had a reputation for violence. Apparently, he had made examples out of many whom had tried to test him, but she never saw that side of him. He had always been nothing, but supportive of her and although she knew that it was a bit much to ask, she could really use his support now. She didn't want to be halfway around the world by herself. She needed someone and since Merci probably already knew all of the bullshit that Dom had taken her through she didn't have to be embarrassed about it with him. She had hid her problems behind her smile for so long, that she had built up a false reality for others. Everyone thought Dom was the perfect man. With Merci she could be real. She snatched open the door and stepped into the hall.

"Merci," she called after him as he stood thumbing through his phone, waiting for the elevator. He looked up at her.

"Can you stay?" she asked. "In St. Tropez I mean...with me?"

'Merci hesitated and she immediately knew that her question was out of line. She recanted instantly. "You know what? I'm sorry. This is inappropriate. You're his friend. I don't know what I was thinking..."

'She walked back toward her room.

'Merci knew he should say no. Dom was his friend. They had

come up from the sandbox together. He couldn't side with Noni, even if he thought his friend was wrong. *This nigga carrying her like she's just any other chick. This is his wife,* he thought, sympathizing with Noni. *It ain't yo' job to play captain save-a-hoe. That's his business,* he thought. Merci looked at her with apologetic eyes and said, "Take care of yourself Noni."

'She nodded and then retreated to her room, mortified.

'

Chapter 12

MERCI

Behind the privacy of the closed elevator doors, Merci leaned his head back against the wall, conflicted. He didn't mind Noni's company, he wanted to be her shoulder to cry on, but it was against every code he had ever learned. Wasn't nothing G about playing sucker to his best friend's wife. He had always kept a strict line in the sand with Noni that he didn't cross. Their chemistry was too organic and Merci had recognized that upon their first meeting. He had to come correct. He valued his friendship with Dom too much to ever cross those lines, but he had known years ago that Dom would never treat Noni the way she deserved to be treated. He should have pulled Dom's coat tail then. He had known how Dom's actions would tear down such a jewel of a woman, but he hadn't and now they all were living with the consequences of his silence.

The Past

'"Everyone quiet down. You don't want Dom to hear the party before he even walks in," Noni said. She checked her Rolex watch. It was a quarter to seven. He would be there any minute.

'"Merci!" she called, summoning him from across the room. "Have you heard from Dom today?" she asked. "He doesn't suspect anything does he?"

'He could see that she was eager…nervous about the surprise birthday party. She had planned it for months. She had made Merci drive back and forth from Ohio to Detroit every weekend until every detail was attended to. He laughed at her anxiety.

'"Relax ma," Merci said. "The hard part is done. You put all of this together for him. Rented out an entire yacht without him knowing. You look beautiful; all of his people are here. Now all you have to do is wait for him to show up." He stopped a waiter that was passing by and grabbed two flutes of champagne. He extended one to her. "Have a drink. You earned it."

'She took a sip. "Thank you for being such a great friend. Without you, I would have gone crazy," she said. She checked her watch again. "Where the hell is he? The boat is supposed to leave at 7:15," she said.

'"Noni, you're in charge. You paying the captain. He'll leave when you say it's time to leave," Merci said.

'She nodded and then scurried off to busy herself with more stuff that didn't need to be done. He smirked as he shook his head and pulled out his phone. He didn't say anything but Dom was unusually late. He dialed his number.

'"What up bro?" Dom answered on the first ring.

'"Happy G day my nigga," Merci said. "What you got up for the night?" he asked, pretending as if he didn't already know.

"'Daddy, hang up the phone. You could be putting those lips to better use."

'Merci's eyebrows rose as he said, "Who is that?"

"'Nobody special, just a little birthday entertainment," Dom said with a chuckle. "Oh shit," he groaned. "Mami know what to do with her mouth."

'Merci's temperature rose as he looked at Noni working the crowd across the room. "You fooling Dom. Don't you think you getting a little reckless?" he asked. "It's your birthday nigga. You don't think your *wife* will wonder where you are?"

"'Gone with all that Merci, you fucking up a nigga vibe," Dom said. "Let me get into this and I'll hit you back." Merci heard the girl giggling in the background before Dom ended the call.

"'This stupid mu'fucka," he grumbled as he watched Noni. Her beauty radiated across the room. He anticipated the disappointment to come because he knew that there was no way Dom was going to drop what he was doing to come attend to Noni. Merci couldn't tell her. He could only hope that Dom came to his senses and got there soon. Knowing him he wouldn't even wash the next woman's pussy off himself before getting in bed with Noni. Dom had always been a ladies man. Merci didn't expect a platinum band to change his antics, but as he stood watching more and more time go by, he couldn't help but feel sorry for an unsuspecting Noni.

'With every half an hour that passed, Noni's face showed more and more heart break. Finally, the guests began to leave. It was clear that Dom wasn't showing and she apologized on his behalf, feeling embarrassed as everyone stared at her sympathetically.

'Merci walked up on Noni. "I'm sorry for wasting your time Merci," she said, vision blurry from her watering eyes. One trailed down her cheek and Merci wiped it away with his thumb.

"Don't cry," he said. "I'm sure he just got caught up," Merci said, covering for Dom.

"Yeah," she scoffed. "Is he cheating on me Merci?" she asked, cutting straight to the chase.

"No, ma," Merci replied. "He would be a fool."

She shook her head, distressed. "I just need to go home. I'm so pissed I can't even think straight," she said.

Everyone on the boat had left except for the captain and the crew. The event coordinator walked up to them. "Mrs. Meyer, if your party isn't happening, I'd like to let the staff go home," the woman said.

"Who said the party wasn't happening?" Merci said, stepping in. "Tell the captain we're ready to sail." He snapped his fingers at the live band that had stopped playing. They came to life as he grabbed Noni's hand.

"What are you doing?" she asked.

"You paid for a dinner on the river, you're going to have dinner on the river," Merci said. He pulled her onto the dance floor and she placed the side of her face onto his chest as the swayed back and forth to the sounds of band's rendition of 'Nothing Even Matters.'

As soon as he pulled her close it was like they clicked into place. She fit perfectly in his arms like two long lost pieces of the same puzzle. The tension in her shoulders eased as they danced.

They were silent, but it was a comfortable solace that filled the room. It was like they were in their own little world. When the song ended and the band picked up the tempo the two of them still swayed slowly, lost in a trance that felt so right in the moment. It took a few seconds for them to pull away from each other.

"Want to go for a walk?" he asked.

She cleared her throat. "Yeah, I could use some fresh air. The deck is right out here," she said. She kicked off her five inch heels and walked barefoot as she took his arm, leading the way.

They leaned against the railing and looked up at the luminous night sky as the sound of the boat breaking through the stillness of the water provided the sound track.

"Thank you for not leaving," she said. "After being stood up, it feels good to not be alone. I find myself feeling lonely a lot nowadays. I guess the honeymoon's over," she joked, completely embarrassed.

"He's wrong for the way he's carrying you Noni," Merci said. "Any man would be lucky to have you."

"If that's true than why am I going through this? Why does he not come home at night? Why do I find bitches numbers in his phone? Smell perfume that I don't wear on his clothes?" she asked, tearing up.

"I can't answer that," Merci said. She shook her head in disgrace as she turned to head back inside.

"I'm sorry. I'm a mess. Excuse me," she stepped away from him but he grabbed her arm, pulling her back toward him…into him. Their lips met and he kissed her so passionately that it took her breath away. She melted into his arms as his hands cupped her face. She moaned it felt so good. His kisses were breathing life into her.

"No," he said, stepping back. "We can't do this. I'm out of line." His voice was stern but still she stepped back into him, kissing him.

"This is wrong Noni," he whispered as he pressed his forehead against hers, but she didn't reply with words. Instead, she kissed him.

"Why can't he be more like you," she whispered. "Why can't he see me the way that you see me?"

Merci stopped and wiped her gloss off his lips. "That's not the problem, ma. The problem is that you don't even see you, the way I see you. If you did, you wouldn't even tolerate a nigga treating you the way he do," Merci said. She lowered her head, ashamed of the type of woman she had become. Before Dom, she was independent and she didn't take any shit from anybody. Since marrying him she had become a doormat that he walked all over.

She leaned over the rail, planting her face in her hands as she sobbed. Her tears were the hardest thing to watch. He pulled her close once again and lifted her chin. "Smile," he said.

And just like that, simply because he had asked, she did. "This is how it felt when I first met Dom. Just like this," she whispered. "How is it that you're making me feel like this?"

"You're supposed to give the energy that you receive from a person, Noni. I'm just giving you what you give me. It's called reciprocity. If a nigga give you shade, you give shade. If he shows you love, you show love. Stop giving so much if you're not getting anything back. You deserve better."

The Present

Merci remembered that night like it was yesterday. It had played in his mind many times over the past few years. It was after that evening that Merci began to pull away from Dom. Although they still did business, their friendship had changed all because of the feelings he had felt that night on the boat. He hadn't wanted to ever get so close to Noni again and he definitely couldn't bear witness to her repeated heartbreaks. If Dom was any other nigga, Merci would have just cuffed his girl, but he couldn't. This situation was different and Noni was off limits. He threw his belongings into his luggage. He needed to be on the first flight back to the states because if he stuck around too long he would forget where his loyalties lied and go after what he wanted.

Chapter 13

TAT

At first it started as a game. An innocent flirtation back and forth between her and Dom that had gone too far. Now she was so deep in that she didn't want out. Her love for Dom had turned her loyalty to Noni into jealousy. She hated her and as she called Dom's number for the fifth consecutive time, panic filled her. *He's probably laid up with that bitch right now,* she thought, inciting herself up to the point where all she felt was rage. She hated Noni for having what she knew Dom would never give her…his last name. She had the title. She was his Mrs. and Tatiana despised her for that. When she gave Dom a baby she thought it would be enough to sway him away from Noni. *She can't do for him what I can do for him,* she thought as she ended the call in frustration. *I gave him a son. I gave him his seed. He will eventually see that our family is more important than his marriage.* For nine months she had waited for the day their son made his arrival. She was sure that Dom would leave Noni alone for good after he saw Thomas. To her dismay, he hadn't and even worse he didn't even allow her to give their baby his last name. Everything seemed to be about Noni. They tip toed around each other, pretending that their affair didn't exist when all Tat really wanted was for him to claim her. "Be patient," he had told her. "I have to wait until the right time." He had said. Tat had been patient long enough. She was tired of playing this game. She was driving herself crazy trying to one-up Noni at every turn. She wanted to cook better, dress better, keep her body up better, fuck him better, suck him better...just be better. She was in competition with a woman that didn't even know about the game being played. It was mentally exhausting.

'Tat knew that all she had to do was spill the beans to Noni. If she told her about her affair with Dom, Noni would leave him. The things that Tat had to say would ruin their marriage, but she feared that Dom would never forgive her if she spoke out. "I just have to be patient. I have to let him leave her on his own," she whispered.

'The sound of her son crying caused her to close her eyes in frustration. "All this fucking crying. All you do is cry, cry, cry. What the fuck is wrong with you now?" she screamed as she went into the bathroom where she had left him, soaking in a tub full of bubbles. Baby Thomas was so much work. Having him, without having Dom there, was the world's worst torture. She was never the type to even want children, but when she had gotten pregnant with Thomas all she saw was a means to an end. A baby was a way for her to win in her silent battle against Noni. She never thought of how hard it would be to be a mother, she only thought of how rewarding it would feel to be Dom's main girl.

'Tat grabbed a towel and pulled her toddler out of the water and dried him off. Every time she looked at him she felt resentment. Yes, she loved her child but her plan wasn't unfolding in the way that she had expected. The everyday grind of motherhood overwhelmed her. There was always something to do. A diaper to change...a meal to make...a cry to soothe and where the hell was Dom? She didn't realize that this was the bed she had made. Laying up with a married man was always disastrous. Now that the excitement of their affair had passed, she was forced to lie in it. 'Tat stood to her feet, wet baby dangling off her hip and picked up her phone. With one hand she sent a text to Dom.

You've got ten minutes to call me back before I call Noni and tell her everything.

'She was sick and tired of Dom playing her to the left. She knew that some women forgave infidelity. Tat and Noni had been friends long enough to know that Noni would give her marriage another chance while flushing their friendship away. Noni would probably even forgive Dom for Thomas. After all, they had set her up to the point where Noni adored the little boy. She had no idea that she cared for a child that her husband had fathered outside of their union. So yes, Tat knew that Noni would be pissed and eventually get over that as well. The one thing that Noni wouldn't look past was the truth, however. As she dressed Baby Thomas tears welled in Tat's eyes. *Her ass won't be so quick to forgive him once she finds out I'm HIV positive,* Tat thought. Tat placed her son in front of the television and turned on some cartoons. She hated for him to see her cry.

'She rushed to her room. She hated to even think about it. Tat knew it was her karma. She hadn't even told Dom yet, partly because she wanted to give it to him; partly because she was too afraid and embarrassed to have the conversation. Tat didn't even know where she had contracted it. She very well could have gotten it from Dom, but seeing as how Noni wasn't sick she doubted it. She knew that once it was revealed he would hate her. That was something that you couldn't take back. No amount of apologies would make up for ruining his life, but after his anger passed she was sure he wouldn't leave her. Where would he go? He wouldn't be selfish enough to stay with Noni. Tat knew she would be his only option and she would take Dom however she could get him, sick and all. She wasn't crazy. Just desperate...desperate for the man she loved to love her back by any means necessary. She sat down on her bedroom floor and opened her nightstand drawer. Prescriptions filled it. She took twenty different pills every day just to keep the disease from getting worse. She had to worry about taking anti-retroviral meds, keeping her t-cell count up, and not compromising her immune system. It was all just too much. On a good day she felt normal. Her medications kept her weight up so she looked normal. Everything was under control, but then there were the bad days. Sometimes she would be so sick that she couldn't pull herself out of bed. Her weak legs couldn't even carry her to the bathroom to throw up when she had to. It was up and down. A constant rollercoaster that derived from the war going on inside of her body. This battle wasn't even the worst part. It was the mental part of it that defeated her. The fact that she was living with HIV. She was so embarrassed and so afraid that some days ending it all felt like the only reasonable thing to do. It was so much more than she had asked for. Sleeping around, hopping from man to man, had been fun. She had done the most in her younger years in the quest to hook a man with money and when she had gotten pregnant by Dom she knew she had hit the jackpot, but now she was paying the ultimate cost. She grabbed the bottle of water off the nightstand and closed her eyes as she began to pop the pills in her mouth. One by one she swallowed them all. She closed her eyes as she thought back to the day her world came to a standstill...the day she first found out.

The Past

"Housekeeping!" the hotel maid called through the door waking Tat and Dom from their liquor induced sleep.

"Hmm," Tat groaned, completely hung over as the sun shined through the hotel's drapes. "What time is it?" she asked as she rolled over to grab her phone.

"Fuck!" Dom said as jumped out of the bed.

"Housekeeping!" the maid called again.

"We're good!" Dom shouted back as he began putting on his clothes in a frenzy. "Fuck! Why did you let me fall asleep?"

"Because this is where you're supposed to be anyway," Tat said with an attitude as she sat up in bed. Her head spun and she immediately let her body fall back against the plush sheets. She felt like crap. Her stomach churned as nausea tickled the back of her throat.

"Damn it!" He was flustered, she could tell but she didn't care. He checked his phone. "Noni blew me up last night," he said.

"Somebody's got some explaining to do," Tat teased as she rolled over onto her stomach and crossed her feet at the ankles. "You're already in trouble. Why don't you just come back to bed and show up later. You might as well let me send you off right. You ain't doing nothing but rushing home to an argument," she said.

"I've got to go," Dom said as he grabbed his wallet and his car keys off the dresser.

"How am I supposed to get home?" she asked as she sat up seriously. The pounding of her head caused her to wince as she swept her messy hair out of her face.

Dom opened his wallet and pulled out a few hundred dollars and tossed them in her direction. They fluttered in the air before finally landing at the foot of the bed.

It was in moments like these that she felt like shit. She didn't mean anything to him. There was no anticipatory kiss at the end of their dates, no promises to call later, no walking her safely to her door.

"Call a cab or something," Dom said.

"Oh so now that you've fucked you're good on me?" she asked with an attitude, ready for a confrontation with him. He gave her no kick it however. At the moment all he could think about was getting home to his wife.

"I don't have time for this." He was out the door without even a goodbye.

"Happy birthday to you too muthafucka!" Tat shouted as the hotel door closed shut behind him.

Tat had known about the huge celebration that Noni had planned. She had been invited, but she couldn't stand to be in a room with the two of them. Seeing Noni and Dom standing arm in arm, watching him fawn all over her, seeing the smile on Noni's face. It would have made her sick, so instead she foiled the evening. She had shown up to the funeral home just as Dom was getting off of work and offered to take him out for one birthday drink. One drink, led to two, which led to three, which led to her head in his lap as they drove to the nearest hotel. She stood up and the uncontrollable urge to throw up overwhelmed her. She had been waking up for weeks feeling sick and depleted of all energy. She rushed to the bathroom but barely made it before her stomach erupted. She was dizzy and she clung to the porcelain toilet for dear life. Suddenly, another urge hit her and she stood to her feet. Her bowels felt like they were boiling and she had no control over herself as she released them. Her legs were too weak to climb up off the floor and she felt disgusted with herself. It was like suddenly she felt like her body was breaking down, as if it were betraying her for betraying it for so long. *What the hell is wrong with my stomach?* She thought. She had never been this sick. This wasn't a normal hangover. This shit was crucial. It was a good thing that Dom had left because she wouldn't have wanted him to see her this way.

"Housekeeping!" the same maid called out before actually entering the room. Tat was sitting with her head bowed as she felt her stomach turn again.

"Get out!" Tat screamed as she picked up the small trash can and threw it toward the maid who was peeking inside.

"Do you need help miss?" the woman asked. A look of concern mixed with disgust was on the maid's face and Tat's face flushed in pure shame. She was horrified. "I'll get help," the woman said, flustered.

Tat was hot and sweating as the room spun again. The last thing she remembered was thinking, *why is it so hot in here?*

She woke up in the emergency room. Her clothes had been disposed of and an IV ran through her left arm. She was so mortified that she just wanted to snatch that shit out and go home but before she could even contemplate the thought, two women walked into the room. Both wore white coats so she knew they were doctors. A blonde and a black woman, both middle aged, wearing very serious expressions on their faces.

"Tatiana Gray, how are you feeling?" the black doctor asked.

"Better. So much better. I'm sorry. I don't know what happened. I just felt sick and I..."

"Well a number of things contributed to you feeling ill. I'm Dr. Scott. This is our grief counselor Dr. Taylor," she introduced.

"Grief counselor?" Tat asked as she sat up in her bed. "What's... happening right now?" she looked back and forth between the two women, waiting for answers.

"There are quite a few things going on with you right now," Dr. Scott said.

"For one you're 16 weeks pregnant."

LOVE BURN

The news hit Tat so hard that she stopped breathing as her mouth fell open.

"Say what now?" she said. She didn't know how this happened. She and Dom wore condoms.

"Do you use condoms?" Dr. Scott asked.

Tat's mind was all over the place as she tried to think back. She couldn't believe what she was hearing. "Pregnant?" she whispered. Her thoughts shot to Dom. A smirk crossed her face. *He's been trying to get Noni to give him a baby forever. Once he finds out, he's mine. He's finally going to leave her,* she thought.

"Ms. Gray?" Dr. Scott said, interrupting her reverie. "Condoms, do you use them?"

"Most of the time," she replied, wondering how the hell she was carrying a child inside of her. Dom was always so careful. *Except that one time,* she thought. She could pinpoint exactly the date that she got pregnant. They were both too wrapped up in lust and he had sexed her unprotected on his desk at the funeral home.

"Have you noticed any changes in your body? Any bad colds, any rashes?" Dr. Scott asked.

'Tat frowned. Their questions were out of left field. "Umm yeah. I mean I caught a few colds. A few sore throats, why..." she began to stammer. "What does this have to do with me being pregnant?" She looked at the white woman. "And why is a grief counselor here?"

"Well Ms. Gray we drew blood to confirm the pregnancy and we discovered that you are HIV positive, " Dr. Scott said. Tat went deaf instantly, as a burning feeling filled her chest. She could see their lips moving, but she heard nothing. It was like things began moving in slow motion.

"It's wrong, it's wrong, it's wrong," she kept whispering. Over and over she told herself.

"'There are programs...support groups...'"

"'It's wrong!' she shouted.

"'It isn't wrong,' Dr. Taylor said, finally speaking up. Tat balled her fists as a flood of regret filled her eyes. She beat her fists against her thighs. "So stupid," she scolded. "It has to be wrong," she sobbed. She was inconsolable.

"'There are measures you can take to ensure that the chances of your child contracting the disease are minimal," Dr. Taylor said. They were so clinical in their delivery, as if they hadn't just told her that her life was over. She began to pull at the IV, snatching it out as she swung her legs over the side of the bed.

"'What are you doing?' Dr. Scott asked.

"'I'm going home! I don't know what kind of bullshit hospital this is, but I don't have it. I don't have that!" she screamed. Dr. Scott hustled over to the bed and pressed the call button, summoning nurses to the room. "I need a sedative, now!" she said as soon as one entered the room. Tat fought them, tooth and nail, as she tried to run away from her truth. If it hadn't been for the needle the doctor stuck in her arm she would have bulldozed right pass them. Instead, her body went limp as she fell into the doctor's arms, completely out of it.

"'Let's get her up to psych. It'll take her a couple days to accept this. We'll place her on a 72 hour suicide hold," Dr. Taylor said.

'The nurses placed her on a gurney and tied down her hands as they wheeled her away.

The Present

Tat swiped the tears from her eyes as she finished stuffing her prescriptions down her throat. It was a daily routine that she would never get used to. She wished she could go back and do things differently, but that was the one thing about life...there was no reliving it. She just had to play with the cards she had been dealt and one thing was for certain she didn't plan to be in the game alone. She would get Dom, one way or another.

Chapter 14

NONI

Noni lay drowning in the luxurious white covers as she stared at the ceiling. The pit in her stomach was still there and she knew that it wouldn't go anywhere for a while. She missed her husband or rather her ex-husband and she couldn't help it. No matter how bad he was, he had been hers. Now she had no one and it was the loneliest feeling in the world. She pulled herself out of the bed and forced herself to shower. She dressed simply in fitted blue jeans and a matching denim shirt, accessorizing with a couture hat and nude heels. She didn't bother with make-up. She simply covered her eyes with oversized sunglasses. She grabbed her cross body purse and then went to grab her phone. She thought about calling him. It felt so strange to not check in with him. She had been accountable to him for so long that true freedom felt abnormal. She dialed his number, her hand shaking with every digit that she touched but before she could press the green call button there was a knock at her door. She tossed the phone on the bed and then went to answer it.

"You stayed," she said, surprised to see Merci's face.

"You asked me to," he replied. "When have you ever known me to tell you no?"

She smiled and it had been so long since she had genuinely done it that the grin felt foreign on her face.

"You eat?" Merci asked.

She shook her head.

"Come on," he replied as he extended his hand. She held up a finger, gesturing for him to wait. She went back in to grab her room key and cross body. She reached for her phone and then paused. *He doesn't deserve to know where you are,* she thought. Noni took a deep breath, grabbed the envelope that held her divorce documents and then exited her room. She walked into the hallway and grabbed Merci's hand. Even the simple way he intertwined his fingers with hers made her feel better.

"Thank you for staying," she said as they stepped into the elevator.

"You're welcome," he replied.

'When they stepped off the elevator, Noni headed towards the hotel restaurant. Merci stopped walking.

"'You're hungry right?" she asked as she looked at him in confusion.

"'Yes, but we didn't come half way around the world to stay on the resort. We're eating authentic French food, taking in French views," he said as he nodded for her to come back to him. "Trust me."

'She smiled and then said, "Okay, hold on. I just need to do one thing." She went to the concierge desk and handed him the divorce envelope. "Can you mail these for me?"

"Yes ma'am, right away," he replied.

"Thank you," she said sweetly. She hurried back to Merci and squinted her eyes at him curiously. "Why do I feel like you're about to have me ripping and running all over St. Tropez in my Loubs?" she asked.

'He winked and then led her out of the front door where a driver waited for them. Merci escorted her to the car. "Where are we going?"

"'Sightseeing," he said. "Now get your difficult ass in the car and stop asking so many questions."

'She laughed and got inside as he made his way to the other door. They drove for an hour and Noni didn't say a word. She just looked out the window at the beautiful coastline. It wasn't until they pulled up to a tall, historic looking structure did she speak.

"'What is this place?" she asked.

"'It's the Portalet Tower. It was used back in the day to defend the city," Merci said as he stepped out of the car. Noni exited and immediately stumbled on the un-leveled pavement.

"'It's amazing. The view from the top must be gorgeous," she said.

"'Let's find out," he said.

"'I'm going to break my neck trying to climb up there," she said as she pursed her lips.

"'Hop on my back," Merci said.

"'Boy I will break your back!" she said as she laughed from the gut. "I'm twenty pounds heavier than that skinny girl you met five years ago."

"'There's nothing wrong with your weight ma, chill out," he replied. "It's either your feet or my back. The name of the game is self-preservation." He gave her a charming smile and Noni rolled her eyes as she hopped on his back.

"'Oh shit!" Merci said as he pretended to break down. She quickly hopped off and hit him playfully.

"'See! You got jokes! Nope, I'm good. I ain't going," she said, laughing.

"'I'm just bullshitting with you," he said, playfully. "Come on." She hopped back on and he started up the path to the top.

'He carried her as if she weighed nothing, effortlessly. "Why are we the only people here?"

"'I paid to have it shut down for the day," he said. "Ticket sales are limited every day to preserve this thing. They don't want too many tourists here at once. So I purchased every ticket for today," he explained.

'Her arms were wrapped around his neck and her mouth near his ear. She didn't say anything, simply because she didn't know what to say. By the time they reached the top he was covered in sweat and winded.

"I'm sorry," she said with a laugh as he peeled out of a layer of his clothing, leaving him in a fitted, V-neck t-shirt and jeans. She hopped off his back as she looked at the picnic that had been set up at the very top. It overlooked the dark blue hues of the rolling ocean.

"It's all good ma," he said with a wink.

"You really didn't have to do all of this Merci. You being here is enough," she said.

"That's your problem," Merci said. "If you accept the bare minimum from a nigga then that's what he'll always give you. Come on.. have a seat."

He floored her into speechlessness as she followed him to the blanket that had been carefully placed on the ground. It was beautifully arranged with wine glasses, a big wooden basket filled with fruits, cheeses, fresh bread, and smoked meats. It was simple, but so very thoughtful and she smiled as he poured her a glass of wine. Being around Merci was so easy, it always felt so good, which is why she had avoided him for years. After they had shared one kiss years ago, she always made it a point to be absent whenever he was present. She had liked it a little too much. It had felt a little bit too good and she was always the type to avoid trouble. But here today, she was so grateful for his friendship. He made her feel good about herself, as if she was worthy of love. Merci looked at her like she was a rare jewel. He was handsome as hell, rich, and a little cocky. She had seen him change women with the days of the week. She was no stranger to his womanizing ways, but with her, he was exclusive and in tune with her needs. He was the type that would make exceptions for her, canceled plans for her, and who made her feel like she was the only girl in his world and they weren't even in a relationship. He did all this through their friendship. She could only imagine how special he treated his woman.

"I signed my divorce papers," she said as she sipped from the glass.

"I'm sorry," Merci replied, sincerely.

"Yeah, I don't know if I am anymore," she said as she diverted her gaze toward the water. "I'm just all out of fight. I've fought for our marriage from day one. Love shouldn't be this hard. It should feel effortless, you know? Easy like Sunday morning, not hard as fuck like a miserable ass Monday." She chuckled, but she was serious. Lately, being with Dom had been like mixing oil and water. All of the things he had promised...the type of love he said he wanted that day on the beach years ago...he had gone back on all of it. His word was just that...words. They meant nothing to Noni anymore. "I almost called him this morning. I'm so used to having this other half...this partner to talk to daily. It feels weird. Like I don't even know how to be me without him anymore."

"You'll learn that there is beauty in your solitude, ma. Just because he was around you every day doesn't mean he was ever truly there for you. There's a difference in a nigga that keeps you around because he loves you and one that wants to hold onto you so that another man can't have you," Merci said. "A lot of times with men we get a beautiful woman and we get used to her. We deal with the PMS, we see the attitude, the everyday process of it all, and we start taking it for granted. It's not intentional, but it happens. It becomes a problem when it turns into neglect and disrespect though, ma. Only you know when you've had enough."

"'I had enough a long time ago," she admitted. "I was just too afraid to leave."

"'Afraid of what?" Merci asked.

"'Myself I guess," she replied unsurely. "Afraid of going back to being lonely."

"'Are you lonely now?" he asked.

"'No," she replied with a meek smile. "In this moment, I'm content but you can't stay by my side forever. You being here is the only thing keeping me together. I know I'm asking a lot of you. You're his friend. You really shouldn't even be on my side."

"'I'm here because it's where I want to be, ma. It's no secret that you and I have had moments in the past that we shouldn't have, Noni. I've kept my distance from you for a long time because of the shit I feel whenever I'm around you. Your face..." he paused, not knowing if he should even open the can of worms that they had buried.

"'What?" she pushed.

"'You just do something to me, ma. When I'm around you I feel something. When I see you with Dom it makes me sick to my stomach. He's my nigga and I can't stand to see him with you. What type of hater shit is that? I'm not built with that disloyalty shit in me. I don't move like that, but when it comes to you I can't be happy for him. Especially not when he's not doing what he should do. When I see tears in your eyes because of him... I don't know I'm probably not making sense. You just do something to me Noni and I'm not proud of that," Merci admitted.

'She lowered her head, flattered, as her heart raced. "You make perfect sense," she replied. "I wish that I could just be yours."

"'I wish a lot of things ma," Merci replied. The wine had lowered their inhibitions. Things that they wouldn't normally say to one another were flowing from their lips. The truth was surfacing...a truth that scared them both because it was too wrong to even be considered.

"'What do you wish?" she asked.

'He stood and walked over to the edge of the tower. His brows furrowed as he overlooked the water. The ocean was so dark, so deep...like the feelings he had inside of him. He struggled in this moment...in every moment he spent around Noni. She was his best friend's wife and he had a thing for her that he hadn't been able to shake, despite his best efforts.

'Noni set down her wine glass and stood to her feet, as she joined him at the edge of the tower. "What do you wish Merci?" she asked.

'She was directly in his face, standing so close to him that there was no space in between.

"'I'll tell you a wish and then you tell me yours," she said. "Right now I wish that you could kiss me."

"'I can't," he whispered, as he closed his eyes, as she stood on her tip-toes to lean her forehead against his.

"I wish you weren't his," Merci said, opening his eyes and staring directly into hers.

"I wish I had met you first," she replied.

"I wish you knew what you deserved," Merci said.

Her heart was racing so fast that she could barely breathe. His lips were so close to hers.

"I wish you would just kiss me," she said.

"I can't," he resisted.

"I wish I could do more than that. I want to kiss you everywhere, ma. Your lips, your neck, your breasts, your clit, your toes. I wish I could hear you call my name. I wish I knew how you felt, wrapped around me…how warm and wet it can get?" he whispered seductively.

Noni's eyelids fluttered in ecstasy as she soaked her panties. Merci was bringing her to mental orgasms as she felt an electric shock vibrate between her legs. If his words alone could bring her to this point she wondered what he could do if those words ever turned to actions. She shuddered from the thought alone. Noni hated that she was so loyal to Dom. Even when he treated her like shit, stayed out for nights on end, had bitches texting his phone…still she remained true. She was a slave to that loyalty and right here…at this exact moment in space and time, she wished her character wasn't so true. "I wish you could love me," Noni said back.

"You don't have to wish that ma, I've loved you for years," he replied, being completely honest with her for the first time ever. Merci had always kept his feelings in check for Noni out of respect. It was a shame that the universe had brought her to him in the form of the forbidden. Shit felt like a cruel joke that he could be so close to knowing real love, but not be able to indulge in it. He had never felt the way he felt towards Noni.

'The chemistry between them was so real that it intensified everything around them. The sun seemed brighter, the smell of the sea bolder, the sound of the winder sharper. God, she wanted this man. Have mercy on Merci because he craved this woman. It was more than lust or at least the intoxication of the wine was making it feel as such as they both silently talked, urging themselves not to let this thing go too far. They were walking on the edge of a ledge called betrayal, praying that they didn't fall off.

"'I wish all of these things could come true," she said, tears in her eyes. She desperately wanted a man like Merci. Dom had disguised himself as a man like Merci.

"'They can't,'" Merci said.

"'I know,'" she replied. A tear fell from her eyes. She already knew that what they both wanted they could never have and still it devastated her.

'He cleared his throat and took a step back from her. "Maybe we should head back," he suggested.

'She nodded as he walked off in the direction of the car, leaving her head spinning. They say the best way to get over one man was to get under another one, but a situation like her and Merci could never exist. It was wrong on so many levels and she knew it, but she couldn't help but want it so badly.

'Noni knew that she couldn't keep Merci in St. Tropez with her for too long. If he stayed, it would only be a matter of time before they gave into temptation. *Lord, please stop me from raping his fine ass,* she thought in amusement. *I need Maya and Tat out here. They can talk some sense into me before I end up in bed with my husband's best friend.*

Chapter 15

DOM

Dom's entire world was in disarray. When Noni was at home, under his thumb, right where he needed her to be, he was fine. It wasn't until she had packed up her things and left did he feel sick. It was then that he realized how much she held him down daily. He didn't know right from left without that woman. He hadn't called Josiah yet. He was trying to give Noni a chance to calm down and come to her senses before he admitted that he had taken a loss. Dom knew Tat had no idea where Noni was. He had called Maya and even her Gram trying to hunt her down. He had no idea where she was or even where to begin looking. He doubted that she would truly leave him for broke, but the more time passed, the more worried he became. Josiah wasn't taking any shorts. He would want his money in full and on time. Dom didn't have time to wait out Noni's temper tantrum.

'Feeling his back against the wall, Dom reached for his phone. Tat had called him over ten times, but he had no energy for her antics. His life was turned upside down, partly because of her, but mostly because of his inability to be a good man to the woman he owed the most…his wife.

'He sent a text to Merci. If he couldn't come up with Josiah's money there would be gunplay and he would need Merci and his shooters at his side in Detroit when it was time to go to war.

'Get with me asap. Fucked up the paper. 911.

NONI

"Oh my God, please answer the phone," Noni whispered as she waited impatiently while Maya's phone rang. Upon arriving back at the hotel she had rushed to her room. She was almost afraid of what would happen if she stayed in Merci's presence too long. His charm was irresistible and her attraction undeniable.

"'Bitch you better have a good excuse for why you haven't been answering my calls! Dom's ass has been calling me every hour looking for you! Where are you?"

"'I left him," Noni said as she plopped down on her bed. "And now I think I'm about to sit on Merci's face!!!" she wailed in distress.

"'Wait? Say what now? Bitch!!!! No!!!!" Maya said. She was tripping and Noni had to laugh at her reaction. "You've been fucking Merci fine ass? I knew it! That's why you never wanted to hook me up with all that sexiness!"

"'No! I haven't," Noni said. "I'm in France on a trip that Dom planned months ago. He invited Merci and Merci showed up. We've been drinking and talking. He listens to me, you know?

He's sooo fine," Noni moaned. "Maya he gone take me down! He gone get my panties."

'Maya's laughter filled the phone as Noni closed her eyes and shook her head in disgrace. "Nigga, he literally makes me feel like I'm a 16 year old girl with a crush. I need you to get your ass on a plane and fly over here before I fuck him! All it's going to take is one more glass of wine and for him to whisper one more thing in my ear before I literally hop on his dick. Save me!"

"'I say go for it bitch. Dom's dirty ass deserves it. How many bitches has he fucked since y'all been married?" Maya replied.

"'Don't encourage me Maya," Noni said, finally being serious. "I sent my divorce papers back. It's over."

"'Aww boo, I'm so sorry," Maya said. "I know how hard you tried to make this work."

"'And I took all of the money from our accounts. Even money he didn't know I knew about. I emptied it all and hopped a flight around the world," Noni said.

"I don't know why you did that? You don't have a grimy bone in your body. You know you're not going to spend that man's money. I would, but you wouldn't. You'll feel too guilty about it," Maya said, knowing her friend.

"I know," Noni said. "I'm just so mad. I wanted to do something drastic to get his attention and let him know I'm not playing, but after spending one day with Merci I just feel like saying fuck Dom. There is something about the way Merci looks at me Maya, I just…oh my God," she sighed as she searched for the words to describe how he made her feel.

"I remember you saying this same thing about Dom five years ago Noni," Maya said sympathetically. "You can't fuck with Merci. They're friends and they are street niggas, Noni. Your ass will have them beefing over you. The shit could just get ugly. I'm all for a revenge fling, but not like this."

"I know…I know…see that's why I need you here! You're the voice of reason. Can you please just come? I could really use my girls. Call Tat. Tell her too. Tell her to bring Thomas. His adorable face will cheer me up," Noni said.

"I have to work," Maya said. "I can't just up and…"

"Please Maya," Noni urged. "I'll buy the tickets and everything."

"Bitch you not about to spend Dom's money on me!" Maya laughed. "How about you bring your ass home and face your husband? I'll have your back when you get here. I've got you, Noni. Through the tears, the laughs, the hurt and confusion. If you leave him or if you go back…doesn't matter…whatever happens, you don't have to go through it by yourself, but you do have to stop running, boo."

A knock at the door stopped Noni from responding. She held the phone to her ear as she went to open it. It was Merci. Everything that Maya had just said to her had gone through one ear and out the other because as soon as she saw his face she said, "It's him, I've got to go." She ended the call when she saw Merci's face.

"You left your purse," he said as he handed it to her.

She took it from him and he walked inside, directly into her space. They stared at each other for what felt like forever before he spoke.

"You're leaving him?" Merci asked.

"I told you. I signed the divorce papers," Noni said.

"I need to know if you're sure," Merci shot back. "Or are you just mad for the moment, ma?"

"I don't know," she replied.

"Because the shit I'm thinking about doing to you, I shouldn't be thinking if you're going to go running back to him," Merci explained. "I've known him for decades, Noni. You've been with him for five years. I'm giving up a friend. He's fucked up, but he's like family to me. Don't play me as a tool for you to get back at him. There has been a lot of women. We've never let any come between us. You're going to divide us, ma. I know that and you're worth that, but I have to be certain that you're sure."

"'I'm not sure of anything right now, Merci. My life isn't my life anymore. I have no guarantees to make you. No promises. My heart and my head are numb…so broken and confused from being mishandled," Noni whispered, breathlessly. "I do know that the only relief I get from this pit in my stomach is when you're around me…when you're directly in front of me…when you hold my hand…touch my face," she paused as he put a palm to her face. She leaned her head to the side, into his open hand and closed her eyes. "This is the only time the pain stops."

'Merci's phone buzzed and he pulled it out his pocket. "It's Dom. He wants me to call," he said.

'Noni's eyes widened. She didn't know if it was hope, fear, surprise, or nervousness that filled her or all of the above. Merci noticed the change in her eyes.

'He knew that being with Noni would ruin everything that he had built with Dom. They got money together, the long way but once a woman came between two men there was no going back. He was willing to take that risk if she was, but he could tell by the look in her eyes at just the mention of Dom's name that she was still on Dom's hook. She was Mrs. Meyer. She had worn the title for too long. She was still in love with Dom, he could see it in the eager look in her eyes. She resented Dom's ways, but Merci could see that she wasn't done…no matter what her mouth said.

'He picked up his phone and dialed Dom's number and then stepped into the hallway.

'Noni paced nervously. She wanted to put her ear to the door to spy on the conversation, but she didn't. She knew that Merci would be honest with her about the call. Was he professing his love for her? Did he tell Dom that she was in St. Tropez? Were they even talking about her? Ten minutes passed and finally Merci knocked on the door.

"'You cleared his accounts," Merci said. He wasn't accusing or asking, just stating what she had blatantly neglected to tell him.

'She nodded her head. "I was pissed."

"'It's not his money to take, ma," Merci revealed. "He owes that to our connect."

' "I had no idea," she replied. "He can have his money back, Merci. I wasn't going to spend it anyway."

"'You need money?" he asked.

"'No, I just took it okay! I knew that would hurt him more than me leaving so I transferred the funds into my personal account," she explained.

"'This shit is messy, ma, I don't rock like this," Merci said.

"'He can have the money. I just want out," she whispered.

"'Do you? Because when he called you lit up? Like you was relieved. You're his wife. There's nothing wrong with you wanting your marriage to work. I want you, but I don't want you like this. Not on no rebound type shit," Merci said, conceding because he knew it was the right thing to do.

'Noni frowned, confused. How had it come to this? To Merci saying he wasn't down to do whatever it was they were doing. She didn't want to lose this…she didn't even know what "this" was yet, but it felt so good and anything that felt this good couldn't be wrong. Right? Or nah? She was confused. Dom didn't deserve her. But was she giving up on her marriage too quickly? Her husband? The man that she had vowed to love forever for better or worse? Agh! She felt like screaming and the confusion was evident on her face.

"'You need to go home, Noni. We almost made a mistake here, but we didn't. Shits all good over here, away from it all, but when we go back home you're going to cling to what you know and all you know is him," Merci said.

"'This isn't what I want," she whispered, devastated.

"'Then tell me Noni, what do you want? Whatever it is you can have it from me? I'll give you whatever. What? You want me? If the answer is yes we can fly back together and I'll cut it to Dom. Straight up, like shorty rolling with me," Merci said, fearless, bossing up on her in a way that made her adore him even more. He could see how uncomfortable even the thought of that altercation made her. "That choice is too much pressure for you, Noni. I can see it all over you. I think you need to find you first. That shit with Dom is too fresh. I'm falling back."

"'I can't just go back to seeing you once every few years," Noni said.

"'Yeah well I can't see you every day," Merci replied. "The shit you make me feel is transparent, Noni. I can't hide that. I can't be your little side nigga, ma, I'm looking for a queen. I don't want what's left over of you after you've given it all to him. Right now you're programmed to Dom, I need you programmed to me."

"'So we just pretend like St. Tropez never happened for us? Like you never said what you said and I never did what I did?" She hugged herself sadly. He approached her and kissed her forehead.

"We put it in our memories, ma. Just like the boat ride. You give Dom back his money. I'll have something transferred into your accounts. I don't want you dependent on his paper. If you ever want to leave you leave even if you not coming to me. I'll supply the mad money and when you've had enough you can use it how you see fit," he said. "You ever need anything you know how to reach me."

He walked out and Noni sat on the edge of her bed. She cried but she wasn't sure what was causing her tears at this point. The fact that she was at odds with Dom or the fact that she couldn't have Merci? Either way, it hurt and she had no idea what to do. One thing was certain, she couldn't stay in St. Tropez forever. It was time for her to go home. She had no idea what type of secrets and lies was waiting for her when she returned.

Chapter 16

NONI

Noni sat on the hotel balcony, sipping wine, as the hint of burnt orange and burgundy began to show as the sun arose in the distance. She hadn't slept. All night she had lay in bed, her mind spinning. She was so confused that she wasn't sure if her emotions were real. She had felt something with Merci… something that stirred her soul. He had awakened a part of her that had lain dormant for five years. Around him, she felt like the sun because everything else revolved around her. Merci catered to needs that she didn't even realize she had. Where she was insecure he provided confidence, when she was weak he gave her strength. In her darkest moments, Merci had been a light to her. He catered to her…appreciated her and realized that her imperfections were the things that made her perfect for him. There was only one problem, she wasn't for him. She was another man's wife and she was contemplating if she wanted it to remain that way. She sat weighing the pros and cons of her marriage. These days there was more bad than good, but she tried to remember the times before all of the bullshit had diluted their marriage. She wished that she could stay here, with Merci. On the other side of the world they flowed perfectly. Inside this bubble of happiness, where only the two of them mattered, they could cross the line and ignore their loyalties to explore what they were feeling. Once she stepped foot back in Detroit, what she felt for Merci was forbidden. She didn't know if she even wanted to give this feeling up. If Dom had been better to her...if he had lifted her up...appreciated her...than this would have never happened. He hadn't however. He had beaten her emotions down so low that now she was susceptible to the idea of satisfaction elsewhere. Her heart had been infected with a disease called Merci and she didn't know if she wanted him out of her system. Noni finished her wine and then walked back into her suite. Her bags were packed. All she had to do was get on the plane and go home to her husband. They could work this out. They had before, but she knew what the end result would be. He would get his act together for a few months at most and then she would find a phone number or a condom, or smell the scent of another woman's perfume on his clothes. He would do something to betray her all over again. Noni slipped into her clothes and nervously made her way to Merci's room. She kept telling herself to turn back. *Just go back to your room, get your bags, and go home,* she thought. She couldn't. Merci wanted her. It wasn't his words that told her so, but his actions and she couldn't deny the truth. She wanted him too. It wasn't the physical things he did to her, but the mental ones that had her falling. She had only experienced this type of emotion twice in her life. She had married the first man that made her feel this way. Could she really let Merci just walk out of her life and pretend it had never happened? She took the elevator to his floor and hurried to his room. She knocked, anxiously.

"'Merci, open up. It's me," she called through the door. She knocked rapidly, desperately. "Merci, please."

'The door opened and Noni stepped back in surprise when she saw a housekeeper appear.

"'Oh, umm, the man who was in this room? I'm looking for him," Noni said.

"'He has checked out. I'm preparing this room for turnover," the housekeeper said as she pushed her cart out into the hall. Noni rushed inside and looked around at the room. The bed was neatly made, the towels replaced, his bags were gone. Disappointment filled her as a slight ache crept into her chest. *He's gone,* she thought. It was too late. Merci had already checked back into reality and as she turned back to head to her room she knew that she had too as well. It was time to go home and deal with Dom.

TAT

"'Why haven't you been answering my calls?" Tat asked as she stood on Dom's doorstep, holding a sleeping Thomas in her arms.

'She frowned as she looked him up and down. His disheveled appearance was uncharacteristic. He reeked of cognac. He was so drunk that it was coming out of his pores. "You okay?" she asked.

"'What I tell you about coming by here unexpected," he snapped.

"'Relax. I know Noni's not home. She parks her car in the same spot every day. It's empty," Tat said. "You gone make me stand out here all night or you gone let us in?" she asked.

'She pushed pass Dom and walked into the luxury home. She looked around with her nose turned up. Dom had put her up in a comfortable three bedroom home, but she couldn't help the jealousy that she felt when in the custom mansion he had built for Noni. Everything inside was top of the line from the subzero appliances to the imported furniture. It was all five-star. *Always the best for Noni,* she thought bitterly. *What about us?* She couldn't help, but feel like she should trump Noni by now. She had given Dom a baby. His first. Didn't that count for anything? She had made the fatal mistake that so many other women had before her in thinking that a baby was the way to a man's heart. Thomas couldn't and wouldn't make Dom love her. It just wasn't how the game of hearts was played.

"'Where is your whack ass wife, anyway?" Tat asked. She couldn't help but throw shots.

'Dom closed the door and leaned against it as he took the glass of cognac he held and tipped it towards his lips. He swallowed all of the brown liquid in one gulp. Wincing, he somberly replied, "She left me."

'It took everything in her to hide her delight. *It's about damned time,* she thought. "You look like shit," she said.

'Dom mugged her as he walked by her and reached for the bottle of Louis that sat on the bar top behind her.

'Tat's eyebrows raised in annoyance. *I don't know why this nigga in here tripping over Noni.* "Where can I lay him?" she asked.

'Dom reached and took his son from Tat's arms. "Come on baby boy," he whispered as Thomas stirred in irritation. Dom kissed the top of his son's head as he carried him up the steps to one of the many guest bedrooms. He laid him down, silently wishing that this could be his son's home every night. How much easier Dom's life would be if this was a little boy he shared with Noni. How much more special the experience would feel. Instead, it was bittersweet. His heart felt like it had been through a shredder. Not knowing if Noni was ever coming back was much worse than the sting of her taking his paper. He just wanted her home. If he could turn back the hands of time and take back all of the bullshit he had taken her through, he would, but that wasn't how life worked. Once the moments had passed there were no taking them back. He had done this cruel act of betrayal and now he had to live with it. The fact that he was hiding it was even worse. He could never truly have a happy day because he feared that at any moment his true intentions would be exposed. That was half the reason why he stayed out in the streets so much instead of coming home to nurture his marriage. His guilt ate away at him and Noni knew him so well that he was afraid she would sniff out his sins if he was around her too long. *Where ever you are? Come home ma,* he thought.

'Tat crept up behind him and placed her hands around his waist, reaching for his manhood.

"'Gone with that shit," he said as he shook her off. He wasn't in the mood, but Tat was determined. Her sex was her only power over men. She wasn't sharp enough to manipulate with her mind. She needed her body as a tool of persuasion.

' He walked out of the room and she followed him persistently.

"'Aww, you're mad because your wife left your cheating ass alone," she teased in a baby's tone. Usually Dom could handle Tat's mouth, but tonight he felt like slapping her head off her shoulders. He grabbed her roughly and pushed her against the wall in the hallway.

"'That's right. I like it rough daddy," Tat moaned. She reached for his manhood again. "I just want to make you feel better. Your bed is empty, let me fill it for you Dom." As she spoke she rubbed all over his crotch, awakening him as she felt him harden in his pants. "Oh my goodness, you're so big," she moaned. Just the feeling of Dom's bulge rubbing through the fabric made her wet.

He was a beast in the bedroom and he was a fiend for good loving. He was stressed and she had the perfect stress reliever. He had no idea he was playing with fire every time he laid down with Tat. "Not here, I want to do it in your bed," she whispered.

'Dom knew it was wrong, but he wasn't equipped to deal with the pain that Noni's absence had caused. He was in his emotions and he didn't like it. Getting into another woman was the only way he knew to take his mind off Noni. His heart told him that this was fucked up. He was about to smash his wife's best friend in their marital bed, but his ego urged him forward.

'Dom picked Tat up by her waist and she wrapped her silky legs around him as he carried her effortlessly to the master bedroom.

'He tossed her onto the bed as he pulled his shirt over his head and stepped out of his pants.

'She stripped, slowly, giving him a show. Tat had always been petite but the war that was waging within her body was causing her to look frail. She kept her sweatshirt on, only removing her jeans and panties in an attempt to hide her thin frame. Dom grabbed a condom from the nightstand.

'"We don't need that. I want to feel you," she said as she leaned back on her elbows as she spread her legs.

'Dom didn't respond as he ripped the condom open. She had caught him up once. He wasn't trying to have it happen again. The last thing he wanted was for her to pop up pregnant again.

'Tat instantly caught an attitude. He was adamant about strapping up. She needed leverage. She didn't want Dom to have an option when it came to dealing with her. She was HIV positive. If she gave it to him, he wouldn't have a choice but to stop messing with Noni for good and commit to her. Or at least that's the twisted way Tat planned to force his hand.

'"Let me," she said as she took the condom and placed it in her mouth.

'Dom smirked. *It's freak shit like this that make it hard to tell her ass no,* Dom thought as he watched her roll the condom onto him, using only her skilled tongue. He didn't see her bite tiny holes into it before she put it on him. Tat was willing to stop at nothing to get him, even if that meant destroying his entire life.

Chapter 17

NONI

Noni entered her house. She didn't even bother to bring her bags in. She wouldn't be staying long. The entire flight home she had built up her nerve to stick to her guns. She was leaving Dom. She had said it many times before, but this time she was serious. *No matter what he says, I'm over this,* she thought, coaching herself as she put her key in the door. She entered and half expected Dom to be waiting by the door. She was ready for World War III; prepared for confrontation but all she was met with was silence. Noni made her way through the home. She had decorated every inch of it. The paintings on the wall, the color of the carpet, the furniture, the scent…it was all her. She had fallen into the comfort zone of it all, but she had played herself by staying. She hadn't wanted to lose all of this. The luxury, the routine of the life she had built with Dom. It wasn't that she couldn't stand on her own two feet. She was educated. She could go out and start a career that would finance her tastes, but Dom had made life so convenient. Life here, was already established. Life without him she would have to figure out. She would call the shots and she had allowed him to lead for so long that the thought of it had caused her to sacrifice her self-respect. She shook her head. She wasn't even that girl.

This was never supposed to be her life. Taking bullshit from a man in the name of love, in the name of money. It was the reason why she had worked so hard to obtain her Master's degree in the first place. She never wanted to be this type of woman, but ironically she had become exactly what she feared. The walking mat to a man with money and power.

'The sound of soft cries startled her. They sounded so foreign in her house. She frowned as she followed the sound to the guest bedroom. She cracked open the door, peeking inside.

'"Thomas?" she said in confusion as she walked over to the big bed and sat down next to him.

'"Nono, Nono," he whined. It was the nickname he had given her. She scooped him up in her arms and instantly mummed his cries.

'"Aww come here auntie baby," she said. "What are you doing here? Huh? Where is your mama?" She spoke soothingly as she rocked back and forth. She spent so much time with him that her presence alone was enough to calm him. "There you go," she whispered. "Go back to sleep. It's okay. I've got you baby boy."

'She turned and Tat stood staring at her, speechless, her eyes wide in shock.

'"Surprised to see me?" Noni asked her brow raised. She took in Tat's appearance. She was half dressed. Her sweatshirt hung off of her shoulder seductively and it was barely long enough to cover the bottom of her voluptuous behind. She wore no bra. "What the hell are you two doing here?" Noni asked as she continued to rock Thomas. She trusted Tat so deeply that she didn't even have malicious thoughts regarding her presence. The toddler cuddled into her soundly. He was so comfortable in Noni's arms.

'"I...I...um," Tat stammered trying to find words. This was the moment that she had been waiting for. She could come clean. She could tell Noni exactly what she and Dom had been up to.

She could throw the affair in her face and end Dom's marriage for good. All she had to do was open her mouth, but as she watched Noni with her son, looking down at him so lovingly Tat grew teary eyed. She had awoken to the sounds of his cries and had gotten up to comfort him, but Noni had gotten there first. She always seemed to beat Tat to the punch. She had been first in the friendship race for years. She was the first to fall in love, the first to make it out the hood, the first to finish college, the first to get married. Noni was winning the race of life and Tat couldn't help but envy her. Tat's envy didn't motivate her however, it ruined her but as she looked at Noni and her son she realized that Noni genuinely loved Thomas. She had from the very first moment he was born. It would destroy their bond when she found out that Thomas was a child that Dom had fathered. Tat wasn't ready for her son to lose that yet. Honestly, now that she was standing in front of Noni, Tat didn't know if she was ready to lose her as a friend either. Not just yet at least, not in this moment. She knew that the truth was her weapon, but for some reason she couldn't unleash it. She had threatened Dom for months that if he didn't let Noni know, she would, but now she understood his struggle. He couldn't and for the first time since sleeping with her best friend's man she thought about what the truth would do to not only Noni, but to them all.

'Noni laid Thomas back into the plush bed and then turned to Tat. She nodded her head toward the hallway.

'Tat followed and then Noni turned around. "What are you doing here?"

'"My...my...my water is cut off at my place," Tat lied off the top of her head. "I came by earlier to ask you if the baby and I could stay for a few days. You weren't here, but Dom said it was okay. He told me what happened, Noni. Are you okay?" '

'Noni shook her head. "No, not really. I signed my divorce

papers. I need to talk to Dom. I'll give you some money to get your water cut back on in the morning." Noni said.

'A burst of joy exploded inside of Tat when she heard about the divorce, but she couldn't show it. Her nerves were on edge. She had been caught off guard, half naked in Noni's home. She wanted to tell Noni that she was the woman in Dom's life, but now just didn't seem like the time. The angel and devil on her shoulders pulled her in different directions but tonight, the good Tat nodded as she breathed a sigh of relief. Noni started down the hall toward her bedroom. She stopped. "And Tat?"

'Tat turned around. "I don't ever mind if you and Thomas stay here but don't walk around like that," Noni said. "Put on some clothes."

'Tat nodded. "I was just coming from the bathroom. My bad Noni. Good night," she replied before retreating into the guest room.

TAT

'Tat tossed and turned all night as she thought of Noni, lying in the spot next to Dom. *The smell of me is still on the fucking sheets,* she thought bitterly. She had wanted to expose everything to Noni, but deep inside she knew that losing Noni as a friend would ultimately damage her. Noni's life wouldn't be the only one to change after everything came out. Tat's would as well. It had been so long since she had allowed herself to see Noni as anything other than competition. She had forgotten the bond that they had shared once upon a time. They had been on the come up together until Noni started college. It was then that Tat began to feel inferior. When Noni married Dom, Tat's jealousy only grew. Suddenly, Noni was sitting on a throne, spending money by the boatload and Tat was still struggling. Still clubbing, still scheming, still broke, still living the same life as they had when they were young and dumb. She faulted Noni for this, but in actuality she should have faulted herself. She hadn't grown. There was no elevation. So instead of going out and making her own way she took Noni's piece of happiness. Jealousy had turned her disloyal and instead of celebrating her friend's highs, she did everything in her power to contribute to the lows in Noni's life. It was friends like her that made enemies the lesser evil. Tat was a snake in Noni's grass.

NONI

'Noni stood over Dom, watching him as he laid out across crumpled sheets of their king sized bed. The satin gold sheets clung to his body making him resemble a Greek God. She hit his foot, stirring him out of his restful sleep. He shot up, ready to protest, but when he realized it was Noni waking him his heart dropped in his stomach. A nausea overcame him as he scrambled backwards in the bed, placing his back against the headboard and raising his hands in defense. He looked around for Tat, but only saw an empty space where she had lain. "Noni baby you're back," he said, sighing in relief as he stood. He pulled her into his arms, cradling her head against his shoulder as his eyes scanned the room nervously. The condom wrapper lay on the floor at his feet. He stepped on it, discreetly covering it. *Where the fuck is Tat?* He thought trying to piece his thoughts together. "You can't leave me, ma. I need you. You can't do me like that Noni. You know I'm nothing without you," Dom whispered as he breathed erratically from the nerves that wrecked him. He had just sexed another woman in their bed, hours before. He thanked God that Noni hadn't decided to pop up in the middle of their sexual escapades. Even still, with Noni and Tat under the same roof he was sure this was the day that his shit would hit the fan. He held onto her tightly, afraid that this would be the last time he would ever embrace her. He knew Noni well enough to know that once she found out, her hatred would run so deeply that their marriage would never recover. She wasn't the forgiving type, especially for a trespass such as this.

"'Dom, stop," she said as she placed her hands firmly on his chest and pushed out of his embrace. He reached for her again. "Just stop!" she shouted, her voice firm...serious as she slapped his hand away.

"'I signed the papers. Your lawyer will be receiving them soon," she whispered, her voice cracking.

'Her words slapped him, stunned him as his brow furrowed. He never thought that she would pull the trigger on their divorce. He had cheated repeatedly, lied to her as if lies were the new truth...and still she had stuck around. For five years she had put up with his games. He had sent the divorce papers as a scare tactic. The threat of losing him for good was supposed to force her into complacency. She was supposed to accept the piece of him that he had given her. No, it wasn't one hundred percent, but half of a man was better than no man. Or at least that's what she was supposed to believe. He had no idea where this new backbone had come from, but it was uncharacteristic for her to stand up to him. "You sure this is what you want? This is how you want to play it? You just gone say fuck me? You gone give up on us? On the past five years?"

'Noni could hear the contempt in his voice and it only angered her. *Is this nigga really mad about it? After all he has put me through he has the nerve to act like I'm the one who led us to this point.* "Me?" Noni asked, exasperated. "This isn't my play Dom. This is your doing. You pushed me to this point. What else am I supposed to do? How much more am I supposed to take from you?"

"You're supposed to hold me down Noni. I ain't perfect but..."

"But nothing Dom. Who is the bitch that sent me this text from your phone?" she asked as she held out her cell for him to see. Dom looked at the text. He cringed as he grit his teeth in anger. Tat had been playing games. *She must have sent that while I was asleep. I'm going to fuck her up,* he thought. *No wonder Noni left.* "Who sent it Dom? Which one of your ho's did you stand me up for? You're mad at me for signing papers that you sent to me. You dog me out and just expect me to stick around. Well I'm not doing it anymore. I can't," Noni shouted.

"Lower your voice," Dom stated harshly.

"Why? Because Tat is here? This is my house and that is my friend! She ain't worried about you! I will yell, shout, hoop, holler all up and through this bitch! If you wanted to save your pride you should have kept your dick in your pants. You don't want people in our business than keep people out of our house. You told her she could stay, so now she gone hear this! That's the problem. I've been too nice to you. You cheat and you lie and I just smile and take it. I keep up appearances to make you look good. When I should have just been getting at your ass every time you disrespected me," Noni was shouting at the top of her lungs. She was so livid she could feel the veins popping out of her forehead as she spoke. This blow up had been a long time coming and she was finally getting everything off her chest. She cocked her head to the side as she frowned. "And I appreciate you being nice to my home girl, but next time she knocks on our door and I'm not here, send her to a hotel." Noni's frustrations were at an all-time high as she mumbled. "She's a grown ass woman with a kid and her water cut off." She shook her head in disgrace. "I don't understand why you wouldn't just get them a room for a couple nights anyway? What you thought I would call her and she would tell you where I was?"

'*What the hell is she talking about?* Dom thought, taken off guard by Noni's rant. He didn't know how Noni had come to the conclusion of why Tat was present, but he would roll with it. It was a better excuse than he could muster up at the moment. Noni was beginning to ask questions that Dom wanted to steer clear of. If her wheels started churning enough, Noni would starting doing math. One plus one would begin to look like two and she would figure out that there was more going on here than what met the eye. He would do anything to distract her from coming to the conclusion that he and Tat were together. "Well where the fuck were you Noni? Where did you go? Where you been Noni? What nigga done put a battery in your back? Huh? And where the fuck is my money?"

'Merci's face flashed in her mind and Noni's courage dwindled as guilt flooded her. Within the blink of an eye Dom had turned the tables. He was the king at flipping shit. The real problem between them was his inability to be faithful but here he was putting her in a position where she felt wrong. He was a master at manipulation and now instead of being on the offense, Noni was forced to defend her decision to flee.

'"You're going to leave me and take everything I built? Huh, ma? That's you? I didn't peg you as a bird, but the first thing you do is fly off with my bread when you get hot at a nigga?" Dom asked. "You didn't walk into this marriage with shit. You was broke. I gave you everything."

"You son of a bitch," she responded. "I don't have anything because you asked me not to work. You didn't want your wife out all day. You wanted me here, cooking meals and making babies. Barefoot and pregnant."

'Dom smirked. "Yeah and you couldn't even do that right," he said. Dom knew it was a low blow. When the words fell out his mouth he instantly wished that he could chase them down, but there are two things in this world that you can't get back...words once spoken and time. He could see the damage that his emotional bullet had caused. It was the issue in their marriage that they had never addressed and the way that it had come out of his mouth was so malicious that Noni recoiled. Noni gripped her stomach as if he had knocked the wind out of her. She had been pregnant many times, but she bore no children. Her body just couldn't hold onto another life. Her womb wasn't strong enough. Every time she got excited about the possibility of becoming a mother, nature would cruelly rip her dream from her. The blood would always be her first indication that something was wrong. It would seep out of her and there was nothing she could ever do to stop it. It was like trying to hold water in her hands. It always drained out as did every baby that she had ever attempted to bring into the world. Eventually she stopped trying. To avoid the disappointment... the anguish...the embarrassment of yet another miscarriage, she told herself she didn't want children, but they both knew it wasn't true. For Dom to pull that card on her was more than wrong it was cruel and it made her hate him. The slap she delivered across his face was so swift that he never saw it coming.

"Noni, baby, I'm sorry. I didn't mean that," he whispered as he watched her turn to leave.

'"Words spoken in anger are truth," she whispered. It was one of the things her Gram had told her long ago. "I'll have your money wired back to your account tomorrow morning," she said. "I'm done."

'She stormed out and walked directly into Tat who stood, looking like a deer in headlights.

'"I...I heard the shouting. I was just um," Tat couldn't even form an entire sentence.

'"Mind your business Tat," Noni spat as she brushed past her.

'Tat stood, stunned as she stared at Dom who was slipping into his clothes.

'"Noni!" he shouted. He tried to go after her but Tat stood in the door, challenging him with her eyes.

'"What the fuck you running after her for? I dare you to make the wrong move in this mu'fucka," she threatened in a low tone through gritted teeth.

'It was in that moment that Dom knew he had made the ultimate mistake. Tat wasn't worth this. The damage he had done to his marriage with Noni over her was for nothing. The two women didn't even compare and Tat felt like she had so much leverage that she was getting out of pocket. They weren't even in the same league. Dom reached out and grabbed Tat's skinny neck, pushing her against the wall. "Bitch I should snap your neck for that shit you pulled with my cell phone. You deleted the text you sent to her so you didn't think I would find out. Get this shit through your head. You're not my wife. You keep threatening me with this shit. You gonna tell...you gonna expose me, but you had your chance. Tonight was your chance to air all this shit out and what did you do? You covered your ass. You ain't telling her shit you understand? I fucking hate the day I laid eyes on your simple ass. If it wasn't for that little boy in that room I would put you in the dirt," Dom said. He walked past her and raced after Noni but by the time he made it outside all he saw was her illuminated taillights as she sped down the street.

"'Damn it!" he shouted. He had never lost his cool with her like that before. There were certain lines that he had been careful not to cross with Noni over the years. He knew that her miscarriages were a touchy subject and he felt like a scumbag for using them against her. He sat on his porch, defeated, as he buried his head in his hands. He didn't know what to do. He was about to lose her. She was slipping through his fingers like water and there was no catching her.

'Dom was almost to the point of tears as he thought of life without Noni. He knew that he wasn't shit, but selfishly he couldn't let her go. Dom would rather see her hurting with him than happy with someone else. He wanted to be a good husband one day and he only wanted to be that to her. He just didn't have it all together at the moment, but it didn't mean that he liked who he had become. He was a broken man but still at the end of the day he wanted to be her broken man. He didn't give a damn about the women he slept with, especially Tat. This thing had gotten so far out of hand he was just drowning in it. Tat was like quick sand. The more you struggled to get out of it, the deeper she pulled you in. Fed up, Dom stood to his feet. *I can't let this bitch break up my marriage. I can't lose my wife,* he thought. He had seen the determination in Noni's face. She was serious this time. He had tried her one too many times.

'He stood to his feet and walked back inside. When he reached his bedroom he found Tat back in his bed, more comfortable than ever.

"'You talk to me like that again and I will ruin your life," she said. "Now come here." She spread her legs wide open, revealing her pink center as she let her fingers explore her depths while her thumb massaged her swollen bud. It was her sexual prowess that had lured him in originally. It was how it had started. Noni was a love maker, she was soft and reserved, a bit shy in the bedroom. She pleased him but Tat was a certified freak. There were no rules with her, no restrictions. When she was in his bed they fucked, there was nothing romantic about it. She was animalistic and took Dom anyway he felt like serving her. Tat gave a porn star a run for her money, but after the climax there was nothing else she could provide. There was no depth. She was a pretty face, with bomb pussy, and a bum bitch's motive. It had been all fun and games until she wound up pregnant. Now, she was a nigga's worse nightmare. Usually seeing her spread wide open in front of him would entice him, but today her audacity sent him into a fury.

'Fed up with the threats, with the games, and with her bullshit, Dom stormed over to her. "Get up," he said, the bass in his voice threatening.

"'What?" she asked, confused.

"'Get up and get your ass out," Dom demanded.

"'I'm not going any…."

'Before she could even finish her sentence Dom had grabbed her by one of her legs and was dragging her out the bed. She hit the floor with a loud thud as he pulled at her. "Get the fuck out!" He shouted, enraged as she pulled back, trying her hardest to stay.

"'No! I'm not going nowhere!" she screamed.

'She kicked and hit him with all her might as he dragged her across the floor. "Get your shit and get the fuck out. I don't give a fuck what you do. This foul shit between me and you is over."

"'Dom no! Stop! I'm not leaving! You can't throw me out like a piece of trash!" she screamed as she began to cry. She clawed at the floor, at the chairs, at the legs of tables…anything she could hold onto as he pulled her through the house.

"'Bitch get your ass up before I hurt you," Dom said, panting when he finally reached the front door. He had broken a sweat and he was heaving from the exertion of pulling her through the massive house.

"'I'm not leaving," she cried as she sat in a heap on the floor.

'Dom picked her up and pulled her, kicking and screaming out onto the front porch. "Get the fuck off my property," he said angrily.

"My baby is in there! Give me my baby!" she cried as she stood to her feet and tried to bum rush back inside. Dom pushed her away, forcefully, causing her to stumble.

"That's my baby bitch. You're done using him as a pawn. I'll tell Noni myself before I let you control me with this bullshit another day. Take your dusty ass home," he said spitefully. He slammed the door, locking her out.

Tat stood to her feet, sobbing and embarrassed. *Karma is a bitch Dom, you just wait and see. Nigga I got yo' ass,* she thought bitterly as she retreated to her car and pulled away into the night.

Chapter 18

NONI

Noni sat in the parking lot of the bank for an hour before she decided to step foot inside. She thought about taking Dom's money. She thought about leaving him for broke and disappearing from his life for good, but she knew that she would never go through with it. She wasn't cut that way. Noni had never been the wife to get into Dom's business, especially his street business, but she knew that if he didn't pay Josiah this money that danger would come knocking at their door. Dom had betrayed her, but she could never be vindictive enough to do something that would get him hurt. For that reason alone she climbed out the car and walked into the bank to transfer the funds back to Dom's account.

She walked up to the teller.

"Good morning, I need to transfer funds from my account into my husband's account," Noni said as she sat picked up the pen and began to fill out a bank slip.

She removed her driver's license and slid it across the counter. When the teller saw the amount she frowned.

"I need authorization for this amount," the woman said.

Noni nodded. "Do whatever you have to do," she said. The woman walked away and shared whispered words with an elderly white man who Noni assumed to be the branch manager.

Within seconds the man came over to her. "Ma'am could you come to my office. This is a substantial transfer and the activity on your account is rather unordinary considering that you just transferred these funds not too long ago," he said.

"It's my money. I can transfer it as much as I want. Is there a problem?" she asked.

The man came from behind the counter and held out his hand in the direction of his office. "Please ma'am, this way," he said.

Noni frowned and followed him. Once inside, he closed the door and she took a seat in front of his desk. "I don't understand why this is necessary," she said, displeased. She wasn't in the mood for this today. She just wanted this done and over with. She wanted everything regarding Dom to be done and over with.

"Where are you employed?" the man asked.

"Excuse me?" she shot back.

"Just making conversation," the man said with a nervous chuckle as his eyes darted to the door behind her. Noni followed his gaze and her heart skipped a beat when she saw a man in a black suit standing outside the office. There were two police officers by his side.

"What is going on here?" she demanded as she spun in her seat. She stood.

"Please, these men just have some questions for you," the branch manager stated. "They're from the IRS."

"What type of questions?" Her frustrations were evident as the men walked into the office.

"Ma'am I'm agent Marx with the internal revenue service. We have frozen your accounts. I need you to stand and come with me," he said.

Noni was completely blindsided. Her heart raced because in the back of her mind she knew that Dom wasn't all the way legit.

The fact that she had moved so much money at once had thrown a red flag for the government and now she was caught with dirty money.

"I'm not going anywhere," she replied, fear filled.

"We can do this the easy way or I can escort you out of here in cuffs," Agent Marx replied. "The choice is yours."

Tears filled Noni's eyes as the agent grabbed her elbow and led her out the bank.

"You are a stay at home wife. Is that accurate Mrs. Meyer?" Agent Marx asked as he sat with his hands folded across the table.

"Yes," Noni answered.

"Your husband is Dominick Meyer?"

"Yes," she replied.

"What does your husband do for a living?" Agent Marx asked.

"He owns several funeral homes, investments...he is self-made. He is a business owner," she responded defensively.

"Self-made?" Agent Marx asked as he looked at her suspiciously.

"Yes, is that a crime?" she shot back in irritation.

"How much does your husband make annually, Mrs. Meyer?" Agent Marx pressed.

Noni wearily squinted her eyes. "Am I under arrest?" she asked.

"No, not yet, but we'll be watching," Agent Marx said as he stood from the interrogation table. "And until you or your husband can prove that you earned the $10,000,000, your account will remain seized by the federal government. You see, I have a knack for catching drug dealers and I have a feeling about Mr. Meyer. I believe this money was earned illegally and

I'm going to do everything in my power to see that he doesn't get to spend a dime of it."

"I don't have anything else to say without my attorney," she answered. She looked straight ahead into the mirror that hung on the wall. She was sure there was someone standing on the other side, studying her, analyzing her.

Agent Marx chuckled. "What a faithful, loyal, wife you are," he said. "When you're ready to cut a deal, I'll be here. You can either watch Dom's ship sink or be on board when it goes down, either way, we're going to get him."

Noni stood to her feet. She was trying her best not to reveal her fear. She snatched her hand bag off the table and stormed out of the room, grateful that she was even being allowed to leave.

She fought the urge to run out of the building. The last thing she needed was to make herself look guilty. *How am I supposed to get home?* She thought, frantically. She exited the building and walked down the street a few blocks, wanting to put as much distance between herself and Agent Marx as possible. She slid into a diner and found a seat at a booth. Her hands were shaking so badly that she clasped them together and closed her eyes for a brief second in an attempt to gain her composure. *What did I do? What did I do?* She asked herself. Acting out of anger had caused her to mess with Dom's money in the first place. Now she had attracted unwanted attention and she had no idea what to do. It was crazy because Dom was her biggest enemy, he had broken her heart, and he had made her feel worthless, but he was also the first person she thought to call now that she was in trouble. He was her rider, her shooter. When she needed muscle he was her one man army. Dom's infidelity wasn't a measure of his love for her. He loved her like crazy, probably more than he had ever loved anyone in his life. He would move mountains for her… pull triggers for her. Whatever she needed, he would be there.

It was the simple things that he couldn't seem to deliver on. He was a man with a disabled mentality toward love and marriage. He had harmed Noni to her core but if anyone else misplaced one hair on her pretty little head, Dom would end them. He had disrespected her so many times, but he gave no passes when it came to how the outside received her. It was the twisted mentality of a man who didn't truly know how to love. She was his queen and he defended her honor. Right or wrong he rode for her. She retrieved her phone from her handbag and called him without hesitation. She wished that she didn't need to but relying on him when she was in trouble was instinct for her. It was automatic.

He answered on the first ring. "Dom, I..."

"I have to tell you something Noni," he said interrupting her. "I don't deserve another chance with you baby, I know this but I swear to God, if you give me one I'll be straight up with you from this day forward. I have some things I need to come clean about...some shit I've done..."

"Dom! I think you're in trouble...we're in trouble," she said, stopping him from his confession. The only thing that was on her mind was the ten million dollars that the IRS had seized.

He heard the distress in her voice. "What is it, ma?" he asked.

"I don't have your money. I went to the bank to try and transfer it back. The IRS was waiting for me. Federal agents escorted me out the bank. They questioned me Dom. They seized the money," she said, rambling.

"Stop talking," he said.

Noni immediately closed her lips.

"Where are you?" he asked.

"I'm at some diner, off Woodward Ave. I'll text you the name of it. Can you come get me?" she asked.

"I'm on my way," he replied.

Noni had never felt such relief as when she saw Dom's car pull into the lot of the diner. He got out the car and she walked outside. They stood awkwardly in front of one another, neither knowing exactly what to say.

"Are you okay?" he finally asked.

She nodded.

"You know I love you right?" he asked.

"I don't know that," she replied. "Not anymore I don't."

"And that's my fault," he said as he leaned back on the hood of his Escalade. "I haven't shown you how much you mean to me in so long that you can't remember that you're everything to me Noni. I don't give a fuck about the money. I can replace that. I can't replace you. It's taken me some time, but I'm realizing that. I just want to love you like I did in the beginning, ma. I want to prove it to you."

Noni could feel her resolve wavering. He did this to her every time. He would fuck her over and then apologize so sincerely that she questioned why she had even tripped in the first place. The intensity of the highs and lows of their relationship made her crazy.

"Who is she?" Noni asked. "I want the truth Dom. I can't keep giving you the benefit of the doubt. I know you're cheating on me, probably with multiple bitches. Who is the bitch that text me from your phone?" she asked. "I tell myself that these women don't matter. That they will never measure up to me and that they can't do for you what I do. Lately, I've been getting the feeling that it's deeper than that. It's feels like I've been replaced and if you connected with another woman like that it's going to kill me.

That's what I fear most. I can forgive a one-night stand, but an affair is different. Please tell me the truth. Have you fallen in love with someone else?" she asked. "Who is she?"

"She's nobody, Noni. Some random girl," he replied. He immediately felt like scum for lying, but after hearing her fears how could he tell her the real? No, he wasn't in love with Tat, but yes it was serious. She was the mother of his child. It didn't get any more serious than that. He couldn't change what he had done. The evidence of his sins had been born in the flesh, but now that he knew Noni's limits he had to keep the truth from surfacing. "She's just some chick I picked up at a bar one night. She's nothing. I'll dead that. I'll dead it all, I promise," Dom said. He was knee deep in his own dishonesty, but he could tell that his words were persuading her to give him another chance. "You're made for me Noni. When you picked up and left I was lost. I don't know what life is without you anymore. Come back home ma. Take care of your man. I do dumb shit and I've made a lot of mistakes, but one thing that has never changed is how much I love you."

Her mind and her heart were at war. She knew what needed to be done, but when Dom said things to her like this she turned putty in his hands. "I just need some time."

"I'll give you all the time you need but you can't just be out here unprotected. I'll handle the fed shit, but until I can get Josiah his money, it's going to be a problem. Anybody who knows me knows that you are my weakness. Shit ain't sweet Noni. If you want to leave me, I understand, but at least wait until after I take care of this situation with my connect. Once it's safe if you still want to go, I'll accept that."

Noni nodded as he extended his hand. She took it and he pulled her into him, closing his eyes as he kissed her forehead. "I'm sorry."

Her eyes watered as he escorted her to the passenger side and opened the door. It was then that she noticed baby Thomas sleeping in the back seat. "What is he doing here?" she asked. "Where is Tat?"

Dom wished he could just come clean. The secrets that he was keeping were weighing him down, but Noni wouldn't accept this mistake. She wouldn't forgive a baby outside of their marriage. He had fooled her into loving Thomas by having him pose as their God child. All of the elaborate stories he had weaved in order to keep both his wife and his son in his life would be the same ammunition she used to kill their marriage. She wouldn't accept this and as he opened his mouth to tell yet another lie his eyes misted slightly in regret. Everything in Dom just wanted to come clean. She was his best friend and he couldn't even share the joys of fatherhood with her. He couldn't experience his firsts with her, his fears, his goals as a father because he was playing the role of parent with someone else. That fact caused him to become so emotional that he pinched the bridge of his nose to stop the tears from welling in his eyes. He cleared his throat as he answered, "She woke up this morning to go to the water department to see about having her service cut back on. I told her I'd watch him for the day."

Noni smiled. "Sometimes I think that is where we went wrong. You're so good with Thomas. You would make a great father and I can't give you that."

"I don't need that from you Noni. You're enough," he assured.

"Then I need you to act like I'm enough," she replied, seriously. "No more hoes on the side, no more bitches calling your phone, no locks on your cell, none of that Dom. If you want me to even begin to trust you again you have to be honest. I need transparency." This conversation was like a broken record. She had laid out her terms of forgiveness so many times before. Not even Noni knew why she kept going back. She felt like a slave to her own loyalty. She was trapped by her affection for him. No matter how apparent his lies were she always wanted to see the best in him. Giving him the benefit of the doubt allowed her to hold onto her marriage a little bit longer, but in her gut she knew. This needed to end, she just wasn't strong enough to stay away from Dom. Whether she was loving or hating him, he evoked an emotion so strong out of her that it made her throw reason to the wind. It was passionate and she was so full on him that she feared if he weren't around her life would lack purpose. It was pathetic that a woman with so much potential had become so wrapped up in a man. Without him she felt worthless. A woman with degrees and wit and intelligence had made a man her everything. Now she was nothing more than an accessory to his lifestyle.

Noni was setting the tone for him to continuously disrespect her. She knew it, so did he. It was a sad routine that they had become quite used to and neither had the strength to end their marriage for good, so instead they wallowed in a mediocre love.

Chapter 19

DOM

Dom waited anxiously inside the abandoned warehouse as he saw a tinted SUV pull into the space. Dom didn't know what to expect. He owed a debt of ten million dollars. A debt that he could not pay. Dom knew the rules of the street. He had killed men for much less, but he knew that delaying this inevitable meeting would not help matters much. Josiah knew how he got down. If he just gave him a little more time, Dom could make the money back. He just hoped his old friend would be patient. Lupe exited the car and immediately got down to business. "Dom, good to see you," Lupe greeted as another goon exited the car behind him. The driver stayed behind the wheel.

This day has been a long time coming," Lupe said. "You're inevitable exit from the game. Business has been good with us, no?"

"It has," Dom said.

"We've been straight up with you, eh?" Lupe asked.

"You have," Dom agreed.

"Then tell me. Why wouldn't you call us when you ran into trouble, Dom? I hear that you've run into some trouble with the federal government," Lupe said.

"My problems aren't your problems," Dom said, standing his ground.

"It is when you can't pay what you owe," Lupe said. "Where's our money?"

"I need to speak directly to Josiah," Dom said.

"You speak to me," Lupe insisted. "You knew the terms of the agreement. Ten million to buy your way out of the game. Anything less and…"

"And what?" Dom asked, challenging Lupe. "Nigga don't forget who you're talking too."

"Don't forget who you owe," Lupe stated. "There is a price to pay. If you can't pay it…"

Dom was taken off guard as one of the goons came up behind him and placed a plastic bag over his head, pulling it so tightly that Dom couldn't breathe. Dom jerked his head back, head butting the goon and then snatched the bag off his head as he gasped for air.

Dom rushed the goon, pulling his gun and popping two in his belly.

Lupe drew on him and Dom turned simultaneously.

"What is this about? You never came here to get paid did you?" Dom asked as he breathed heavily.

"Your wife got picked up by the Feds. You're accounts are seized. You know too much about us. We eliminate our problems before they even get to our doorstep," Lupe said. "It's nothing personal."

Dom frowned. Josiah thought he was snitching. He knew there was no remedy to that. If Dom didn't squeeze on Lupe, Lupe would end his life.

BOOM!

Dom didn't hesitate. He laid Lupe down where he stood. The driver skirted off as Dom aimed at the truck as well, but he couldn't get off a good shot. Dom grit his teeth as he rushed to his car. He had just killed a member of a Mexican drug cartel, nephew to the boss, there would be hell to pay. This time, Dom just may pay with his life. He had started a war and Josiah had the bigger army. It was a beef that he would eventually lose.

"You are such a big boy Thomas. Yes you are," Noni said lovingly as she placed the sliced apples in front of him. "You want to stay another night with Auntie Nono?" she asked.

Thomas nodded his head and gave her the biggest smile. Noni couldn't help but to smile back. "Well your mommy is being a baby hog. She is coming to get you, but I promise to come see you soon okay?"

"Okay," he answered.

Noni's phone rang and she put it on speaker when she saw that it was Tat.

"Hey hun. What's up?" Noni asked.

"I'm outside. Bring my baby out so I can go," Tat said. Noni frowned.

"What the hell wrong with you?" Noni asked. She heard the attitude all in Tat's tone.

"Nothing Noni. I'm just tired and I'm ready to go. Can you bring him out?" Tat asked.

"Yeah a'ight," Noni responded as she pressed end. "She can be such a bitch," she mumbled as she rolled her eyes. She gathered

Thomas' things and placed them in his bag before scooping him out of the chair.

"I love you man. I'll see you next time," she cooed. She inhaled his scent, loving the way he smelled. She wished she had a baby around full time. She always felt so full of love whenever Thomas was around. "Let's go give you to your grumpy mommy. She could have at least come in to help with your stuff."

With a toddler holding one hand and a diaper bag hanging off her shoulder she walked him outside.

Tat got out the car and Thomas took off running in his mother's direction.

Rat, tat, tat, tat, tat...

Gunshots rang out from out of nowhere as a black SUV pulled up directly in front of her house spraying automatic weapons.

"Thomas!" Noni shouted as she attempted to run in his direction, but she was forced to the ground from the bullets flying in the air. She laid down, face in the grass as she covered her ears. It wasn't until she heard the sound of tires screeching on pavement did she look up. Time seemed to stand still when she saw Thomas laying in a pool of blood.

"Noni! Help me!" Tat said as she ran to her son.

"No! No!" Noni screamed.

"What do we do? What do we do?" Tat was hysterical as Noni picked up Thomas' limp body.

"Open the back door!" Noni shouted. She slid into the backseat as she cradled Thomas in her arms. "Get us to the hospital Tat. Hurry!"

"'Is my baby going to die Noni? Please don't let my baby die? Is he breathing?" Tat asked as she pulled out into the street.

"'I don't know! There's so much blood. Just drive!" Noni

shouted frantically. She hoped and prayed that this baby didn't die in her arms.

'When they arrived at the hospital Tat ran in to get help. An entire team rushed out to pull Thomas from Noni's arms.

'Noni was covered in blood. Everything had happened so fast.

"You have to call Dom," Tat said. "Get him here. Dom has to come."

'Noni nodded in agreement, silently questioning why Dom's presence was so urgent to Tat but Noni needed him as well. She picked up her phone and with shaky hands she dialed his number.

'He answered on the first ring. "Dom, you have to come… we're at Beaumont hospital. Thomas has been shot."

Chapter 20

TAT

Noni and Maya sat consoling Tat as she leaned over in her seat with her head buried in her hands. She was a wreck. She was so distraught that her body quaked as she sobbed.

"It's okay boo. He's going to be fine. Dom is going to find whoever did this. The doctors are going to take care of him," Maya said as she looked at Noni skeptically.

"Tat? Honey? Look at me," Noni said gently as she knelt in between Tat's legs. She cupped her friend's face in her hands as wrinkles of concern creased her forehead. Tat looked down at Noni while sniffling loudly. The clear tears stained her face as she looked Noni in the eyes. "He's going to be fine. You just have to be strong for him. We're here for you. Dom is out looking for the niggas that did this. Just be strong. Let's pray for him, okay?"

"God don't got no blessings for me," she mumbled.

"I'm not no bible thumper either Tat. You know the last time I've been to church, but it doesn't stop me from talking to God when things are out of my control. Let's just ask him to bless that little boy in there," Noni urged. She held out her hands and Tat and Maya held onto her.

"What do I say?" Tat asked, her cries causing her voice to crack.
"Whatever is on your heart," Noni said.
Tat squeezed Noni's hand as guilt coursed through her. Tat didn't deserve a friend like Noni. Noni was too pure, too good of a person to even be surrounded by Tat. Here she was holding the hand of the woman whose husband she was sleeping with.
Tat closed her eyes. "God please don't take my sins out on my baby. I know I haven't been the best mother, the best person, the best friend, but judge me. Don't judge him. Please forgive me," she whispered. "Amen."
"Amen," both Noni and Maya said in unison.
The doctor, a man in a white coat came over to the group. His face was grim and Noni anticipated bad news, bracing herself for whatever he was about to deliver.
"Is he okay?" Tat asked, eagerly as she stood to her feet. She was a ball of nerves as she held her breath waiting for the answer.
"One of the bullets hit both kidneys. The organs are failing. We've placed him at the top of the transplant list, but it would help if we could get a match from a parent. We could do the surgery as early as tomorrow morning if either yourself or the father is a match," the doctor explained.
Suddenly the air in the room thickened and Tat found it hard to breathe as she turned to Noni. Fear resonated in her stare and Noni frowned.
"This is a good thing Tat. If he gets a kidney he'll be okay, right?" Noni asked, looking at the doctor.
"All you have to do is get tested," Maya added.
"I can't," Tat whispered as she shook her head back and forth. Tat knew that her HIV status prevented her from being a suitable donor. "I'm not a match. Our blood types are different."
"And the father?" the doctor asked. "Is he a possibility?"
Tat grimaced as she clenched her teeth and closed her eyes.

This was the moment that she had plotted on for years. The moment of clarity. The moment of truth. She had always thought it would be the bullet that she used to kill Noni with, but instead it felt like she was about to commit suicide. Noni was good to her. She always had been and she was about to repay her with the ultimate act of deceit.

"Tat? What about Thomas' father? We know you don't fuck with him like that but..." Maya stopped talking when she noticed Tat begin to shake her head.

"I'm sorry, I'm so sorry," she said to Noni.

Perplexed, Noni looked at Tat in concern. "Sweetie what do you have to be sorry about. It's okay, Tat. We'll just contact Thomas' dad and..."

"It's Dom," Tat whispered.

Noni's back straightened and she let go of Tat's hand as the words stunned her into silence. She blinked slowly as her confusion spread across her face.

"Thomas' father is Dom," Tat repeated. "I'm so..."

SLAP!

Tat never saw Noni coming. Noni's follow through was so nice that she knocked Tat to the floor from the force alone.

"Noni! No!" Maya hollered as she tried to break up the fight, but Noni's grip was strong.

"Bitch. You. Have. Lost. Your. Entire. Mind. His daddy is who? My Dom?"

BOP!
BOP!
BOP!
BOP!

Noni was beating that ass in a rhythm as she delivered blow after blow to Tat. Tat had no wins against Noni's rage. She dragged Tat all over the waiting room as the two scuffled. It took two security guards and Maya to finally get Noni off of Tat and even then she had a firm hold of a fistful of Tat's hair.

"Get her off me!" Tat screamed.

Noni maneuvered her way out of the holds of security and swiftly followed up with another blow to Tat's face. She was going for broke. Had Tat been any other woman, Noni wouldn't have reacted this way but Tat was her friend. She was her confidant. She had told her things that no one else knew.

The security grabbed Noni and shook her firmly. "Ma'am, if you don't leave we're going to have to call Detroit Police in and they are going to arrest you," the man said.

"Noni, let's go," Maya said. "She's not worth it."

The crowd that had formed catered to Tat because Noni had left her bloody and slumped.

"Where's my bag?" Noni asked, frantically as she made her retreat.

"I have it Noni, let's get out of here," Maya urged hastily pulling her toward the door.

Noni stormed out enraged.

When she made it to the parking lot the contents of her stomach exploded and she rushed to a nearby bush as she threw up. She was sick. How could they? Dom and Tat? None of it made sense. All of a sudden she remembered odd glances between the two of them. Instances where they had been a bit too friendly with one another. She wondered how long it had gone on. *At least two years apparently,* she thought.

"I could have killed her Maya," Noni spat as she stood to her feet.

"I wouldn't have blamed you," Maya said in shock as she shook her head in disgrace.

'Noni was trembling with rage and hurt. There was so much angst inside of her that she ached. Each time her heart beat she wished it would just stop because surely death was more peaceful than the turmoil that had entered her life.

'Noni had foolishly given Dom chance after chance after chance. She had believed him when he promised to change. Now she wished she had left him years ago. All of the times she had forgiven had been for nothing. He kept making her relive this pain. Each time she caught him up the wound grew deeper and this time it had murdered her deep down in her soul.

"I have to go talk to Dom," Noni said.

'Maya frowned. "You're shaking Noni. You're in no condition to drive," she said.

"I'm good," Noni said. "You don't even know how good I am Maya. This was the nail in a coffin full of lies."

"What are you going to do?" Maya asked.

'Noni leaned against her car and then doubled over. It was just too much to bear as she tried to calm the uneasiness in her stomach. She swiped her face as she stood up and blew out a deep breath. "I don't know," she said, honestly.

'Noni hated the way Maya was looking at her. *She pities me*, Noni thought. She could tell just from the sympathy in Maya's eyes. Noni felt pathetic.

"You call if you need me? Don't hesitate Noni," Maya said.

'Noni nodded. She sat down inside her car, started the engine, and drove away, leaving skid marks on her path as she made her escape.

MAYA

'Maya walked back into the hospital. She couldn't believe the events that had just transpired. The three of them had been friends for so long. This was a betrayal that she would have never expected and she felt personally slighted as well. *If her ass would do this to Noni, she wouldn't hesitate to do it to me*, Maya thought. She found Tat, sitting alone in the waiting room. The commotion had calmed and Tat sat with a pack of ice pressed against the side of her face.

"'Don't look at me like that," Tat whispered. "You don't understand."

"'You're damn right I don't understand," Maya replied with contempt. "Noni has had your back through everything!" Maya shook her head. She didn't know what to say. She was just disgusted.

"'You don't think I know that!" Tat replied.

"'Shut your ass up. Your son is laying up in this hospital clinging to his life because of you. You're a horrible friend and even worse mother. You deserve all the pain that is coming your way," Maya said. She was screaming so loud that she didn't even notice Dom enter the room.

"'That's enough," Dom said, surprising Maya. She turned to look at him. "What the fuck is wrong with you?" he asked, confronting her. "Whatever is going on, this isn't the time or the place."

"'You're right," Maya responded sarcastically. "Your first born son is in there fighting for his life."

'Her words were a punch to the gut and Dom's eyes widened in alarm.

"'You ain't shit," Maya said. "You know I don't think Noni would have ever left you. Like ever. She said she was going to and she even signed the papers, but she loved you so much that she was just going to keep coming right back. Not this time. Not after what the two of you did. You're a grimy motherfucker Dom. She will never get over this."

'Panic flowed rampantly throughout his body. "Where is she?" he asked.

"'Far the fuck away from you," Maya shot back. She began to walk out as Tat stood to approach Dom. Maya stopped as if she had forgotten something. "Oh yeah and Tat?" she called out as she turned around.

'Tat looked at her curiously. "What else could you possibly have to say?" Tat asked with an attitude.

"'I forgot one last thing," Maya said. She marched back over to Tat and grit her teeth as she threw one final punch. "You dirty Bitch!" she growled as her fist connected. Maya was a ride or die type of friend. If you crossed Noni, you crossed her. There was no question as to which side she stood on.

'BOP!

'Tat lunged for Maya, but Dom broke them up as Maya stuck up her middle finger before walking out.

'Dom turned to Tat and grabbed her by both shoulders. "What did you do?" He firmly asked as he shook her. She snatched out of his grasp.

"'What I had to do!" she shouted back. "The bullets tore up his kidneys. He needs a transplant. I'm not a match," Tat explained. "The doctor came out and told me this and you weren't here. It just slipped out."

'So many thoughts circled through Dom's head. He was worried, about his wife, about his son, about what the revelation of his affair meant for the future of his marriage. "I've got to find her," Dom said.

'Tat grabbed his arm. "You've got to get tested and see about our son! That's what you have to do! Fuck her!"

'Tat hated the fact that not even her son came before his wife. It was the cons of being a man's mistress. Nothing she did, not even giving birth, would put her above his real life at home. Dom was so conflicted that his heart felt like it was being torn in half. Although Tat meant nothing to him, his son was one of two people whom he loved most in the world. Noni was the other. His natural reaction was to go after her. He wanted to explain…to apologize…to beg her not to leave him, but Thomas needed him.

'He grit his teeth. He wanted to leave the hospital, but he couldn't. Not when death was knocking at his son's door. He picked up his phone and dialed Noni's number.

"Who are you calling?" Tat asked, enraged. It was then that she realized it wasn't Noni who she hated. It was Dom. It was his devotion to his wife that enraged her. When she was around Noni alone she felt nothing but regret. Noni was a good friend and Tat loved her, but when she thought of Dom loving her, jealousy turned her heart cold. "Our little boy is laying up, dying and you're calling her?!" Tat screamed on him.

"Lower your fucking voice in this hospital. I wouldn't have to check on her if you had kept your mouth closed," Dom said. "She's my wife."

"He's your son!" Tat argued.

Dom was stuck between a rock and a hard place. "I'm here ain't I?" he snapped. "Where is the doctor?"

Tat went to retrieve the doctor as Dom continued to call Noni. He got no response. Each time it just rang repeatedly before finally going to voicemail. His heart beat erratically from the fear of facing the consequences to his actions. She always answered for him. Always. She made it a point to always keep him in the know of where she was and who she was with. Lately he had lost his hold on her. He could feel their bond breaking under the stress of his deception. Why had he taken her for granted? Why would he jeopardize someone he was so afraid to live without? All he could think of was her. Even now in the moments when his son lay fighting for his life, Noni's face invaded his worried thoughts. *Damn,* he thought. Losing her would be his life's biggest failure. He couldn't in good faith go into a surgery without making sure she was okay. Dom reached out to the only person he trusted that he knew could help. Merci.

I need you in Detroit like yesterday, fam.
Shit is bad. Call me.

Chapter 21

MERCI

Merci received the text and he instantly ignored it. He hadn't spoken to Dom since the ordeal with Noni. In fact, he wanted to put as much distance between he and Noni as possible. When he thought of Dom, he thought of her, and the thought of them together caused a rage inside of him that was inappropriate. He had attempted to put his feelings for her to bed when they had returned home, but he found her breaking into his thoughts often. He couldn't be the man who fell for his best friends girl. He was fighting hard to deny himself of her, because he knew that if he really wanted her, he could have her. He and Dom had decided long ago that they would never let pussy come between them. There was too much of it out here to let one woman divide them, but Noni was more than just an attractive lay. He knew it. He had felt how their souls had aligned. It was like when they were together the Earth stopped spinning, everything stopped moving. That type of chemistry was hard to ignore. Distance was the only way that he could ensure he didn't violate the code. As long as she wasn't in his presence he wouldn't be tempted by her aura. He was trying to be a loyal friend, but here Dom was, asking him to seek her out. Dom was proving why he didn't deserve Noni, but still Merci knew it wasn't his place to save her. *Fuck it, that nigga gon' have to clean up his own mess,* Merci said.

He deleted the message, but Dom was calling his line moments later. He sighed as he hesitantly answered.

"What up bro?" Merci said. "I just saw your message. Everything smooth?"

"I fucked up man. Bad this time. I need you to come check on Noni," Dom replied. Merci frowned.

"What you mean, check on her?" he asked. He knew Dom and he had never heard the vulnerable tone that he was using now. Dom's voice quaked with emotion and Merci could tell that he was on the brink of a breakdown. Whatever had gone down, it was serious and Merci's mind instantly went to Noni's wellbeing.

"What happened?" Merci asked.

"Man, bro, it's bad," Dom admitted.

"You out here fucking with these hood rats when you got a good girl at home. What now? She find a condom in your pants, a phone number or something?" Merci asked.

"I've been fucking with Tat. The shit with Josiah has gotten out of hand. He sent niggas to my house blazing. We have a two-year old son. He got hit…"

"Nigga what the fuck is wrong with you?" Merci said, astonished. "You put a baby in that bitch? That's your wife's home girl! That's foul in itself but you didn't have enough fucking sense to strap up?"

"I know, nigga, I know. The shit's bad. My boy got hit. The bullets tore up his kidneys. Noni found out about all of it. I'm on my way into surgery and I can't reach her. I just need you to come find her for me, man. I'm fucked up in the head. I can't think straight. She gon' leave me behind this shit bro. I know my wife. This is gon' be the death of us," Dom said.

Merci grit his teeth as he thought of the amount of pain that

Noni must be feeling. "Nigga, you wilding," Merci said. "I'm a man so I know how it is. New pussy is fun, but it don't beat loyal pussy." Merci paused and shook his head. " This is fucked up." He could only imagine how Noni had received the news. "You got your wife out here playing the fool. You giving her friends room to sit back and laugh at her. Fuck was you thinking?"

"It just got out of control, man. I've been trying to keep this shit from her since the day he was born. I've tried to stop fucking with Tat, but she had me by the balls. I was just trying to hold onto Noni as long as possible. I knew this would be the blow to end it all. I'm fucked up. I need you to find her," Dom said. He had no idea what he was asking and Merci closed his eyes, feeling conflicted. He couldn't go after Noni because he knew what would happen if he found her. He wasn't trying to go down that path.

"Find her and then what?" Merci shot at him.

"I don't know," Dom admitted. "I just need to make sure she's okay." There was a pause on the line before Dom continued. "I've got to go see about my son. Just do me this favor, my nigga. I owe you."

CLICK.

"This mu'fucka," Merci grumbled as he tossed his phone in his passenger seat. He turned his car around and made his way to I-80 east. He didn't even go to his home first before heading to Detroit. He told himself that he wouldn't cross the line with Noni...that he was just going as a favor to Dom, but deep inside he knew... that she needed him. This was a heartbreak that no woman should have to endure. He wouldn't push up on her, but he did need to see her to make sure that Dom hadn't destroyed her.

NONI

Noni drove for hours. She was surprised she hadn't crashed due to the tears blinding her vision. She had no destination. She was just driving as thoughts of her failed marriage haunted her. She sat inside of her car, gripping the steering wheel as she overlooked the lights to the Canadian bridge. A part of her thought about driving her car into the depths of the river in front of her. She just wanted the pain to go away. Nothing, not even the loss of her pregnancies had hurt this bad. At least through her infertility issues she had Dom by her side, but in this situation he was the enemy. He had aligned his loyalties on the other side…she had never even suspected that the other side was Tat's. She had cried on Tat's shoulder about Dom's infidelity when all along Tat had been the cause of it. The air in the car was suddenly so thick that she couldn't breathe. She climbed out and placed her hands atop of her head as she gulped in fresh air. Her lungs felt like they were closing. She just couldn't get enough air as she struggled to breathe. The scenery in front of her began to spin and she closed her eyes. She was panicking. The thought of the next step in her life frightened her. Her anxiety was real. She walked over to the railing that separated her from the water's edge. The moon illuminated off the dark water and the soothing sound of the Detroit River accompanied her tears. She pulled out her phone.

28 missed calls.

'Everyone had blown her up. Dom had called numerous times, but she simply let it ring. She didn't even have the energy to button his ass. She just wasn't ready to speak to him. What could he say? There were no words that could make this better. Maya had called, even her Grams had called, but she didn't want to speak to anyone. For reasons even unknown to her, she was humiliated. She had allowed this man to play her. For five years she had been more than faithful. She had been the dutiful, submissive, wife while he was out acting a fucking fool. Embarrassment filled her. Shame suffocated her. How had she allowed this to happen?

'Noni stood staring up into the sky until the moon turned into the sun. She was so exhausted from crying. She had spent every minute of the pass twelve hours going over the past five years of her life. Now everything was beginning to make sense. Every lie she remembered, every time Dom had told her something that didn't quite sound right she had swept it under the rug…given him the benefit of the doubt, but now all of his indiscretions were out. What had been done in the dark had finally come to light and it was more horrific than she had ever imagined. Her suspicions had been milder than the truth. *He got her pregnant. While I was trying my hardest to give him a child, he had one with her,* Noni thought. It was the ultimate slap in the face. It was a blow so mighty that it made her sick. She had thrown up so many times that there was nothing left on her stomach. She was so weary…so tired…so drained. All she wanted was to sleep, but she knew what she would see when she closed her eyes. Images of Tat and Dom, entangled in throes of passion filled her imagination. Tat knew what Dom felt like. She knew his thickness. The sounds he made. How long he lasted. Noni turned and made her way back to her car. Her thoughts were driving her crazy and she just wanted to get home.

'She was in a zombie state. Noni was just going through the motions. She was behind the wheel and her foot was on the accelerator, but her mind was somewhere else. She never saw the light change red. She was driving on autopilot. By the time she heard the horns it was too late to do anything. She went through the intersection full speed as a car slammed into her passenger side.

'The force of the crash sent her car flipping. Her body jerked left, then right. The car landed on its roof, leaving Noni crushed in an upside down position. Noni was in shock as she blinked and saw a red hue cover her eyes. *Why is everything red?* She thought. She reached up with a shaky hand and touched her forehead. She was in shock and when she brought it away she saw that the red hue that had suddenly covered her world was in fact blood. She fought the urge to close her eyes. They felt so heavy and she didn't know if it was from the sleepless night or from the crash, but slowly her lids lowered. Blackness. It enveloped her until she felt nothing. The last thing that crossed her mind was, *death would hurt less than life right now. Please God just take it all away.*

"Now I should just knock you clean out this hospital bed."

Noni's eyes slowly fluttered open and she saw her Gram standing over her, scolding her.

"He hurt me so bad Gram," Noni whispered as she shook her head hazily.

"I know baby. Maya told me everything," Gram replied as she rubbed the top of her head gently. Maya stood and came to Noni's bedside.

"You scared us girl. Your car is totaled. You're lucky to only have a broken wrist and a concussion," Maya said. "You might have a scar for that cut on your head, but you're alive. Most people don't walk away from car accidents like that. What were you doing out there that early?"

"I never went home," Noni replied as she lifted her arm, noticing her injured wrist. "My head was so clouded. I was crying. I wasn't paying attention. I just flew through an intersection."

"Whenever a man is making it hard to think straight, that means it's time to let him go Noni. You don't lose your sanity for anyone. Your peace of mind is valuable. You don't wreck your brain trying to figure out why he did what he did or when or how. Liars weave the stickiest webs and you're caught up in Dom's. You break free. Consider Tat the unlucky one. She is the one bonded with him for life. If he did the woman that he married this way what do you think he has in store for her? She didn't win, baby. There is no such thing as losing a bad thing. You give them away. Dom was no good. Give his ass to that trifling heffa. He wandered in her yard like a dog now let him shit all over it. You lock your gate and don't let that dog back in."

Tears fell from the corners of Noni's eyes as she listened to her Gram's words. "I was so stupid."

"You're supposed to be able to be stupid for the man you love. That's where the trust comes in. Us women are all trusting and naïve. Stupid in love I call it. You don't even know how much trust you are putting into a man until he breaks your heart. The right man wouldn't take advantage of that," Gram said.

"I just want to sleep," Noni whispered. "I'm tired."

"You're high," Gram replied with a chuckle and a pat on Noni's uninjured hand. "Enjoy it baby and rest."

A knock on the door caused Noni's eyes to open wide.

"Uh uh," Maya said as she saw Merci enter the room. "If you're here for Dom you can keep it moving Merci. She don't want to hear shit he has to say." Maya turned to Gram and said, "Excuse my language."

Gram shook her head. "You're so pretty, but you have a filthy mouth," she said to Maya. She then turned to Merci. "Don't you bring no bullshit in my granddaughter's room. You tell that nigga to go straight to hell."

Maya covered her mouth in shock and said, "Gram!"

Merci smirked at the feistiness of the old woman and replied, "I'm not here for Dom, ma'am. I just wanted to check on Noni."

"Oh," Gram replied. "Well that's more like it. We'll give you two some privacy."

Gram and Maya walked out the room, leaving Noni and Merci alone.

Merci stood still for a moment as he looked at Noni.

"How did you know I was here?" Noni asked.

"I called your phone. Your home girl answered and told me about the accident," he said.

"You drove all the way here just to check on me?" she asked.

"Dom asked me to come," Merci revealed.

Noni leaned back and looked at the ceiling as she shook her head. "He shouldn't have put you in the middle of it," she said. "He has a baby," she whispered. It was like those words were a trigger for instant tears. She couldn't stop them from falling.

"He is sitting in this same hospital, at the side of some kid that I didn't even know was his. They had me playing God mom. Buying toys and babysitting while they were fucking with each other behind my back," she whispered incredulously. "How did I not see the signs?"

Even Merci had to admit that it was fucked up. This level of deception was cruel in every way. This was beyond being unfaithful. This was disrespect and a form of hate that Dom had bestowed onto Noni.

"I'm sorry you have to go through this, ma. It isn't what you deserve," Merci said, choosing his words carefully.

"Have you seen him?" Noni asked.

Merci nodded. "He's getting tested to see if he's a match for Thomas' kidney transplant."

"I hope he dies," Noni said.

"No you don't," Merci replied.

"Can you get me out of here?" Noni asked. "I just want to go home."

Merci frowned. "You look pretty beat up. Maybe you should stay for a day."

"Merci please," Noni said. "I can't be this close to him or her or that baby. I just need some space."

Merci nodded as he went to retrieve her doctor. Within half an hour he was wheeling her out of the hospital. He placed her in the passenger side of his car and drove her home. She was silent, consumed by her thoughts. Merci let her be. He knew she had plenty to work out in her head. She didn't need him adding more onto her plate. When they arrived she looked over at him.

"I should have stayed in St. Tropez," she said. She was so damaged that there was an ever present mist in her eyes. She was drowning in sadness. It oozed off of her like an infection. Her heart was broken and he could see it. He wanted to mend it. It was instinctive for him to want to save her, but if he hadn't been sure before he was now. Anything that they possibly could have shared no longer had a chance. To become involved with Merci would be disastrous. He would be her rebound and that wasn't his style. "I came to your room that morning and you were gone. You didn't call me after that. You just came back and forgot about me."

Merci reached out and moved a stray hair out of her face. "I didn't forget, Noni."

There were those tears again. Fleeing down her face. "It feels like I'm dying Merci."

"But you aren't, ma. You're strong. You're one of the good people. Everything will get better with time," he assured.

"Can you stay?" she asked. "The only time I'm ever better is with you. Please stay with me. I just want to feel something other than this pit in my stomach."

"I can't," he replied. "The fact that he can hurt you like this means that you belong to him. I don't want what doesn't belong to me. That ain't my style ma."

She smiled as she looked down at her hands as she pulled at her fingers nervously. Looking back up at him she replied, "You're everything Merci. Why can't he just be like you."

"Because he ain't me," Merci replied. "I better get you inside."

He walked around to the passenger side and helped her out of the car. She winced as she walked by his side. Her body ached. She was so sore and her wrist ached. The slight headache pounded behind her skull.

He walked her inside and carried her up the stairs. She stopped him when he went into the direction of her bedroom. "I don't want to sleep in there," she said. Merci took her to one of the guest rooms and placed her on the bed.

"You good?" he asked.

She nodded. They stared at each other for a minute straight without speaking. Their energy wasn't the type to make either of them shy away. They enjoyed looking into one another's eyes. She was searching for a sign that he wanted her and he was searching for strength within her.

"You're so fucking beautiful, Noni," he said.

"Then why won't you rescue me from this pain?" she asked.

"If I'm everything you say I am why won't you just make me yours?"

"You think I don't want you?" he asked. "I want every part of you ma, but how that work when another nigga still capable of making you cry? It's complicated. He's my best friend. You're his wife. That shit don't look right. It don't feel right," Merci explained. "I can't save you ma, you have to save yourself. You have to be woman enough to walk away from a nigga that's not for you. If I pull you away, you're just gonna go right back. Maybe not right away, but eventually the hold Dom has on you will make you go back to him. Its unfinished between you two."

"Oh, it's finished," she said. "I'm done."

"Are you?" he asked. "Because it sounds like you want some get back to me, ma. What? He fucked with your friend so now you feel like you want to fuck with his? Eye for an eye?" She didn't answer because no matter how many times she assured him she knew Merci wouldn't believe it. "Look, we agreed in St. Tropez that this couldn't happen," he said.

"No, we didn't. You agreed. I came to tell you that I wanted you, but you were already gone. You didn't even say goodbye," she argued.

"So you mad at me for leaving or you mad that you didn't get to leave Dom before he dropped this bomb on you?" Merci asked.

She pinched the bridge of her nose in stress. Her head was pounding. This was too much.

"Just rest ma. You have a concussion...your wrist is shattered. All this back and forth is only making it worse," Merci said. He disappeared from the room and a few minutes later came back with a tall glass of water and a prescription bottle. "Here is your pain medication," he said. He opened it and placed one pill on her tongue. He handed her the water. "You call me if you need anything."

She didn't respond. She wouldn't even look at him. He knew that she was taking her anger out on him, she needed someone to focus on. He could take that.

"I'm sorry, about everything," he said as he turned to leave.

"Me too," she replied stubbornly, slightly upset that he wasn't willing to be the bandage that would cover her emotional wound.

"I've got some business to handle. I'll check on you later, a'ight?" he said.

She nodded and then watched him leave.

When she was alone the reality of the situation hit Noni like a ton of bricks. Yes, she was hurt. Dom had broken her. Tat had betrayed her, but as she sat with tears flowing down her face she knew...she had contributed to the bullshit too. She had allowed Dom to do this to her. Years of threatening to leave without backing up her words had trained him how to treat her. Forgiveness was a double edge sword. She had forgiven infidelity time and time again. Even when she didn't believe his lies she had accepted them to avoid conflict. Each time she did, it only contributed to his disrespect of her. He knew that she wouldn't go anywhere. She had stayed already through hell and high water. She had endured too much. Why would he stop hurting her if he knew that there were no repercussions to his actions? *I did this to my self,* she thought. It was like a light bulb had gone off in her head and suddenly the sadness that she felt turned to extreme rage. She was seeing red as she heaved...her breaths rapid, her stomach hollow, and her mind racing from the trauma that had just hit her. Her peace of mind had been shattered. Destroyed. Like a mirror that had been cracked, there was no putting the pieces of her back together again. This sham of a marriage had changed her and she knew that she would never go back to being the Noni she was before.

Noni grabbed the pills on her nightstand and twisted off the top. She poured one into her hand and then hesitated before pouring them all out. She took them one by one, until there was nothing left. If Merci wouldn't numb her pain, then she would do it herself…one way or another she was going to make it stop. She just wanted everything and everyone to go away…for good.

Chapter 22

DOM

Dom sat on the hospital bed as the nurse wrapped an elastic band around his upper arm.

"We're going to draw blood so that we can make sure you're a match for your son's transplant," the nurse said as she prepared to put a needle in his arm. Tat watched anxiously. She wondered if the same disease that was slowly killing her flowed through his veins. She hoped that it didn't, at least not yet. She needed Dom healthy so that he could save their son. What bad karma it would be if her own actions contributed to the death of her child. She had been trying for months to give Dom this monster. She had schemed and lied and plotted, partly because she didn't want to go through it alone. Now here she was, scared to death that Dom's blood would come back positive. If that happened her son would die and it would be no one's fault but her own.

The doctor stepped into the room, interrupting the nurse. "We no longer need to run your blood work Mr. Meyer. We've got a donor that is a more suitable match. The donor is the same age and blood type so the kidney will be a better fit. Our team is going to retrieve the organ. I've scheduled surgery for this evening."

The nurse disposed of the needle and untied Dom's arm. He stood to his feet.

"Where are you going?" Tat asked.

"I'll be back before he goes into surgery," Dom said.

"You're going to her aren't you?" Tat shouted.

The doctor and nurse hurried out of the room, not wanting to be in the middle of the confrontation that was brewing.

"Don't worry about where I'm going. I'll be back before they begin. Hit my line if anything changes," he said as he rushed out. He immediately called Merci.

"Where is she?" Dom asked, concern filling his voice.

"There was an accident Dom. She was upset and she tried to drive. Totaled her whip," Merci explained.

"She's here? At the hospital?" Dom asked as he stopped walking abruptly.

"Doctor's fixed her up and I took her home. She has a broken wrist and a concussion," Merci informed.

Dom didn't even say goodbye before he hung up the phone and rushed to his car.

Dom made it across town in record speed, but when he pulled up to the palace he had built for Noni he hesitated before going inside. He couldn't justify his actions. Nothing he could say would make him seem like less of a bad guy. He could only imagine the pain that Noni was going through. He took a deep breath and exited the car.

He entered the house and the quietness inside sent a chill up his spine. It was too still...too peaceful. He had sparked a war in his marriage. Where was the yelling? The screaming? The outbursts of rage and hurt? He had been sure that he would walk into a battle zone but instead all her heard was silence.

"Noni?" he called as he went from room to room on the bottom floor searching for her.

No answer.

He raced upstairs and headed for their bedroom. He was sure that she was packing her clothes, perhaps even his clothes in an attempt to put him out. He cracked open the door and saw her lying there, so peaceful and he just wanted to watch her for a moment. This was his baby girl…his love. He had done so many things wrong. Not even he understood why he had jeopardized what they had. Tat or any other woman could compare to Noni. She had hooked him at hello five years ago. He had simply forgotten that she was the woman that every man wanted. Now he was at risk of being without her. He walked over to the bed and sat on the edge. "Noni," he whispered. "Wake up baby."

She didn't move.

"Noni," he called again.

He noticed the pill bottle that she still gripped in her hand and he reached for it. When he discovered it was empty he panicked.

"Noni!" he shouted as he lifted her body from the bed. She was limp in his arms and her body felt cold. He placed his head near her mouth and felt shallow breaths coming from her. It wasn't even enough to make her chest move so he knew that she was fading. "Noni! Baby wake up! Wake up, Noni!" he shouted as he frantically lifted her from the bed. He carried her to the adjoining bathroom and placed her in the shower. He just needed to shock her system. He needed her to open her pretty eyes. He needed her to curse him out…yell at him, slap the fuck out of him, anything, but die on him. His actions had caused this. He had pushed her to this. The loneliness, the betrayal, the secrets, the lies, the disrespect, the deceit…*damn did I do this to you ma? Did you do this because of me?* He thought as tears clouded his vision. He turned on the cold water and blasted it over her entire body. It stunned her, causing her to stir, moaning as she came too.

"There you go baby, wake up," Dom said. He sat her up. She had taken so many pills that they had her on cloud nine. She was groggy and weak as he turned her on her side. "You've got to throw that shit up Noni," he said. He stuck his fingers down her throat as far as they could go until finally she erupted. He did it again, this time bringing up even more bile. He forced her to throw up until nothing, but dry heaves came out. She cried as she fought him.

"Don't touch me," she wailed.

"I'm sorry baby. I'm so sorry," he pleaded as he removed her soiled clothes and cleaned her up, rinsing the mess down the drain.

He turned the water to warm and rinsed her from head to toe, massaging her scalp as he let the stream cleanse her hair. He blinked away tears and then scooped her out of the shower before carrying her back to their bedroom.

"You're okay. Everything is going to be okay," he whispered as he placed her back in bed.

Her eyes were lazy. She kept blinking, trying to follow what he was saying, but all she wanted to do was sleep.

"It will never be okay," she whispered.

"Yes it will baby. I promise. I'm going to make it right," he assured. She turned on her side and he laid down behind her, wrapping his arms around her to hold her tightly. He knew what he had to do. It would pain him, but when his back was against the wall and he was forced to make a choice, it would always be Noni. She was his wife. His rib. Now that he realized exactly how fragile she was without him, she had to come first. It was the way things should have been all along.

MERCI

Merci walked along the Riverwalk casually as the reassurance of the burner resting against his hip kept him calm. He carried a large duffel bag on his shoulder as he thought of the sacrifice he was about to make. He hadn't ever officially met Josiah. The introductions had never been made. Josiah had inquired about him many times before but Merci preferred to be the nigga getting money in the back. He didn't need the plug as long as his man had it, but now that the winds of change were blowing in it was time that Merci and Josiah met face to face. He wasn't foolish. He knew that a man of Josiah's clout wouldn't come alone. He peeped the Mexican hitters that were sprawled around, pretending to be regular pedestrians. They stuck out like sore thumbs in the Midwest. There wasn't a strong Hispanic culture in Detroit so as he walked along, he picked Josiah's men out of the crowd with ease. Merci wasn't one to be caught slipping either, however. He hadn't come to town alone. He had brought his own shooters. Five young wolves from Youngstown, Ohio were also scattered about, but they camouflaged quite nicely. If anything popped off, Merci wouldn't be outnumbered. This wasn't Mexico, Merci was the home team...he had the advantage. He spotted Josiah. His expensive suit and shiny shoes gave him away. In an industrial city where most made their money in the factories, Josiah's flashy appearance stood out.

Merci went and sat at the opposite end of the bench that Josiah occupied. He placed the duffel bag in the middle.

"You must be Merci," Josiah said, without looking his way. Instead he looked out at the Detroit River. "I must say I was surprised to get your call."

"The hit you put on Dom's wife and son," Merci said. "I want it lifted."

Josiah chuckled slightly as he sat back and crossed one leg over the other. "Now why would I do that? Dom killed my nephew. He owes me money," Josiah said.

"There's five million dollars in the bag," Merci said.

"That's not enough," Josiah replied sternly.

"That's a gift," Merci shot back. "A symbol of my appreciation for you lifting the hit."

"Why are you here? I have requested your presence many times and you always declined to get in bed with my kind. Why is it you're sitting here instead of Dom?" Josiah asked, finally looking at Merci.

"Because I love his wife," Merci said honestly.

"Ahh, and the plot thickens," Josiah replied in amusement.

"You don't have to accept this," Merci said. "But I think you're an honorable man. Women and children have nothing to do with the business between men. Am I right?"

Josiah simply shrugged but Merci had his ear. "You call off the hit and give Dom a pass, I'll acquire his debt. You give me the same deal you gave him. 5 years. We can do business and at the end of the term I'll pay you back the ten milli with interest. You know my flip. You would have never agreed to meet me if you didn't know how I move through em'. But my people got to be safe. Noni, has to be off limits," Merci said. "Because at the end of the day if the talking don't fix this, I'm prepared to take this that other way too. Neither of us want that. Why make it bloody when I can just make you rich."

Merci could see Josiah's jaw tense. "The blood of my nephew… somebody has to pay for that," Josiah said.

Merci could have easily thrown Dom under the bus, but he wasn't built like that. "Nah nobody on my end pays for that. That's your men's fuck up. Where were the people you paid to protect him when the shit went down? Your people aren't on point. Look around," Merci said as he paused. "My little niggas could chop this shit up right now because your people are sloppy. Lupe's death is on you, not Dom."

"I can't promise that if I see Dom again that I won't kill him," Josiah said through gritted teeth.

"You won't see him. You will do business with me from this point forward," Merci assured. "Do we have a deal?" Merci asked.

Josiah nodded and it was done. "I'll be in touch."

Merci stood to his feet and began to walk away. Before he got too far, Josiah called him. "Why not just let me kill Dom? I can have my revenge and you get the girl."

Merci turned and replied, "That's not how I want to get the girl." *She's got to choose for herself,* he thought. He walked in one direction and Josiah walked in the other. Merci had just given up most of the stash he had been saving for years. He had only kept enough to cop his first shipment from Josiah, but it was worth it. He would pay any amount of money to keep Noni safe. Even if that meant putting it all on the line for a woman that belonged to his best friend.

Chapter 23

NONI

Noni awoke and the pounding headache that plagued her instantly made her wince in pain. Dom sat in the chair across from her, staring at her with concern. She pinched the bridge of her nose, embarrassed as she tried to think of an excuse that would make her seem less crazy.

"You took an entire bottle of pills," Dom said. His tone was more worried than angry. "Is it that bad, ma? Did I push you this far?"

"Yes," she replied. "I gave you everything. Every part of me Dom and I trusted you. Even when you showed me the real you, I still built you up in my head. I still treated you like the man I wanted you to be instead of the disloyal asshole that you are. She was my friend and you got her pregnant. Then you got me sitting here babysitting, throwing birthday parties, buying clothes, and spending time. You concocted this whole story, this entire lie when all along you're the father! Yes, it's that bad, Dom! It feels like I'm dying." She was trying to convey her torment to him, but no words could express the sorrow she felt. So many times she had given him the benefit of the doubt when she should have just trusted her instincts.

"I'm sorry," he said, hanging his head low as he rubbed the top of his head in distress.

"Stop saying that!" she hollered. "You're not sorry. You're just sorry you got caught. You should have told me! From the moment you found out, you should have come clean. Maybe then I would have believed your apology, but now...now you just look like a liar." She shook her head. "I don't even know you."

"You're the only one that knows me, Noni. You're the only one that matters," he said.

"But you gave her the baby," Noni spat.

"I don't even want that baby!" he burst out. Shame filled him as soon as he said it, but it was true. It was the ugly truth that he had buried deep down inside of him because he knew how fucked up it sounded coming out of his mouth. "I love him Noni, but I don't want him like this...with her...I wanted a son with you. Shit just got so fucked up," Dom explained. "I wanted to tell you so many times, but I couldn't. I was just trying to hold on to you for as long as I could."

"Well now you can let go. I can't do this anymore," Noni said. "You're never going to change and to be perfectly frank, Tat is exactly who you deserve. A no good, dirty, trifling, second place ass bitch like her is your perfect match."

"I want you," Dom said.

"I want a faithful husband, bitches want their edges back, niggas want the bag," she popped off. Her mouth was getting slicker the angrier she got. "We can't always have what we want, can we?"

Dom was speechless. He had no response. He didn't know how to relieve the hurt he had caused.

"Fuck you. Just leave." Noni spat.

"There has to be something I can do," Dom said. He wasn't above begging. Anyone else he would have dismissed without a second thought. Not this woman. Not his strength. She was worth putting in work for. It was too bad that he was only just now realizing it.

At that moment, Noni hated him, but oddly she still didn't want to lose. Suddenly, she felt like she was in a race for Dom's heart, as if she had to compete with Tat for his affections. She couldn't just make it easy for Tat. If she turned Dom away, he would end up with Tat and Noni couldn't let that happen. She would hold onto him simply so Tat couldn't have him. It was backwards logic and it was the thinking of a broken woman who had been mistreated one too many times. The moment she felt she was in competition with another woman was the moment she was supposed to throw in the towel, but her ego wouldn't allow that. She had been with Dom so long that she would be damned if she let a bum bitch like Tat come along and destroy the life that they had built. Noni didn't even want to hold onto Dom for love. This was about winning. This was about not losing to Tat. This was about possession and entitlement. If this was the 'for better or worse' that they had spoken about in their vows, Noni would have to endure. Right? She didn't even know. She was so hurt that she wasn't thinking clearly, but her moment of indecision was enough for Dom to weaken her resolve.

"I'll cut her off, ma. I won't speak to her. It'll just be about me and you," Dom said. "We can get back what we lost. Just let me prove it to you." Dom crossed the room to sit on the edge of the bed. "I know I've fucked up, but I do love you, Noni. I love you and I can change."

She fixed her lips to tell him no, but his cell phone rang, interrupting her. He looked down at it and the guilty expression on his face told her who it was.

"Is that her?" Noni asked.

Dom nodded. "I told her to call me if anything changed with Thomas. He's having surgery tonight. I won't talk to her. You can handle everything regarding Thomas, ma. This can work if you just give us a chance."

"Give me the phone," Noni said as she snatched it from his hand.

She answered. "What do you want?" she answered.

"What do I want? Not you! Where is Dom?" Tat demanded.

"Bitch my husband is unavailable. In fact, he will always be unavailable to you. You'll be dealing with me from now on," Noni said. "Now what do you want?"

Noni knew Tat long enough to know that she had gotten under her skin.

Tat hung up the phone and Noni passed Dom's cell back to him. "You're changing your number. If she needs something she can call me," Noni said.

If Noni knew any better she would just take her losses, but the looming feeling of failure was causing her to make bad choices. Had she really tried everything to make their marriage work? Maybe now that the truth had been revealed they could work things out.

"What did she say?" Dom asked.

"She didn't say anything," Noni snapped. "She hung up the phone."

"I have to get to the hospital," Dom said. "Will you come with me?"

Everything in her wanted to tell him no. She wanted to say fuck Dom, Tat, and their love child, but she couldn't. Thomas hadn't asked to be here. He hadn't asked for any of it. *He's still the same little boy that I've always loved,* she tried to convince herself, but she knew that it just wasn't true. Nothing would go back to the way it used to be. With this much hate in her heart it was impossible. Resentment had settled so deep into her soul that it had turned her cold. Noni was a woman scorned.

It took everything in Noni to control her anger as he walked into Thomas' room holding Dom's hand. If looks could kill he would be circled in chalk.

"What the fuck is she doing here?" Tat asked.

"Now isn't the time or place," Noni replied.

"Where is Thomas?" Dom asked.

"You would know where your son is if you weren't so busy chasing behind this bitch," Tat said. "The doctor already took him into surgery. All we can do is wait."

A knock at the door caused them all to turn. Merci entered the room. Noni's eyes widened and she dropped Dom's hand as their eyes met. She could tell he was surprised to see her there, but he quickly recovered as he walked over to Dom and shook his hand. He pulled him into a brief embrace.

"Thanks for coming," Dom said.

Merci nodded. "He went back already?" he asked.

Dom confirmed with a solemn nod and Merci took a seat in one of the chairs. Noni avoided Merci's eye contact. It wasn't until she saw him that she felt foolish for sticking by Dom. *Why am I even here?* She thought. *Trying to prove a point to this simple bitch and this disloyal ass man.*

"Why are you even here?" Tat snapped, voicing Noni's thought's. "Everything is out in the open, Noni. Ain't no more sneaking, no more hiding what Dom and I are to each other," Tat started.

"What you and Dom are to each other?" Noni interrupted. "Do you hear your fucking self, Tat? What you are? To my husband? You're nothing to each other! You understand? You are nothing. If it wasn't for my God son..." Noni paused. "Oh wait, excuse me... my step son," she added sarcastically. "He wouldn't even be in your presence. You have no words for him. You need money for Thomas you contact me. I'm his wife. You're his whore."

"Whore? Whores don't get houses paid for honey. I'm his family. Thomas is his family. I gave him what you couldn't with that rotten ass womb of yours."

"You gave him all that and he's still sitting over here with me, loving me. Must suck to know that you can push a baby out for a nigga and that still ain't enough for a man to make you number one. You bum ass bitch," Noni said nastily.

"Chill out," Dom whispered to Noni.

Noni snaked her neck as she looked at him like she was crazy. "Don't tell me to chill. You better tell your side bitch to chill. You're lucky my wrist is fucked up or I would drag your ass," Noni threatened.

Merci stood to his feet and exited the room without saying a word. Noni could tell by the look on his face that he was bothered. She waited a few minutes before she stood to her feet. "I can't be in here with her. I need some air. I'll be back," Noni said.

"You didn't belong in here anyway. You're not his parent," Tat said.

Noni paused but instead of getting mad she replied, "You're right."

She rushed out of the room and down the hall searching for Merci. She knew that he was headed toward the exit and she hoped she could catch him before he pulled away.

NONI

"'Merci!" Noni shouted as she ran out of the hospital after him. He kept walking as he pulled the Mercedes key out of his pocket and unlocked his doors.

"'Merci!" Noni screamed. She caught up to him as he opened his door. She stood between him and the interior of his car, blocking him from leaving.

"'Are you mad at me?" she asked.

"'Nah, I don't feel nothing for you, ma," Merci replied, his tone of voice even as he looked up at the hospital. "You better go back. I'm sure Dom needs you. You're back with him, right?'"

' "Merci? What would you have me do?" she asked. "He apologized. He is going to cut Tat off. We're gonna start over." Even as she said it, it sounded foolish.

"'I didn't ask you to explain," Merci answered. "If you like it, I love it." He wouldn't look her in the eye and it was killing her.

"Merci please understand," she pleaded.

"'I understand Noni," Merci responded, finally looking at her. "I played my part. I stood in there watching you go back and forth with Tat. You're fighting for your marriage. I hope that works out for you, but I've seen enough, Noni. I'm out."

"'Please don't leave," she whispered, tears coming to her eyes.

"'Noni, go! You on this back and forth shit. Earlier you were asking me to fuck with you, now you here with him on his arm like a trophy. I ain't with it. Do you know what I did for you today? Do you even know what I would do for you?" Merci asked as his face scrunched as he chewed her out. He shook his head. "Fuck it, ma. I'm good." He eased her out of the way.

"'You think I don't wish he were you?" she asked. "I think about you all the time Merci, but you have your morals. You're just as confused as I am. You don't know if you want to be his friend or you want to be my man. He's your best friend and you have this wall up when it comes to me. You want me, but you won't act on it and I can't be alone. So I'm fighting for the only thing I've got... my marriage. Yes it's fucked up, but it's the only thing I have to show for the past five years of my life!" The fear that he was going to walk out of her life forever had her near tears. "That doesn't mean that what I feel for you isn't real. It is."

"You say that, but you don't know what you feel right now, Noni. He broke you. I can see it. You wearing the sadness all over you," Merci replied.

"I'm so damaged Merci. He ruined me to the point where no other man deserves the mess I have become. I want to leave him but I don't want to be alone the rest of my life. I don't trust men. I can't put my heart in anyone else's hands, but I'm too afraid to be alone. So I'm stuck. Stuck in this marriage trying to make the best out of a bad situation," she cried. "I want to love you, but hurt people hurt people. I'm going to hurt you Merci. I'm going to hurt any man I encounter after him because of what he's done. I'm miserable Merci. I can't take it if you're mad at me. I can't take losing you."

'Merci wanted to break Dom's jaw for what he had reduced Noni too. She was a blubbering mess of tears, inconsistencies, and pain.

"Shhh," he whispered as he pulled her into him. "It's okay. Everything is okay, Noni." He wiped the tears from her face.

"I need you Merci," Noni promised.

'Merci's jaw clenched as he looked down at this beautiful woman. Somehow they had crossed a dangerous line, but now that they craved one another, it was inevitable that they act on their suppressed feelings. He caressed her face. "I don't want you to go back in there. Don't cry beautiful," he said as he wiped her tears. "Do you love him?" Merci asked.

"No," she answered honestly. "I love you. Am I tripping? Am I misreading the energy between us?"

'Merci hesitated because he knew once the words were spoken he would be all in. He couldn't have Noni and Dom in his life simultaneously. He had to choose between love and friendship and his emotions for Noni was slowly gaining the advantage.

"You already know how I feel," he said.

"I'm contemplating leaving my husband for you, Merci. I need to hear you say it," she said as she sniffled.

"I fuck with everything about you, Noni. Since the day I met you. You weren't mine to love though, ma. You still aren't," he answered.

'Noni felt herself drawing closer to Merci. He made her feel so lovely…so worthy of the epic love stories she always read about as a little girl. Being with Dom had convinced her that fairy tales didn't exist, but Merci was a real life king, looking to save her. She kissed him and he stood stoic, stubbornly refusing to kiss her back at first, but she kept finding his lips.

'One peck. He turned his head. She turned it back.

'Two pecks. He lifted his head out of her grasp. She grabbed his chin and lowered it.

'Three pecks. Four. Finally he kissed her back. His full lips covered hers as their tongues danced. Neither of them wanted to fight the temptation anymore. So much sexual tension filled the space between them that they could feel each other's heart racing.

"Take me with you," she said.

"You sure this is what you want to do?" he said.

'She nodded. "I just want to be with you," she replied.

'He escorted her to the passenger side and tucked her safely in his car. He then hopped into the driver's seat and pulled away into the night.

'Neither of them saw Tat lurking in the shadows. She had

followed Noni out of the hospital to confront her, but instead she had witnessed something even better and she planned to use it to her advantage.

TAT

That sneaky, lying ass, goody two shoes ass bitch is fucking Merci. She wants to turn her nose up at me like she's so much better. She's just as dirty as the rest of us, Tat thought as she rushed back into the hospital.

"Where's Noni?" Dom asked as she walked into the waiting room.

"It's always about her, isn't it?" Tat asked. "Let me tell you something about your wife. While you were fucking with me, she wasn't twiddling her thumbs." Tat rolled her eyes and began to walk toward their son's room.

'Dom grabbed her by the elbow, stopping her from leaving. "Fuck is that supposed to mean?" he asked.

"Ask her. Seems like you weren't the only one sleeping with somebody's best friend. Don't you find it peculiar that as soon as Merci left, Noni disappeared? Your bitch of a wife ain't as perfect as you thought she was," Tat said. She snatched away from him and walked into Thomas' room. He was still under. He would be for a while but she would rather sit in and look at him then look at Dom at the moment. He stood, piecing together his thoughts as Tat's accusations played over and over in his head. *She wouldn't do that,* Dom told himself. Tat didn't even look at him as she said,

"Go ahead and see for yourself. You know you want to know. Wherever Merci is, that's where she'll be," Tat said.

'By the time she looked over her shoulder Dom was gone. She dropped a tear because she knew she would never be able to hold onto him. It didn't matter what she did. She had given him a baby and he still had no interest in her. Even when her son was laying up hurt, Dom was still jetting out the door to chase after his wife. Tat leaned down and kissed her son's head. "Mama will be back. Rest up," she whispered. She grabbed her handbag and marched out, following after Dom. She wasn't going to let Dom off the hook so easily. It was time for her to get rid of Noni once and for all.

Chapter 24

NONI

Noni swept her hair over her shoulders as Merci slowly unzipped her dress. His fingers caused goose bumps to form on her shoulders and she shivered slightly as he placed a kiss on the nape of her neck.

"'Do you want me to stop?" he whispered.

"'No," she gasped as he released the straps and the dress fell into a puddle at her feet. He scooped her up, as if he were carrying her over a threshold and placed her onto his king sized bed. He undressed himself slowly, his brow furrowed in deep thought. He removed his cuff links first, then his tie, then unbuttoned his oxford shirt. He was trying to convince himself not to do this... trying to remain loyal to a nigga he had known since childhood, but his heart was fully invested with Noni. She made him ache for her in a way that he had never experienced. His loins, his heart, his soul, his mind, every part of him yearned for this one woman. It was as if he had found his purpose and as she leaned back, so beautifully in his bed he knew that he was done forcing loyalty. He just wanted her. This was there first time taking it this far and the nerves that came with making love for the first time were non-existent. There were no butterflies, no anxiety, no shame in the images of their bodies. Noni felt nothing, but contentment. It was like they had done this before, like they were so used to one another that this routine was natural. Their souls had to have mated in a previous life because this all felt too familiar. She had never been so comfortable in her own skin. The look of appreciation in his eyes made her feel like she was the only woman in the world that met his expectations. He started at her feet, kissing her soles as he massaged her legs and took her toes into his mouth. He showed every inch of her attention as he moved to her legs and her thighs, eventually indulging in her essence. When he put his mouth on her spot she arched her back in pleasure. "Merci me," she whispered, her tongue getting tied as she tried to form a sentence that made sense. He feasted on her, unafraid of her womanhood as he placed his mouth on her entire peach. He was in it; nose deep, as his head moved in circles between her legs. He was gentle, but it was a known fact that he was in control. This was his show, she was just attending it. She didn't have to give him instructions to her body. He operated her as if he had been handling her for years. He was skilled at the art of seduction. When he parted her thighs she reached down to feel his strength. *My God*, she thought as she bit her bottom lip in anticipation. She was on cloud nine. They were both caught up in the rapture, so much so that no one was thinking about condoms or protection. He entered her and she gasped from the thickness of him.

'He worked her over slowly, patiently, lovingly and with every intention of satisfying her, before himself. He left her legs quivering at the end. Her arms were around his neck as he hoisted himself over her, staring into her eyes as he planted kisses on her lips.

'"I love you," Merci said.

'"I love you," Noni answered.

'"What do we do now?" she asked.

'"Whatever we want to do, ma," Merci replied. "I don't know

about you, but I want to do this, again and again and again, until the sun comes up."

'She smiled as he kissed on her neck.

"'I'm going to need some nourishment first," she said with a laugh. "Today has been so emotional for me that I forgot to eat."

"'Order a pizza while I hop in the shower," he said. "There's money in the nightstand."

'Noni grabbed her cell phone and saw that Dom had called her back to back to back, on repeat. She ignored him. She didn't even want to think about him. Her night with Merci was too perfect. She didn't want to kill the vibe by thinking about the problems that daylight would bring. She called the pizzeria and ordered the food. She wrapped herself in the bed sheet, before joining Merci in the steamy bathroom. She leaned against the sink and admired him as he let the water run through his dreadlocks.

"'You want to join me?" he asked with a sexy smirk.

'She dropped the sheet and walked over to the shower, but before she could step inside the doorbell rang.

"'Food's here," she said.

"'I'll be right out," Merci said. She rewrapped her body and then rushed to the door.

"'I'm coming, I'm coming, one second!" she called out as the doorbell rang again.

'She pulled open the door and Dom stood staring at her in disbelief. Her entire world crash as she stood face to face with the man who had hurt her, and with the man that she had now hurt. She fixed her lips to speak, but nothing came out as she waited for his reaction. Fear filled her. She could see the disappointment in his face. It was like the sight of her, wrapped in the sheet, obviously basking in the afterglow of lovemaking crippled him. He swiped his hand over his face.

"'I'm so sorry," she whispered.

'Dom grabbed her by both arms and shook her as he shouted, "He's my best friend."

"'I'm sorry!" she whispered. She knew exactly what he was feeling. Betrayal was so painful because it came from those closest to us. She knew this burn all too well.

"'Where is he?" Dom asked, heated.

"'I'm right here, my G," Merci said as he stepped into the room his towel hanging wrapped around his waist. "You might want to let her go or it's going to be a problem."

"'Nigga what?" Dom asked. "This is my bitch."

"'And that's exactly how you handled her, my nigga. Like a random bitch. That's how you lost her," Merci said.

'Dom was so heated that he drew on Merci. He went everywhere strapped. His gun was like his cell phone and in this case he was glad to have it. He pointed a nine-millimeter pistol and trained it on Merci. Malice was in the air.

'Dom had never felt a sting this bad. These were the two people he trusted with his life and they had come together to burn him. This was that love burn. The kind of pain that seared you to the core.

"'You gone shoot me, Dom?" Merci asked, his own temper flaring as he stepped up toward Dom.

'Noni stood with her hands covering her mouth in disbelief. "Dom, don't," she said.

"'Please, let's just go home Dom. I'll leave with you. Let's just go home and talk," Noni pleaded. She knew that Dom wouldn't hurt her, but she wasn't sure how long he would keep his hands off the trigger. She would say anything to get Dom to lower his gun, but she could see Merci was taking her words to heart.

"'You sure that's what you trying to do, ma?" Merci asked. "I'm not beat for the drama. You can't keep riding the fence. If you go back that way, you can stay there."

"'She never left nigga. I'm home," Dom said arrogantly.
'Just as things were about to escalate Tat walked into the house with a sinister smirk on her face. "Well, well," she said, facetiously.
'Noni instantly saw red. "You brought her here?" Noni asked.
"'I followed him here," Tat said. "But I'm not here for him. I came to talk to you, Noni."
Noni shook her head. Tat was testing her. She looked at Dom. "You better get your bitch."
"You stormed up in the hospital talking all that shit, I didn't get one word in. You want Dom, you can have him. I wasn't going to do this in front of a group of people, but since you want to parade in like you're the one calling the shots, I thought you deserved to know…"
"Know what?!" Noni hollered in frustration. "What else could you possibly have to say to me?"
"I'm HIV positive," Tat said.
Dom lowered his gun as the news stunned the entire room. Noni felt the room spin. "I got it from Dom," Tat finished.
"She's lying, Noni," Dom said as all eyes trained on her. "This is what she does! She will do anything to break us ma, don't listen to her."
"I'm lying?" Tat shouted, challengingly. She knew that she had twisted the story. She hadn't actually caught it from Dom. In fact, she was trying to give it to him, but Noni didn't know that. Just the revelation that Tat was sick was enough to send Noni over the edge. Tat pulled out bottle after bottle of prescription pills and threw them at Dom. "Then what is all this for? I'm sick! I'm infected! You son of a bitch!"
Fear seized Noni as she went through her mental Rolodex trying to remember all the times she had sexed Dom without protection. She looked at Merci. "I'm so sorry," she whispered. "Am I sick?" she asked Dom, panicking as she began to gasp for

air. It felt like all of the oxygen was leaving the room. "God, what have you done?"

Tat smirked as she turned around and strolled out the door. She knew that their marriage wouldn't survive this blow. It was only a matter of time until Dom found out his status and came running back to her. Even if he wasn't positive, she was satisfied with the fact that she had ruined his life. If she couldn't be happy, neither would he.

Dom rushed to Noni's side. "Get out!" she shouted.

"Noni, it's not true baby. Look at me. I don't feel sick. I'm not sick," Dom reasoned, trying to convince himself.

"Leave Dom," Merci said sternly.

"Nigga, don't tell me what to do with my wife," Dom barked.

"Just get out!" Noni screamed at the top of her lungs. She rushed to the bedroom and locked herself inside as she slid down the door until her butt hit the floor. She pulled her knees to her chest and sobbed uncontrollably. Suddenly her life was flashing before her eyes. Dom had bed hopped from woman to woman for years and the possibility of something this devastating had never even crossed her mind. She had known about his cheating and she had done nothing to protect herself. *I was so stupid,* she thought. *So fucking stupid.* Moments later Merci knocked.

"It's just me, everyone's gone," he called through the door.

Noni stood and opened the door, rushing directly into his arms, distraught. "What if I'm sick? We didn't use a condom, Merci. What if I have it?"

Merci held both sides of her face and said, "Let's not jump the gun, ma. I know you're scared. We'll go get tested first thing tomorrow. Whatever happens, I'm here."

On the inside Merci was freaking out. This was more than he had signed up for, but he wasn't running. He wouldn't leave her to deal with this news alone. Noni held onto him so tightly that night. Sleep didn't come easy. Peace of mind was elusive. She was too paranoid of what was to come. They both were. She was so grateful for Merci's presence because she was sure that if she was alone, this would have been the night that she took her own life. His love was so unconditional. What he had heard would make most niggas run for the hills, but he was still there, reassuring her that everything would be okay.

The clock struck five a.m. and Noni's eyes hadn't closed once.

"Are you awake?" she asked.

"Yeah ma, I'm up," he responded.

"What if I have it?" she asked, fear filled.

He didn't respond. He just held her tighter and kissed the top of her head. Merci had been prepared to fight for Noni, to ruin his relationship with his oldest friend over her and even deal with her emotional baggage. He never expected this, but he wasn't going anywhere. No matter what happened, he would hold her down. He lifted his eyes to the sky and for the first time in his life he spoke to God.

Please let her be okay. Don't do this to her, he prayed. He had never had to call on his faith before, but in this moment he knew that nothing else would suffice. He had to place this burden in the hands of a power greater than him because it was too much for just the two of them…it was their worst nightmare come true. Merci had finally found someone whom he could lend his heart to. He couldn't lose her yet. Life couldn't be that cruel or could it?

Chapter 25

Noni could see her doctor's lips moving but she didn't hear one word. It was like the Earth was spinning in slow motion and everything around her moved at a snail's pace as she received the news of her test results. She didn't know how her life had become so dramatic. It was like a running soap opera and she was emotionally drained. Noni just wanted to check out for a little while. She was so tired of people taking her for granted. The people who were supposed to be the closest to her were the ones she had to worry about. It was disgusting. Not only had her husband betrayed her, but her best friend had as well. She had endeared her trust to the wrong people and she was left looking foolish.

"Do I have it? Just tell me," Noni interrupted. "I don't mean to be rude, but I don't need the pamphlets or the talks about protection. I'm a married woman. My husband put me in this situation," she said as she turned her head to the side as tears ran down her face. She sniffed and corrected her posture as she cleared her throat. Wiping her eyes she took a deep breath and then stared back at the doctor.

"I'm sorry to hear that Mrs. Meyer. We ran a full blood panel and you did test positive for Human Immunodeficiency Virus…"

Noni's heart twisted in her chest as her stomach hollowed. *I didn't hear her right*, she thought. *This is a dream. I'm dreaming.*

LOVE BURN

This isn't real. Noni reached out for the doctor. She couldn't breathe. The air felt as thick as water as she stumbled forward, tiny specks of color appeared before her eyes.

"Mrs. Meyer. I need you to breathe. You're having an anxiety attack," the doctor said.

Noni just couldn't inhale. She could feel her lungs burning and her mind begged for air, but her body wouldn't comply. She saw the world spin around her and she felt gravity pull her down as she crashed to the floor. Blackness. The darkness pulled at her like a force of nature and Noni hoped that she never woke up. Facing the reality of what the doctor had told her would be worse than death.

When Noni awoke the intensity of her emotions crushed her.

"Relax, relax, just lie down for a few minutes," the doctor said as she handed Noni a cool compress to place on her head. "You hit your head pretty hard when you fell. So I want you to take it easy and just give me a chance to tell you a few things about your status."

"I'm HIV, positive," Noni said. The waterworks came immediately. They came so effortlessly that Noni didn't have a chance to put her emotions in check. There were no sobs, no hysterics, just raw sadness spilling down her cheeks.

"You are, but it's not the death sentence that it used to be," the doctor said. "There are plenty of people who carry this disease that go on to live full, healthy, beautiful lives. If you take the medications and you stay ahead of this thing, you can beat it. You can't cure it, but you can manage it."

Noni felt like her world was ending.

"Manage it? This isn't supposed to be me," she said, a little louder than she intended to. She caught herself and lowered her voice. This wasn't the doctor's fault. This was Dom's. He had done this to her. He had fucked around on her and exposed her to danger. Not only had he given her heartache, he had given her something she couldn't get rid of. "I'm sorry. It's just..."

"I know. It's a lot of information to process right now, but I have something else to tell you. We detected HCG in your bloodstream as well. You're pregnant."

"No, no," Noni cried in alarm. This had to be some cruel joke. She had tried for years to give Dom a baby. They had miscarried so many times that she had lost count. Now when she was receiving the worst news of her life, God wanted to fulfill her greatest wish. This had to be a gift from the devil. She was convinced of it.

"Will the baby have it?" she asked, panicked.

"If we get you started on a course of treatment there is a good chance that the baby will be born perfectly healthy," the doctor informed.

"But there is a chance that it could be born with HIV," Noni stated, harshly as her face expressed sheer devastation.

"This is a lot to think about right now. I can set up counseling for you. There are support groups to help you understand exactly what is happening with your body. I'll need a list of sexual partners you've had..."

Noni stood and grabbed her handbag. "I have to get out of here. I can't...I just can't..."

Noni hustled out of the doctor's office hastily, practically running to Merci's car. When she got inside she wept. She cried so hard that her head hurt. Her fingers wrapped around the steering wheel so tightly that her knuckles turned white. Rage filled her as she put the car in drive and pressed her foot on the gas. She knew she shouldn't be driving. Noni's mind was all over the place. She didn't even notice the other cars on the road. She just heard the sound of the thoroughbred horses revving up as she accelerated the car all the way to the floor. Dom, her husband, the man that was supposed to protect her had ruined her life. This was no longer about hurt feelings and insecure thoughts. Dom had infected her with a disease for which there was no cure. He had given her a monster that terrified everyone and that no one fully understood. He had reduced her to loneliness. No man, no person, would stick this out with her. The fear of catching it, the stigma of being associated with someone who carried it…it would cost her everything. Noni couldn't get to Dom fast enough. The house that she had once shared with him came into view and she lifted her foot off the gas, only to press it down again causing the car to accelerate even faster. She didn't slow down. She didn't brake. She didn't think of who may be inside. She drove into the front of the house full speed. She crashed through the bay window and then put the car in reverse only to drive forward again. She wanted to tear the entire house down she was so livid.

Glass shattered everywhere as Noni's ears rang traumatically as a throbbing pain took over her head from the impact, but she didn't care. There was glass and destruction everywhere.

"Noni!"

She heard Dom shout her name, but she was slightly dazed from the crash and seeing his face as he ran outside only made her want to kill him. She reversed the car once more and turned her steering wheel, aiming directly for him as she pressed the gas. Dom moved out of the way only seconds before she could hit him.

"What the fuck is wrong with you?" Dom shouted as she reversed it again. They were playing cat and mouse as Dom dodged her again. Noni was seeing red. Her head felt wet and she didn't realize that it was blood until it began to drip into her line of sight. She threw the car in park and reached up to nurse her wounds, but froze in fear when she realized that she was afraid of herself. Her blood was now tainted. Noni was infected. Dom reached into the busted driver side window and snatched the keys out of the ignition.

"Have you lost your fucking mind?" he shouted. Noni jumped out of the car and stumbled slightly. She had hit the house full speed and the impact of it all had her dazed.

"Are you okay? Noni, let me look at you," Dom said as he helped to steady her. Noni snatched away from him and without warning, she hauled off and slapped him. Her open hand stung the side of his face, drawing blood as she busted his lip. "I have it. You son of a bitch! I'm HIV positive! You did this to me! How could you?!" she screamed as she attacked him. She gripped the collar of his shirt, snatching at him and banging her closed fists against his chest as she cried hysterically.

"Whoa! Noni! Calm down! Baby! Wait a minute," he defended as he hemmed her up, using just enough strength to subdue her, but not enough to hurt her.

"I swear to God, I'm going to kill you," she said, out of breath as she fought against him. She was like a madwoman as she tried to get out of his firm hold. She was panting in exhaustion as they struggled, but despite all of her efforts, she couldn't do anything until he freed her.

'Her body shook, her legs were putty, and her mind dazed as she tried to gather her bearings. The impact of the crash had knocked the sense out of her and now that she was here, with him, in his arms, his voice in her ear, she broke down. It was crazy how the one that hurt her was also the one she sought comfort in. It was the paradox of womanhood. Her cries were heartbreaking and he held her from behind, still restricting her movements as she spilled her despair onto him.

'Dom looked around at the wreckage. The entire front of their home was torn up. The gaping hole that the car sat in was filled with smoke as the red tail lights flashed around them. Dom knew that Noni had lost her mind. This act of rage was so uncharacteristic of her that it frightened him. He had never seen her like this. In all the years that she had been his, she had never reacted with such reckless abandonment.

"'Shh," he whispered. "Calm down, Noni. Everything is okay."

'Dom's voice in her ear disgusted her. She pulled away from him and spun on him in anger. "I have it Dom," she said, breathlessly still unable to gather herself. "I just left the doctor. I'm positive."

'The revelation smacked Dom in the face as he took a step back from her. Her words felt like a death sentence. He frowned as he swiped his mouth with his hand in disbelief.

"'No, baby, it's not right," he said. Emotion stung his eyes as he shook his head.

"'I heard it from my doctor's mouth!" She shouted at him.

"'Then who the fuck you get it from, Noni?" Dom asked. "I'm negative." He stormed over to the kitchen table and snatched an envelope off the counter. He practically tossed it in her face.

"'What is this?" she asked.

"'Read it. I'm negative," Dom stated.

'Noni froze as her eyes met his. "What?" she asked.

"'You didn't get it from me, so who else you fucking?" Dom shot at her in an accusatory tone. "Better check your nigga, Merci."

'Noni looked around at her mess of a life. Confusion filled her.

"'That just happened, Dom. We haven't been…"

"'I don't know who the fuck I'm even looking at right now. How many niggas you been with since we got married? You stay accusing me of some shit. That's because you out here doing the same dirt. How long have you been fucking my best friend? What other niggas out here shaking my hand then laying up with you?" he asked.

'Noni scoffed at the audacity of his question. He had clearly disrespected her by carrying on with Tat. Now that the shoe was on the other foot he didn't want to wear it. There was nothing worse than a man that cheated on his woman, but played victim when his woman finally cheated on him. Dom was getting a dose of his own medicine and it was bitter as hell. If the stakes weren't so high Noni would have found great pleasure in the destruction of his ego. He had finally felt what it was like to be hurt by her. He had believed her love was solid and for a long time it had been, but neglecting her and beating her down emotionally had left room for another man to come in and nurture her. Dom had done this to himself. She felt no remorse for her actions. "How long have you been fucking mine?" She answered with tears in her eyes. Contempt was written all over him, but it paled in comparison to the disdain and hatred she felt for him. "Ain't so fun when the rabbit got the gun, is it?" she asked. "Bastard."

'Noni turned and walked out of the house, leaving disaster in her path as she left. She spun on her heels, mentally defeated as she added, "Oh yeah, and I'm pregnant you son of a bitch."

Noni stormed out. She heard Dom calling after her, but she just couldn't face him. She would never look at him the same, not now and probably not ever. Everything in her world felt hopeless. She was plagued with uncertainty. Noni had read the papers herself and Dom's test had come back negative. She knew for a fact that she hadn't gotten this from Merci. What they had was too new. They had just started sleeping together. If anything, there was a possibility she had given it to him. *We didn't use protection when we were together,* she thought. This evil was Dom's doing, it had to be. He hadn't loved her. He hadn't respected her body or their bond. Who else could she had contracted it from? *How dare he*

LOVE BURN

insinuate that I've just been out here with random niggas! I'm not a cheater, I don't deserve this, Noni thought dismally.

Noni stopped walking. Her bag was in the car she had just wrecked, her cell phone was inside the bag. She had no money on her and she was too embarrassed to call anyone for help. She sat down on the curb, pulling her knees to her chest as she planted her face in her hands and just... cried. What else was a woman to do after receiving the news that she had? It was a burden too heavy for even the strongest woman to carry. She heard the crunch of gravel in front of her and half expected to see the police in front of her. After the commotion she had caused she wouldn't be surprised if they had come to arrest her. Instead Dom stood in front of her, the sun shone so brightly behind him that all she saw was his shadow as he bent down and picked her up from the curb.

"I'm sorry, baby. For everything. I'm going to make it all okay," he said. She didn't have the energy to fight him any longer. She had to save all her strength for the fight for her life that was to come. As he scooped her in his arms she laid her bloodied head on his chest and sobbed. "How did this happen to me?" she asked.

"You just loved a nigga that didn't deserve you. I was never worthy, Noni," he said, his voice cracking. He was full of guilt over what he had done to her. "We'll figure it out."

"My phone and my purse are in Merci's car," she whispered.

"I'll get it, don't worry about that. Just let me get you out the street Noni. You fucked up the house pretty good," he said with a small smirk. "But we can get a suite somewhere. We can talk. Together we'll figure this out."

Noni didn't protest. She let him tuck her into the passenger seat of his car...not because she wanted him to, but because she had nowhere else to go. She couldn't see Merci loving her after this. Any chance that they may have had was gone out the window the moment her test results had come back positive. HIV was the type of baggage that was too much for anyone. He would look at her differently and she couldn't say she blamed him. Dom was at fault for this, therefore she was his responsibility. She hated him for what he had done to her. Noni's anger for him was so palpable that when he touched her she felt her temperature rise. This was something that she would never forgive. He had done the unthinkable and no amount of apologies would ever suffice.

Chapter 26

"How did we get here?" Noni asked as she sat on the vanity in the hotel bathroom as Dom cleaned the cut on her head.

"'Not we Noni," Dom said as placed a cold washcloth over the deep cut near her hairline. "Me. I got us here baby and you don't know how sorry I am."

'Noni could hear the sincerity in his voice. He meant every word, but it all just seemed too little too late. "You should really be wearing gloves," she whispered.

'Dom looked her directly in the eyes and said, "You're not a pariah Noni. I'll be careful but I'm not afraid to touch you. I just don't understand how you have it and I don't. You're the last person this should be happening too," Dom stated honestly.

"'What am I going to do?" she asked.

"'We're going to get through this. I'm going to get my shit together. I won't lie anymore, I'm going to be faithful to you, take care of you. All of the shit I should have been on, I'll do now, Noni. I'm your husband. I was supposed to lead you. Instead I lost you. You have no reason to believe me. It's all talk right now, but if you allow me to, I'll show you, Noni. I'll be here for you," Dom said.

'Noni was silent as she contemplated his words. She didn't know how she was supposed to feel. He had done her so wrong and disrespected her on so many levels that it was hard to disregard. Did through thick and thin cover this? Did it mean she sacrificed her sanity for the sake of loving him? Did the risk he had taken with her life not matter? How committed was she supposed to be to her vows, when he had not taken them seriously at all? Noni wanted to give Dom her ass to kiss, but it was in this moment at her most vulnerable that she felt compelled to stay. Noni was afraid of the loneliness to come. It was inevitable. She couldn't see any man in their right mind wanting to be with her once they discovered her status and she wasn't the type of woman to keep something like that hidden. Once she disclosed this to Merci he would leave her alone, despite how they felt for one another. This was just too big of a burden and in truth she couldn't blame Merci or any other man for running for the hills. Dom was the only one she could make stay. He was the only one who should stay. Noni didn't know if she wanted to subject herself to a solitary existence or if she wanted to keep the dog ass man who had caused all this. It was a hell of a choice to make and there didn't seem to be a right answer.

"'I need to know how long you and Tat…" her words trailed off as she stopped herself. "You know what, never mind. It doesn't even matter," she said. She didn't even know why she cared. This was about so much more than an affair. Knowing every single detail about his trysts with Tat seemed so insignificant.

"'It matters," Dom said as he stood between her legs, cupping her face in his hands. "I'll tell you anything you want to know."

"'Why?" Noni asked. "Was I not enough?"

'Dom sighed because he could see how he had beaten down this black woman. It had been his duty to uplift her as his queen and he had failed miserably. When he had met her she had been a shining light to his dark world. He had reduced her to insecurity. He had dimmed her. It had never been his intention, but his selfishness had caused him to become a man that he couldn't look at in the mirror. How could he explain that his shortcomings had nothing to do with her? He hadn't cheated because she wasn't enough. She hadn't done anything wrong. He loved her deeply in fact, but ironically he could never do right.

"'You are more than enough, Noni. You are more than a man like me deserves," Dom admitted. "It was never my intention to wrong you. When I met you, I loved you so much. I still love you. That hasn't ever gone away, but I don't know how to love you correctly. I knew that I wanted to keep you. I didn't want any other man to have what you give to me. The way you take care of me. The way you make me feel. It's mine. It all belongs to me. I don't want that to ever go to anyone else. That's why it kills me when I think of you and Merci. Tat was nothing. She was a mistake. I'm not putting it on her because that's some bitch shit. She came at me, pushing up on me, and being extra when you weren't looking. I should have never accepted it. I should have shut it down and let you know what time it was with your friend before it got out of control. But we were fighting so bad and I was resisting you, not wanting to change fully and accept my role as a husband. I didn't know that when we jumped and got married, what came with that," he explained. "You became mine. I was responsible for your mind, your body, your soul and I was still living for me. I was moving selfishly, Noni. You were so headstrong and I love that about you, but it made me feel less of a man at times. Like you didn't need me. Tat was there and she was easy, she was open, and I slipped up. I was so guilty that I couldn't even look at you. So I started staying out all night, fucking with random groupies and eventually with Tat more and more. By the time I wanted to stop, she was pregnant and I just didn't know how to tell you. I knew once you found out, I would lose you. So I gave her whatever she wanted just to keep her quiet so I could keep you in my life as long as I could."

"You should have told me," Noni said in tears as she processed everything he had just told her. It was all too little, too late. "You took my options away from me. You were out here fucking her raw and who knows who else! I'm the one paying the consequence! I'm paying for your sins with my life!"

"You think I don't know that?" Dom asked. "You don't know what I would give to take all this back. It has to be a mistake, Noni."

"It isn't, Dom! Stop saying that stupid shit! I heard it straight from my doctor's mouth," Noni said in frustration as she hopped off the vanity.

"You're pregnant Noni. You can't just give up. We've been trying for a baby for a long time," he said. "There's something the doctors can do. There's medicine or something to keep you healthy. To keep this baby healthy," Dom urged, his voice almost pleading with her.

"How do you know this baby is even yours?" she asked. Noni knew that it was evil of her to even insinuate otherwise. She knew that it was Dom's child, but she just wanted to hurt him…to ail him the way that he had ailed her.

'Her words silenced him and she saw him shrink before her eyes. Oddly, the hurt resonated with her. Even in the middle of devastation she acknowledged his need of her. She hated herself for extending her empathy to him. How was she thinking about his feelings right now? This was a moment when she was fully justified to hate him and she still couldn't commit to that type of disdain, not fully. He had brainwashed her with notions of loyalty for so long that even when he didn't show it, she felt obligated to.

"You telling me you could be pregnant by my best friend?" he asked.

'Noni's eyes misted as she replied, "I wish that I was. Maybe than you would know exactly what it feels like to be married to a total stranger. I don't even know you Dom and even worse, I don't even know myself anymore."

"'Noni…"

"'Just leave Dom. There is no salvaging us. There is no forgiving, no fixing, no nothing. There is no us. The way you've ruined me can't be changed," Noni said through gritted teeth. "Now get out."

'She didn't need to raise her voice for him to get the point. He knew his wife better than he knew himself and the fact that she was calm as she spoke told him that he had lost her. Noni wasn't emotionally trapped by him anymore. He had cheated on her for years and each time she had cried and pleaded, hollered and fussed. She had engaged him and fought for their marriage. That's why when she came crashing through their home in her car he hadn't flipped. She was still reacting to him, still fighting, still raising hell but now, she had regained her self-control. The look in her eyes scared him. It was the calm before the storm. She was about to leave him and although she had every right too, he still felt abandoned. The fact that she sat in front of him, turning him away was a blow to his ego. She minimized his pride and as he stood to his feet he felt an overwhelming pressure to bring her down a notch.

"'Fuck it," he said, harshly. "You sitting in this bitch like you've got options and shit. Ain't no nigga gone want you now. You think Merci gone parade you on his arm knowing you got that shit? The nigga might have been selling himself as a good guy but he ain't got a death wish. You're damaged goods. So you can get the fuck off your high horse." He stormed to the door.

'Noni's lip quivered. His words had hit her like tiny darts. Each insult he hurled at her stabbed her to her core, injuring the little piece of herself that she had left. "Dom?" she called after him as she stood to her feet.

'He turned.

'She scoffed as she smirked slightly. "I see you so clearly now," she said.

"'Good for you, bitch," he shot back, irritated that she had found the nerve to stand up to him after his rant.

"'Bad for you," she paused as she walked to the hotel room door and held it open for him. Dom walked through it and she finished, "bitch!" She slammed the door in his face and then took in a deep breath, preparing herself to tackle her life, alone.

Chapter 27

Notions of revenge ran through Noni's head all night as she lay in the darkness of the hotel room. She alternated between fits of rage and hopelessness. She tossed and turned all night as Merci blew up her phone. He called her repeatedly and each time his name appeared on her phone her heart broke a little more. She knew she had to tell him. They had slept together without even thinking about protection and she feared the consequences of those actions. She couldn't even look at herself, she could only imagine how Merci would see her after she revealed this to him.

'Just when she had opened herself up to love, to something outside of her marriage, life had come crashing down around her. She was forever doomed to loneliness.

'Noni didn't know what to do. It hadn't even been a full twenty-four hours since she found out and already she was breaking under the pressure of it all. The thought of just ending it all had passed through her mind so many times. Who wanted to live with this? What type of life would she have? Noni would be a pariah. It was a hard pill to swallow when she had done everything right. Noni wasn't promiscuous, she wasn't frivolous with whom she allowed to enter her temple and still she had contracted this vicious disease. She had lived her life the right way and played her hand cautiously for nothing. The bitches that fucked freely and often were walking around in the clear while she was rotting from the inside out. It didn't seem fair. Life for her seemed unbalanced as if she was paying for the sins of her mother or perhaps her father. Karma was not a friend of hers. It never had been.

'Noni was so embarrassed that she didn't want to tell anyone, but she desperately needed someone else to talk too. She wasn't clear headed enough to think about the next step. She was standing on the edge of an emotional cliff and it was urging her to jump. She would rather bite a bullet than to accept this slow, lonely, death. Noni looked at the red numbers on the digital clock as they ticked by at molasses pace. She didn't know why she was rushing sunrise, it would only bring with it more sadness. When dawn came she would have decisions to make. No, the darkness of night would do just fine.

'Noni climbed out of bed and walked over to the mini bar, pulling out all the tiny bottles inside. She twisted one open and tilted her head back as she let the burning, clear, liquid slide down her throat. She wasn't a hard liquor kind of girl, but hard times called for such as she opened the next bottle. She followed this routine ten times before a numbness overtook her. It didn't make her circumstances go away, but it did dull the pain and for that she was grateful.

'When the golden rays of morning snuck through the curtains she was beyond faded. She hadn't slept at all and her bloodshot eyes burned from exhaustion. She knew what she had to do. Her life was not worth living, at least not this version of it. The end sounded inviting and she was about to put herself out of this misery. She couldn't deal with this. She had been through some tough times in her life. Miscarriages and infidelity had plagued her soul, but this disease, this death sentence was too much. She didn't want to turn lemons into lemonade. There was nothing sweet about this. It was all bitter days ahead. She pulled herself off the floor where she had sat all night. Her body ached and the bags pulling at her eyes had aged her overnight. She powered back on her phone and the texts and calls that she had missed immediately caused it to go crazy in her hand. She ignored it and called the one person that she knew would have her back through it all.

As the phone rang she tapped her foot rapidly against the floor. Her nerves were working in overdrive.

"'Girl. I'm really going to kick your ass! I've been calling you all night. I went by your crib and there was a fucking hole through the front of your house. Dom answered the door and said you went crazy and that he was done with you. What is going on? Merci hasn't heard from you, Gram hasn't talked to you…"

"'I need you to come get me," Noni whispered as she fought back her tears. Her words were breaking as sobs plagued her.

"'Oh my God! Noni! What's wrong, boo?" Maya asked with true concern in her tone. Noni had cried on Maya's shoulder many times before, but the deep gut wrenching way that her sobs left her, told Maya that this was different. It wasn't just about Noni catching Dom cheating. This was worse and the sound of her friend bawling incoherently put a pit in her stomach. She was afraid of what Noni would say next. She was crying so hard that she couldn't muster up the strength to say actual words.

"'You don't have to talk Noni. Just listen. Dear Heavenly Father, I need you to give my friend strength right now. Help soothe her heart dear Lord and be the light in this time of darkness…"

'Noni was so grateful for Maya. Hers was a true blue friendship. Where most girlfriends gossiped and dug for details, Maya did none of the sort. She was a soul sister. When Noni hurt, Maya hurt and vice versa. Even more importantly when Noni lost her way, Maya prayed for her to find God's guidance.

'The longer Maya prayed the more Noni's heart rate slowed, until finally she was sniffling as her composure was restored.

"'Can you come get me?" Noni asked. "I'm at the Renaissance building downtown."

"'Yeah, of course. I'm on my way," Maya replied.

'Noni hung up the phone and rushed to the bathroom as the mixture of liquors erupted inside of her. She heaved violently as she hugged the toilet. She struggled to her feet and over to the sink to rinse her mouth. When she stood and looked at herself in the mirror, she realized that she looked horrible. She was a direct reflection of what she felt like. She stood there, looking at the dark circles under her eyes and wondered how bad things would get. How much weight would she lose? How frail would she become? How long before she began to look like a walking HIV billboard. She wanted to hide it from the world, but knew that she couldn't. Her phone rang and she knew that it was Maya. She grabbed it and tossed it in her handbag as she made her way out the room.

'When she walked out of the hotel Maya waited in the car, curbside. Noni never looked at her as she got in the car and stared straight ahead.

"'Noni?" Maya almost whispered her name. It was like if Maya said it too loudly, Noni would break.

"'I need you to take me somewhere and I need you not to ask any questions," Noni said.

"'Lips sealed. Where we going?" Maya asked as she focused on the road and pulled away from the hotel. There were certain things that you just did when you were best friends. Maya was ride or die in every sense of the word. She didn't know exactly what was going on. One thing was certain, Noni had been betrayed by enough people in her life and Maya wasn't going to be one of them. So if she needed her to ride out and keep her mouth shut, that's exactly what she would do.

"You said no questions asked, boo, so I'm not going to ask any. I'm just going to make a statement," Maya said as she pulled away from the pawnshop that she had driven Noni too. Maya looked over Noni nervously as she eyed the gun that Noni had just purchased. It sat in her lap, loaded, one in the head and with "a hair trigger" the pawnshop owner had said. "There isn't a nigga in the world that's worth your freedom. You are too beautiful and too good of a person to let Dom pull you down to his level. I know you love him, but enough is enough, Noni."

"You're absolutely right. Enough is enough. I hear you, boo. Just do me a favor and drive," Noni said.

'Maya sighed. She was beyond worried for her friend. There was so much anger and disdain dripping off Noni that Maya felt a palpable heat coming from her. Tensions were high and it was clear that Noni was unstable. They were headed to Tat's house with a loaded pistol and despite the fact that Maya was terrified she didn't turn around.

'She looked over at Noni who stared out the passenger window then glanced down at Noni's phone that sat in the console between the seats. She reached for it slowly, without drawing Noni's attention. It wasn't hard to find Merci's number. He had been calling and texting non-stop. He wasn't the only one. Everyone, including Gram had been looking for Noni since the day before.

'Maya tapped on his name and text him with one hand as she steered the wheel with the other.

'Get to Tat's house now!

'Maya quickly put the phone back and slowed down, hoping that Merci remembered where Tat lived and would be there by the time they got there.

'As soon as Noni got to Tat's house she hopped out the car.

"'Noni, wait!"

'Noni heard Maya calling after her, but there was no stopping her. She stormed to the door and rang the doorbell repeatedly, until she heard the click of the lock on the other side. As soon as Noni saw Tat's face, she pounced.

'Noni delivered a blow so vicious that Tat immediately saw stars, but she didn't have time to react. Noni followed up with another jab to the face, then smacked her with the butt of the gun, sending her flying to the floor.

"'You. Dirty. Grimy. Bitch!" Noni shouted as she dragged Tat. Maya stood back slightly proud of Noni, it was the gun in Noni's hand that terrified Maya. Noni stood to her feet and pointed the gun at Tat. Both women heaved in exhaustion from their grapple and when Tat looked in Noni's eyes true fear seized her.

"'You're going to kill me?" Tat asked vulnerably.

"'You killed me," Noni said back. "I have HIV."

'Merci came rushing through the door at the moment of her revelation and it took his breath away.

'Maya gasped as she covered her mouth in shock.

"'Noni," Merci called to her as he stepped toward her.

"'No!" Noni said as she turned and pointed the gun at him. "Don't come near me, Merci. Don't try to save her. This is between me and her." Merci held up his hands in defense.

"'Noni," he said again, this time his voice commanding her as she looked him in the eyes.

'Hearing his voice caused her tears to race down her face. She never lowered the gun, however. She kept it pointed at a bloodied Tat and then wrapped her finger around the trigger.

"'What you doing, ma? This ain't for you," Merci said.

'His baritone brought butterflies to her stomach. If perfection ever existed he was it. She had almost been blessed with the perfect man. Not perfect in every way, but precisely designed for her. He may as well had come with a label that read, *Made for Antonia Welch*. She wouldn't be able to explore that now, not with disease plaguing her body. Whatever it was that she and Merci had been exploring was lost and it was Tat's fault.

"'You slept with my husband then looked me in the face repeatedly and called me your sister! You were my friend! We got our periods together. We slept over at each other's houses as kids. You were supposed to be my family." Noni said through gritted teeth. As Noni said it all aloud it suddenly dawned on her that she sounded naïve. The signs had always been there. Tat had always been a bit too comfortable around Dom. Noni had noticed how extra Tat was around her husband, but she had given her the benefit of the doubt. Noni had thought the girl code was clear. There was no way she would have ever thought Tat would betray her in that way, but here she was, facing the reality that in fact, Tat had crossed that line. The consequence had been deadly.

"'I'm sorry!" Tat shouted. "Please Noni! Stop!"

'Noni bent over and hauled off to whip Tat once more with the butt of the gun. The sound of the metal cracking against the bones of Tat's face made Maya cringe.

"'Noni, that's enough," Maya whispered.

"'It'll never be enough. My life is forever changed. It won't be enough until this dirty, disloyal, bitch is dead!" Noni shouted deranged. She was blinded by rage and lost in a sea of hurt. She was sobbing now, ugly as ever, as snot and tears covered her face. "You were my very best friend. I prayed for you. I rooted for you. I made your dreams my dreams. I was there when your son was born and turns out he is my husband's son! You had me taking care of my husband's illegitimate child. You made me his Godmother! Do you know how cruel that is?" Noni asked as she clenched her stomach. She was sick. Not only physically, but emotionally this entire situation fucked her up. "Now you're sorry? Now you want to apologize. After you've given me a death sentence. After you have ruined my entire fucking life. Bitch, sorry don't fix this and I'm not forgiving shit. You gone take every single one of these bullets."

"'Nono! Nono!" Thomas screamed excitedly as he ran into the room, calling Noni by the nickname that only he used for her. His little face frowned in confusion as he looked at his mother lying on the floor and at Noni standing over her pointing the gun.

"'Thomas baby, go with auntie Maya. We're just playing cops and robbers. Mommy is the bad guy," Noni said with a quivering lip. Maya hurriedly scooped Thomas into her arms and hustled out of the house.

"'Get that gun out of her hand," Maya whispered to Merci as she bypassed him.

'As Maya rushed out of the house, Dom walked in. Confusion and horror filled his face simultaneously as he assessed the situation in one glance.

"'Noni... baby..." Dom said as he stared at his wife in complete shock.

"'Don't call me that!" Noni shouted as she jabbed the hand holding the gun for emphasis. "It wasn't bad enough that you gave her a baby. You planted seeds in her that belonged to me. Every part of you was mine. I was entitled to the baby you gave her, but that wasn't hurtful enough. You gave me the one disease that has no cure."

"'Look at me Noni," Merci said. Noni's rage calmed slightly as she stared Merci in his eyes. "I don't know this version of you, ma. I know. It hurts. He hurt you. She hurt you, but don't let them take the part of you that I love. If you pull that trigger you'll never be the same. Letting your heater bang is the easy part. It gets hard after that. Your heart don't beat the same after that. It takes a toll on you and it'll turn you into someone that I don't love. Be my love, Noni. Come to me, ma," Merci said. Tat cowered on the floor, trembling and crying. Hoping that Merci's words had an effect on Noni.

Dom saw red. It took everything in him to hold his tongue. He feared Noni would pop off on him. He bit the inside of his jaw as he saw her rush over to Merci. Malice filled him. He hadn't taken care of home. He had run her right into the arms of another man, but the fact that it was Merci, made him want to murder something. Dom had always been "that nigga." Stressing and worrying about his woman straying had never been his type of problem. He had programed Noni from day one to be loyal and that anything less was a character flaw. He had been arrogant to think that one day she wouldn't tire of the bullshit. Merci had been the man to show her something different and Dom's heart seared with anger. Watching another man, command his woman was unbearable. Things taken for granted were things lost. He had practically given Noni away. The pain that occupied his chest was mixed with anger and resentment. Wasn't there some type of honor amongst men? There were seven billion people on the planet. Merci could have…should have…chosen any other bitch. This was a violation and blatant disrespect. Dom was so blinded by jealousy that he didn't fathom that he was feeling precisely what he had burdened Noni with.

Noni clung to Merci so tightly that it appeared that they had conjoined. "Give me the gun," he whispered. "You don't need that. I'm here. Your beef don't belong to you when I'm in the room," Merci assured her. Noni took one step back and lowered her head as she allowed him to put his hands over hers and remove the pistol from her grasp.

Tat climbed to her feet, stumbling slightly from the beating she had taken. "Get out my house, bitch! Get the fuck out!" She was suddenly big and bad now that Noni was no longer strapped, but Noni's patience was non-existent. She may not have had a gun on her but she still had hands. She turned on her heels and gave Tat a two-piece.

"Don't fuck with me!" Noni shouted. She no longer cared about class. Noni hadn't been this reckless since her college days, but Tat had brought out the worst in her. "You gone catch this fade every time I see you, bitch!" Merci grabbed Noni by her waist and Dom held back Tat whose bark was much larger than her bite.

"Yeah, whatever. We'll see. Your nigga still right here with me. He was never your nigga. He belongs to me and my son!" Tat antagonized.

Her words were like alcohol on an open wound.

"Chill the fuck out!" Dom shouted to Tat.

Merci had to grab Noni by her face and force her to look at him. "This shit is a wrap. Let's go," he commanded. He didn't yell and his presence wasn't threatening, but she knew he meant business. Most women would have bucked, but when you found a good man who had nothing but the best of intentions for you, it wasn't hard to submit. Noni followed him out of the house without hesitation.

Dom wanted to protest. He wanted to pop on Merci for having the audacity to court his wife, but he knew tensions were high enough. Now wasn't the time or the place, especially with his son present.

Maya stood at the end of the driveway, distracting Thomas with a game of tag. When she saw Noni emerge from the house, she sighed in relief.

Maya met Noni halfway across the lawn and hugged her tightly. "I'm so sorry, Noni. I'm here for you. Whatever you need me to do, I got you," Maya said.

The pair cried together as they clung to each other right there on Tat's lawn.

"Let me get her out of here," Merci said.

"Of course," Maya said, sniffling as she stepped back. "I'll call later to check on her. Take care of my friend, Merci."

"I intend to," Merci answered.

'He placed his hand on the small of Noni's back as he opened the passenger door for her. Once she was safely inside, he got into the car and pulled away. He didn't know what to say to her. A part of him feared the worst as far as his own health was concerned, but the majority of him felt sympathy for Noni. No interaction between them had ever been this strained. Usually their banter was so fluid, so natural, but today he was at a loss for words. HIV was such a taboo subject. It wasn't easily discussed and the hairs on the back of his neck stood straight up just at the thought of her being infected.

"I'm sorry." Noni finally spoke, breaking the monotonous silence.

'Merci reached over and placed his hand on her thigh, gripping it reassuringly, possessively, as if he was telling her she was still his. "Me too, Noni." His mind was blown by what had just gone down, but somebody had to remain level headed. It wasn't in his nature to lose his cool, so he tried to keep his exterior collected, while his insides twisted in knots.

'Merci had known all along that getting involved with Noni would lead to nothing, but trouble. It wasn't right. She was Dom's wife, which meant she should have automatically been off limits to him, but he couldn't help it. Dom was fumbling the play when it came to Noni. Not many women deserved the best. He had encountered a lot of bad bitches with no morals and no brains. He wouldn't think twice about Noni if she were one of those girls. Dom had fucked over one of the good ones, one of the rare ones…Off the strength of their friendship, Merci should have left it alone and looked the other way, but St. Tropez had changed it all. He wanted her and he had become accustomed to having what he wanted, exactly the way that he wanted it. So he took her. It shouldn't have mattered anyway because Dom wasn't taking care of her the way she deserved. It did matter, however. Apparently, karma was coming for Noni and because it had touched her, it had come for him as well. He was left to wonder if he was afflicted with Noni's burden. Had she passed it on to him? And even if she hadn't, could he love her still, now that he knew? His heart told him he would love her through whatever. He loved her for more than just the physical. Still the stigma of it all terrified him. He didn't know if his love could outweigh the fear.

Chapter 28

Don't
Don't play with her, don't be dishonest
Still not understanding this logic
Aye, I'm back and I'm better
I want you bad as ever
Don't let me just let up
I want to give you better
Baby it's whateverrr
Somebody gotta steppp up
Girl I'm that somebody
So I'm next up

Be damned if I let him catch up
It's easy to see that you're fed up
I am on a whole 'nother level
Girl he only fucked you over cause you let him

The sound of the melodic song played softly throughout the condo. It fit his mood perfectly. It was dark, somber, confusing…and Merci nodded his head to the beat as he rolled up the Kush weed. Normally, he wasn't the smoking type, but after the things he had learned today he needed a mental escape. He sat shirtless on the white leather couch, his dreads hanging freely around his handsome face as he lit the dutch. He pulled the smoke into his mouth, long and hard, then held it up in front of his face, pinching it as he blew out the smoke. He and Noni hadn't exchanged words in hours. What good was conversation when it didn't lead to problems solved. He hadn't asked her one question, despite the fact that he had so many. He knew that it would be pointless. Noni was the victim in all of this. She hadn't asked for any of it and he knew that she didn't know left from right at the moment. He didn't want to burden her with more pressure. He knew that his next move was to be tested. He had to know his status. Everything in his life would be at a standstill until his results came back. Merci had never been this reckless. With every woman before Noni, Merci had used caution. He had always strapped up. Physically and emotionally he always protected himself, handling women with a long handle spoon because he hadn't believed in love. He was always so certain that women only wanted him for the perks that came with him. They were attracted to the lifestyle not the man. It was the cars, the jewels, the respect that he got when he entered the room, that made them want him. They came at him with shallow intentions so he handled them accordingly, without commitment and losing interest quickly. They got what they wanted, a handbag or two while keeping his bed warm at night, but he always strapped up and he never opened his heart to them. It was ironic that as soon as he broke those two rules his life became difficult. With Noni he exposed himself. He let her see him like no one had ever before. He had planted his seed into her freely, thinking that her body was as pure as her heart, but with a dirty nigga like Dom polluting her, Merci had exposed himself. In the brief time that he had expressed his love for Noni, it had already proved to be a mistake.

The weed relaxed him, making everything go numb. Merci heard Noni's light footsteps before her face appeared in front of him.

She stood across the room, wringing her hands nervously, her eyes red from crying.

"Come here," he said. She hesitated and Merci stood to go get her. She jumped slightly when he got close to her. He pinned her back against the wall. He placed the blunt to her lips and she turned her face to the side.

"You shouldn't smoke after me," she whispered in protest.

"You can't pass it through saliva, ma," Merci said. He hit the blunt and then put his lips close to hers before blowing the smoke in her mouth. She inhaled it, closing her eyes and letting it settle inside of her before exhaling.

He held the blunt to her lips and she hit it with expertise.

"Good girl Noni know how to hit the blunt?" he asked in surprise with a raised brow.

"College," she replied with a smirk as she took it from his fingers and took a puff. She tilted her head back and blew it out. "I haven't always been nice Noni." She laughed and shook her head from side to side. "I changed my whole life for that man. I gave him the best years of my life. How do I have it and he's clean?"

"He has to be lying. I know Dom. He would never admit no shit like that. Don't focus on him though, Noni. We just got to take care of you now," Merci soothed.

"We?" she asked. Noni instantly felt guilty. She knew that Merci was too much of a gentleman to walk away from her right now. He was saying these things out of obligation.

"We, Noni," he said as he wrapped four of his fingers behind her neck and caressed her face with his thumb.

"You don't have to do this. There is no way that we can do this now. There's still something you don't know," Noni whispered.

This was it. The other shoe that had yet to drop and it was a heavy one. "I'm pregnant," she revealed.

"By him?" Merci asked as he stepped back. Those words injured him and she saw it on his face.

Noni nodded. "See. My plate is full. There is no room for us right now," she whispered, sadly.

"You just walked into my life. I don't really know how we move forward from here, Noni, but I can say I'm not ready to go back to pretending," Merci said, completely honest. She was the only person in the world that he felt he owed complete transparency too. He trusted that she wouldn't use it against him.

"Pretending?" she asked in confusion.

"Pretending like when you enter a room, my shit don't speed up," he said placing her hand on his chest so that she could feel his heart racing. "Pretending that I don't see you drowning in your emotions because the nigga you with ain't lovin' you right." He pinched her chin.

"Pretending that I don't…"

"Love me?" she asked. "Still. After witnessing what you witnessed today and knowing what is at stake? You still…"

"Love you, Noni," he finished for her. "To my core and you know me, I've never loved a woman but you do something to me, Noni. To not love you is going against my very nature. It's as instinctive to me as breathing," Merci said.

Noni wondered how they had become so passionate so quickly, but some things just felt right. Like finding the missing piece to a complicated puzzle, Merci completed her. There wasn't the issue of who loved whom more, because he valued her just the same. He was safe with her. He didn't have to bring the king pin bravado he showed the streets around her. She wasn't impressed by it and she respected him in his purest form of manhood. His melanin and his testosterone were enough for her to appreciate him. Everything else was just extra. He wore a crown before he ever took over the streets and she recognized that. He would love her forever for that.

"You just need to move on, find somebody with less baggage, no complications. Somebody easy," Noni protested.

"Damn," Merci said. "Dom fucked you up so bad that you can't even recognize when a nigga tryin' to love you." He took the blunt from Noni's hands and backpedaled to the leather sofa. "Get some rest. I'll be right here when you wake up."

Tears clouded her eyes. Merci gave her everything that Dom had failed to. He was consistent and loyal, but most of all he stayed. He stayed without having to take a vow to. He didn't leave her when things got hard and through this most tumultuous test he was solid. He was right. She wasn't used to that. It would take some getting used too. To have someone she could depend on, to lean on when the weight of the world became too heavy…it felt…it felt…she sighed, not even knowing what she was feeling. It reminded her of the way she felt when she first met Dom. It left her breathless, but at the same time it terrified her. She had taken the chance with runaway love once before and she had been burned. To make that mistake twice would be stupid.

"Good night," she said.

"Sleep well, Noni," he replied.

"I'm pressing charges on that crazy bitch!" Tat shouted. "And if you defend her one more time, I swear to God it's going to be like an episode of snapped in here!" Tat was furious, but most of all she was embarrassed.

"Lower your fucking voice when you talk to me. Bitch if it weren't for my son, I would pop your stupid ass myself," Dom said in a tone so low that Tat knew he meant it.

"I'm so tired of your shit! You act like I forced you into this," she said, becoming emotional.

"You're walking around this bitch infected Tat! Noni has it! Tell me something. How is it that she has it and I don't?" Dom asked. "What did you do?"

"I'm taking my son. I'm done with you. It's over. Everything is out in the open now. Ain't shit to hold over my head. Stay away from me and stay away from my wife before you make me put you in the dirt," Dom threatened.

Dom stormed to Thomas' room and snatched him up, along with his cover and carried him out the house.

"You're not taking him! He's still healing from his surgery! He needs to be home with me! Give him to me Dom!" Tat screamed as she clawed at Dom's back and grabbed at Thomas to no avail.

Dom pushed her off.

"Give me my son!" she shouted as she hit his back with closed fists. Tat wasn't a mother fighting for her son. In that moment she was the queen fighting for the pawn that she had used to control the king. Dom was storming out with her leverage and it enraged Tat.

"Get the fuck off me before you wake up my son!" Dom shouted. "Your stupid ass antics. You's a silly ass bitch and I'm not beat for the games no more." Dom carried Thomas to his car, slightly stirring the child awake.

"Shh, go to sleep man," he whispered.

"Help!! He's taking my son! Help!" Tat shouted, ignorantly at the top of her lungs.

Dom grit his teeth as he marched back up to the house. "Fuck is wrong with you?" he barked as he grabbed her elbow and pulled her back inside the house.

She pulled her arm away. "You think you're going to take my son back to your house with your bitch wife?"

"I don't have to explain shit to you. I'm taking him, end of story," Dom said. He turned to walk out the door. Tat could feel herself losing control. She had played the back for so long, waiting to destroy Dom's marriage. She didn't know that exposing everything would put her on the losing end of the stick.

"You're not going anywhere!" she screamed as she attacked him. Tat jumped on his back, hitting him with all her might.

Dom tried to show as much restraint as possible, but his temper rose with every blow that he took. He was like a pot of water, threatening to boil over. Steam was practically coming out of his ears. In that moment he didn't know what he had ever saw in her. Tat hadn't been worth the trouble. She wasn't worth losing Noni. Even the presence of his son wasn't enough to silence the regret resounding loudly within him. The lust that had caused him to betray his vows had stalled and now he was filled with hate.

He turned and pushed her with more force than he intended. Dom didn't realize that things had gone too far until he heard the crack of her skull against the corner of the wall as she fell backwards.

"Tat!" he shouted when he noticed she wasn't moving. His heart dropped and panic struck as he scrambled over to her. "Tat!" he said again. He bent over her and noticed a pool of blood leaking from the back of her head. "No, no, no," he mumbled under his breath. Dom checked her pulse and felt nothing. There was no life left in her. "Fuck!" he shouted as he stood, rubbing the top of his head as stress filled his body. His heart galloped and his stomach hollowed. Dom bent over, placing his hands on his knees as he tried to think of what to do next. The right thing would be to call for help, but she was clearly already gone. With the IRS already on his back, the last thing he needed was to catch a manslaughter charge. Tat had pushed him. She had provoked him and he had lost his cool. He stood and swiped his hand over his mouth. "Fuck, fuck, fuck!" he shouted as he collided his fist with the wall. With every jab he gave the plaster he shattered bones. He was so distressed that he barely felt it. Dom thought about Thomas who was sleeping in the car. *I just took his mother away from him.*

Dom rushed out of the house and hopped into his car. He had to get his son somewhere safe and figure out what to do about Tat. Suddenly Dom felt like he had a noose around his neck and the last leg he was standing on was about to break from beneath him.

KNOCK! KNOCK! KNOCK!

The incessant banging stirred Merci from a restless sleep. He had dozed off on the couch and he sat straight up, panicked as he instantly reached beneath the cushions for the loaded .9mm he kept there.

Irritated, his eyes fell on the clock. It was three o'clock in the morning; too late for anybody to be at his doorstep. Merci stormed over to the door, ready to blow somebody's head off. He wasn't the type to peek through the blinds. Fuck caution. It had taken him forever to ease his mind enough to even sleep. Whoever was interrupting it, deserved to catch lead. He snatched open the door, but seeing Dom standing there, holding Thomas threw him for a loop.

"Is she here? I need her," Dom said.

The way he said it wasn't possessive. It was pleading. The way he clutched a sleeping Thomas in his arms, desperately...with red eyes and a swollen hand...Merci knew there was more at stake than a battle of egos. Before he could respond, he heard Noni's voice over his shoulder.

"What are you doing here, Dom?" she asked. She was as beautiful as ever with her messy hair, long legs bare as one of Merci's Oxford shirts served as a nightgown.

"I need you to watch him," Dom said.

"This shit just keeps getting worse," Noni said as she turned to go back up the stairs.

"Noni please! You're the only person I trust with him. I know you. Despite all of my mistakes, you couldn't ever hate my kid. Please. I wouldn't be asking if it wasn't important," Dom said. He was a mess. She had never seen him so panic-filled. Something was wrong. Both she and Merci knew it.

"Fine," she said as she marched over to him and pulled Thomas from his arms. "Now get out."

Dom didn't respond. He simply rushed out as soon as his son was safe in Noni's arms.

Noni frowned in confusion as she turned to Merci. "What was that all about?"

Merci watched Dom hop in his car and speed off into the night.

"I don't know," he said, a pit filling in his stomach. "I don't know."

"Fuck is you doing?" Merci whispered to himself as he followed Dom through the dark, empty streets. He made sure to stay a few car lengths behind so that Dom wouldn't alter the course. Something was awry. Merci had hustled beside Dom in the streets for too long to not recognize the look of panic on Dom's face. He hoped this had nothing to do with the deal he had struck with Josiah. Merci had to practically sell his soul to clean up Dom's mess the last time. There would be no negotiating with Josiah this time around if Dom had done something stupid. Merci's heart raced. It was the unknown that had him on edge. Merci didn't know what he was walking into, and despite the fact that he and Dom were at odds, he couldn't let his man walk into a lion's den solo.

When Merci noticed that Dom was leading him back to Tat's house he shook his head. "This nigga still on that bullshit," Merci whispered. In truth Merci was filled with guilt for the way things had gone down. He had taken his man's wife, a woman who should have been off limits to him. Merci's love for Noni outweighed his loyalty to Dom. Seeing that Dom was up to the same old tricks lifted the burden from Merci's shoulders. Merci hadn't stolen his bitch, Dom had given her away. *If it hadn't been me, he would have eventually lost her to the next nigga, cuz' this mu'fucka foolin',* Merci thought. Dom stopped in front of Tat's home and then backed into the driveway. Merci pulled over at the corner and parked as he observed. *Why would he drop his kid off if he was coming back to Tat's?*

When he saw Dom pull the heavy duty plastic out of his trunk, Merci knew that there was more going on than what met the eye. He knew that routine well. They had mopped a few niggas up in their day. *He killed a nigga in Tat's crib?* Merci thought. He put his car in gear and then skirted up to Tat's home, parking curbside. His presence startled Dom as Merci hopped out the car.

"Fuck is you doing here?" Dom whispered harshly.

"Nah nigga, what the fuck is you doing?" Merci shot back as he eyed the plastic and duct tape.

Dom wanted to tell Merci to mind his business. There was bad blood between them and Merci was the last person he wanted to ask for help, but Dom couldn't get his mind right. He had bodied niggas before but never anyone close to him. It was fucking with his head and Dom knew that he needed the man he had called a brother, now more than ever before. He swallowed the lump of pride that had built in his throat. "I fucked up, man."

Dom was losing his grip on reality. It was like life was spiraling out of control. He had once kept each part of his life compartmentalized. Tat was separate from Noni. Noni was separate from the streets. The streets were separate from his legit businesses. Merci was separate from his wife. Everything had run like a well-oiled machine, but somewhere he had fucked up. All the balls that he had been juggling had crashed to the ground and he was left with nothing.

"What did you do, Dom?" Merci asked.

"I killed her man," Dom said as he sat on the front step and planted his face in his hands.

Merci walked into the house and when he spotted Tat's lifeless body on the floor he closed his eyes. *This nigga ain't even this sloppy. Fuck is he doing right now?* Merci asked. It was a tragedy all around. This woman had birthed Dom's seed and he had taken her life. Merci could see from the blood pooled beneath her head that it was an accident. He knew that whatever had gone down had occurred in the heat of the moment because Dom was smarter than this. If Dom had wanted Tat dead, he would have paid someone to do it and she would have never been found. This had been a mistake. His heart went out to the lost girl on the floor, but he knew that as many lives as she had ruined that her death was nothing but karma. That much Merci was sure of.

He walked back outside where Dom was seated on the porch.

"Shit happened so fast. She was acting a fool while I was trying to get Thomas out of here and I just blacked out on her. I pushed her and her head hit the wall," Dom explained.

"You stay out here. I'll take care of it. Give me the keys to the funeral home. Follow me in my whip," Merci said. He was pissed that Dom had put him in this position, but there was no way he was going to leave him hanging. Circumstance had destroyed their friendship, but there was a code amongst them, even now. This was the side of him that Noni had never met. Only Dom and the streets knew this man. He knew that he wouldn't be going back to Noni tonight. Merci didn't take what he was about to do lightly. There was a personal price to pay for murder. The higher his body count got the more his soul darkened. Merci would need to seclude himself so that he could tuck the bad guy away before he returned to Noni. He didn't want to make the same mistake that Dom had made. He had introduced Noni to the worst version of himself and expected her to accept it. Merci would always be at his best when he was with her, because it was what she deserved.

Merci grabbed the plastic and went back inside as he switched off his emotions to prepare himself for the gruesome job ahead of him.

As Dom turned on the burners to the cremation oven he felt numb. He was erasing all existence of his kid's mother. She had died at his hands and Dom knew that he would have to look his son in the eyes one day and face the repercussions to his actions. He could lie his way through Thomas' childhood, but with maturation would come questions and on that day, Dom knew this ugly secret would be exposed.

"Now that it's handled, I'm up," Merci said as he turned to leave.

"FYI, I'm coming for my wife. So don't get comfortable," Dom stated with a malice-laced tone.

Merci halted and turned around with a smug look of amusement on his face. "Good luck with that man," Merci said simply before walking out. There was no need for a pissing contest. Merci knew that Noni wasn't going anywhere. He wasn't arrogant enough to think that she couldn't leave him. He was just smart enough to know that he needed to put in work so that she wouldn't want to.

His phone vibrated and Noni's name popped up on the screen. He sent her to voicemail as he climbed inside his car and pulled off into the night.

Noni called Merci over and over again, not because she was worried about him, but she was worried about herself. She couldn't be here with Thomas, not now, not after learning his origin. Looking at him, sleeping peacefully, innocently on the couch was making her sick to her stomach. She just wanted Merci to come and take Thomas away. Seeing a kid that was the perfect mixture of her best friend and her husband was too much for anyone. No woman should have to be so strong. There was a sinking feeling within her. Life was drowning her and Noni just couldn't catch her breath. So much anger pulsed through her. She was ashamed of the amount of resentment she felt. Thomas was innocent in all of this too, but she was only human and seeing this living, breathing representation of her husband's betrayal was crippling. She felt like she was trapped inside the room with a stranger, despite the fact that she had known this child for every second of his life. She had been there the day he was born; unknowingly witnessing the beginning of the end of her marriage. Noni's throat was closing. She wasn't ready to be this close to Dom's son. She couldn't remember how she felt about Thomas before the ultimate betrayal had been revealed. It was like the love she had for him had never existed. He sucked up all the oxygen in the room and she couldn't breathe. She gasped for air as she reached out to steady herself against the wall.

DING! DONG!

When the doorbell rang she darted to it, not even looking out the peephole before answering. She was shocked to see Dom standing before her. She had been expecting Merci. It was close to eight o'clock in the morning and she hadn't slept all night, worrying about where he had gone. Noni had stayed up all night, hoping and praying that he was okay...that Dom hadn't gotten Merci into some bullshit. Now, Dom was showing up.

"Where is he?" she asked.

"Don't ask me about him," Dom replied. "You here, in his crib, in his shirt, that shit is fucking me up on the inside, ma. You got to come home. Tat isn't an issue. I swear to God, that's done. It's over. I took care of it. You won't even have to see her face."

"You're drunk," Noni said. "Come back and get your son when you're sober Dom."

'She went to close the door, but he placed a foot inside, stopping it. "I know you're mad at me. I know I fucked up. I've been wrong in so many ways and all I can think about is whether or not, I'll ever get the opportunity to make it right." Dom stood with his hands in his pockets, his emotions building in his eyes as reluctant tears filled them. "I just want to make it right, Noni. I can't erase my son, but I know you can love him. You do love him. You're just upset right now, but you can do this with me. We can raise him. I just can't lose you. You're my sanity, Noni."

'Noni had never seen Dom this vulnerable, and it tugged at her heart's strings. She wished Dom didn't have such a vice like hold on her. She had given 100% of herself to him for five years. She had nothing left for herself. Noni had extended everything and now she was depleted. She didn't recognize that she was always the giver in their relationship. All Dom did was take, take, take... he never replenished the energy and love he sucked out of her so eventually she was left with nothing. She was void of it all. Emotionally, she was on E and because of her HIV status, she was now physically afflicted. Loving the wrong man and putting up with less than what she deserved had led her to destruction. Dom had taken a smart, capable, ambitious, educated, strong, black woman and turned her into a ball of insecurity. Noni could have ruled the world one day, but spoiled love had turned her sour. Day after day of accepting his disrespect had made her feel worthless. For so long she had contemplated leaving, even threatened too, but fear of losing and of the unknown had made her stay with him. She knew exactly what she was getting with Dom. He was a dog ass nigga, but he was her dog. She had invested years with him and it was too much time to throw away. Right? At least those were the thoughts that had prevented her from leaving him alone. He had to love her, somewhere, deep down. He told her every day that he did, but him telling her had never been a problem. It was what he did after he said it that disgusted her. Love is a word of action. It had to be shown in order to be taken as truth and Dom had stopped acting on the word years ago. How he could look her in the eyes and whisper that four letter word with such passion and then go to the next bitch was beyond her. It was a cruel puzzle that she could never solve. He had hurt her repeatedly like no one ever had. Nothing had ever felt so badly, but even still as he stood before her, she was getting sucked back in. Why she was so weak for this man, she didn't know. It was a conundrum as most love affairs are. There was no logic involved where the heart was concerned, but this time her mind was screaming violently. "Dumb bitch!" Noni closed her eyes and took in a deep breath as she willed herself to be stronger this time. She needed as much courage as she could muster because hatred and resentment weren't enough to keep her out of his arms. She had hated him before and had resented him for years and still she had gone back. No, she needed to be brave enough to face the world alone. She had to find her identity again and be satisfied with just being Antonia Welch again. The glistening diamond on her left ring finger and wearing his last name had given her a sense of accomplishment for so long that without it she felt like a failure. She was in an even worse situation now, because not only was she facing loneliness, but now she was infected. There was only a matter of time before Merci realized it wouldn't work out and every man after him would feel the same. Dom seemed to be her only option, but still she couldn't go back. *Be strong, be strong,* she thought.

"'Noni, baby...' Dom pleaded.

"'Just stop," she finally said. "This has to stop. You made your bed and mine, now we have to lay in it. There is no us, Dom. So miss me with all this begging and pleading," she snapped. Her eyes burned with tears and she was shaking so badly that she felt like she needed to sit down, but she was tired of boo-hooing over an ain't shit ass nigga. This was the time to stand up for herself. "I gave you chance after chance after chance and you kept doing the same shit! I'm tired of it. My heart hurts because it's over. I'm sick about it, but guess what? It's nothing new! My heart was hurting when I was in it. You kept hurting me. You didn't care that I cried. You didn't care that you broke me. Your selfish ass still went out and stuck your dick in these nasty ass bitches. Now I have to live with the disease you brought home to me. Tell me something, will your apologies make this infection running through my veins go away? Will it stop me from losing weight? From getting sick? From dying from this shit?"

'Dom was at a loss for words. She was berating him with the truth and all he could do was stand there and take it.

"'No!" she continued. "That apology ain't worth shit to me and neither are you, not anymore." Noni slammed the door so hard that it woke Thomas up. The sound of him whining caused her to roll her eyes. "Fuck this shit," she mumbled. She was sick of it all. She wasn't taking the high road anymore. She pulled open the door and saw Dom heading toward his car. "And come get your kid!"

'Dom looked at her in shock. Noni wasn't playing any games. He nodded his head as he walked back over to her. She could see that her words had stung him. The look of defeat on his face told her she had gotten her point across.

"'Okay, Noni…okay," he said as he walked by her and picked up his son before walking out.

Chapter 29

Waiting for Merci to come home was agonizing. When day turned to night she began to worry, but she refused to call him again. She had tried ten times already and every time the voicemail came on she died a little on the inside. Why should he answer? Why would he want to? Noni had nothing to offer him. The longer she waited the more anxious she became, until finally she decided that she didn't want to wait anymore. Trying to hold onto Merci should be the last thing on her mind. Noni's life was in shambles and she needed to put the pieces back together. She couldn't expect Merci or anyone else to do it for her. Noni packed up what little belongings she had at his place. She wasn't ashamed of her tears now. This was something worth crying over. Noni was walking away from a great love; not because it wasn't true, but because she would only hold up Merci's life.

This is something I have to do on my own. You're too good of a man to leave me at my worst, so I'm walking away from you. I have too much baggage and you deserve to love someone that you can have a future with. I could never express how sorry I am. I love you, but I can't be your burden.

-Noni-

PS…I wish we could go back to St. Tropez.

Noni placed the letter on the bed and then called Maya.

"'I know you're probably tired of rescuing me, but can you come pick me up. I'm at Merci's. I'll text you the address," Noni said as soon as Maya answered.

"'Hi, to you too heffa," Maya replied. "And I'm on my way, boo. Be there in fifteen."

'Merci walked into his place and immediately knew that Noni was gone. Noni had an energy that filled the room whenever she was in it and his home was void of that. "Noni!" he called out as he searched for her. When he entered the bedroom his eyes zeroed in on the folded piece of paper that rested on his pillow. He grabbed it and as he read the words that vulnerable, sinking, feeling that only Noni could make him feel, settled into his stomach. He immediately dialed her line and when she sent him directly to voicemail his anger spiked.

"'You can't make unilateral decisions without talking to me, Noni. Fuck all that shit you talking in this letter. It's bullshit and you know it. You ain't got to wish for St. Tropez, ma. I can give you that, whenever you want. We can have what we had there, right here. You just gotta let me give it to you. You gotta let me love you because I do, ma…I love you. On some vow shit…through sickness and in health, Noni. I ain't just talking. I'll take that walk down any aisle with you, Antonia, if that's what it takes to make you stay," Merci said. He knew he was getting long winded. He didn't want the message to scare her even more, hell the things he was saying was shocking to himself. "Just come back," he finished before hanging up.

'Noni played the message on speakerphone and Maya's mouth fell open in complete shock. "Oh my God, Noni! You have to go back. He clearly wants to be here for you," Maya said.

"'No. I can't ruin his life. I won't," Noni replied. "And first thing tomorrow, I'm getting my number changed. If he keeps calling me, eventually I'll answer."

"'I'm really sorry Noni," Maya said.

'Noni nodded and gave her a flat smile. "Me too," she said. "Me too." Noni stood and headed to the guest bedroom. She didn't even know why because she knew that tonight and every other night after this would be filled with nothing but nightmares.

"'Get up before you sleep your day away child." Noni felt the swat of Gram's frail hand and she thought she was dreaming. The three sleeping pills she had taken the night before had her out of it and as she opened her eyes, Gram came into focus hazily.

"'Am I dreaming?" she asked.

"'Does this feel like a dream?" Gram shot back.

"'Ouch!" Noni exclaimed as Gram pinched her arm.

"'Now get up and tell me why Maya called my phone,

interrupted my stories and made me drive all the way over here to check on you?" Gram inquired.

'Noni sat up. "It's a long story, Gram," Noni replied.

"'Well then you better brush your teeth and wash your face first. Get yourself together and I'll be waiting in the living room. I'll take you to brunch,'" Gram said as she walked out of the room, silver hair glistening in the sunlight that crept through the guest room blinds. Noni thought her grandmother looked so regal in that light and she knew that God had sent one of his prayer warriors to be by her side. Gram was an angel who hadn't yet gone to receive her wings. Noni needed her right now. She pulled herself out of bed and rushed to the attached bathroom so that the shower could knock the sleepiness right out of her.

'Noni emerged to find Gram and Maya sharing conversation over a cup of coffee.

"'I'm ready," Noni announced half-heartedly.

"'Well let's go then," Gram said as she stood and led the way out.

'Noni knew that brunch meant the local buffet. That was her Gram's idea of treating herself. She wasn't hard to please and Noni loved that about her. Over the years Noni had become bourgeois, but today, this was just what the doctor ordered. She didn't care where they ate. She just needed the love from her Gram. Noni always appreciated her time with her Gram, even if she didn't always express it, but this was priceless. There was decades of wisdom inside this little lady and Noni needed to soak some of it up to help her deal with the catastrophic series of events that had recently taken place in her life.

"'So do you want to tell me what's got my fancy pants granddaughter eating at Golden Corral?"

"'There is no easy way to say this. I have HIV Gram and I'm pregnant." Noni whispered it so low that Gram almost didn't hear it. Noni had expected judgment and disgust, maybe even sympathy, but Noni received none of those things. Gram reached across the table and grabbed Noni's hand.

"I don't know what to do. I don't know if I should keep this baby or have an abortion. I'm sad, angry. I want to cry. I want to die..."

"But you aren't going to do any of those things. You're going to fight," Gram said. "In our darkest days we have to pray and you pray hard. You pray for yourself and for your child. You have to hold your faith, because that's the only thing that is going to get you through."

"I swear, I'm trying," Noni said. "I'm trying to keep my faith Gram, but I've been questioning God. I've done everything right. I've honored my vows. I've been a good woman, a good friend and this happens to me? Why am I the one suffering? I'm a good person and I feel like I'm being punished for it. Life isn't supposed to be so hard."

'Gram sighed and she pulled Noni in, grabbing her hands as they both leaned across the table. "I watched you love Dom for the past five years. That love was strong baby...too strong... almost sinful Noni. I watched you place Dom on a pedestal. You worshipped him. God is jealous baby. You put a man before your God, before yourself, before your health and there is a price to pay for that. Now you have to find redemption after it all. It will be hard. It hurts my heart that this happened to you, but this isn't God's doing baby. You had the free will to leave Dom way before this became your story. When he cheated the first time you should have kicked that sucker to the curb and taken him for everything he was worth. You accepted it. You ignored the signs God was sending you about your husband."

"I know," she said, breaking down. "I just loved him..."

"Too much baby," Gram said. "And now it's time learn to live for you. You'll have it a little bit harder now, but you can do it. God doesn't put more on us than we can handle."

'Noni was silent for the rest of the day. Gram had given her enough to think about for a lifetime. Everything Gram had said had been true. Noni had put Dom before everything. She depended on love. She wouldn't do that again. From this day forward she would always protect herself and her heart above all else.

'Dom sat in the middle of his living room, watching the contractors rehab the hole that Noni had left in the front of his house. He wished that the hole in his heart could be fixed just as easily. Dom had so much regret that he was drowning in it. He took a swig of the Louis cognac in his hand. He skipped the formality of a glass. Dom needed the entire bottle to numb this pain. It was ten o'clock in the morning and Dom was beyond drunk. He didn't give a damn about etiquette. He was experiencing so many different emotions that he felt like he was unstable. He had been unfaithful to his wife with many women over many years and it had only taken one affair with one man to bring him to his knees. He hadn't known how strong she was until the roles had reversed and he was faced with the thought of the women he had wed, in bed with someone else.

'The front door opened and Gram let herself in as she walked carefully around the mess.

'"In the kitchen, Dominick. Now," she said without even the courtesy of a hello.

'Dom pulled himself up from the leather chair he sat in and placed the bottle on the table before joining her in the kitchen.

As soon as Dom stood in front of Gram she slapped the shit out of him.

"'You listen here, you little degenerate negro. You're lucky my grand baby didn't tell me sooner about all the bullshit you were pulling. I had a husband like you before. He cheated on me and I put a bullet in his back then laid him to rest before collecting the insurance money," Gram said with a warning finger in his face. "Now if Noni wasn't pregnant, I wouldn't even be telling you this, but it's your baby too. She's decided to keep the baby. Her first appointment is today and I think you should be there to support her." Gram placed a card on the countertop. It was the name and address of the doctor that Noni had chosen. "Now clean yourself up and at least be there for your child. You already failed your wife, but you can still do something about the seed you planted. The appointment is at eleven o'clock. I'm going to wake Thomas and take him with me so that you can go meet Noni at the doctor's office." Gram turned to leave, without giving Dom a chance to respond.

'Dom was a ball of nerves as he sat outside waiting for Noni to pull up. He didn't know what he would say to her or if she would even allow him to come inside, but he had to try. He had arrived a half hour early to make sure that he caught her before she arrived.

'When Noni pulled up driving Maya's car he made a mental note to fix her finances. The feds had seized their accounts but Dom had a little paper stashed for a rainy day. He hopped out and approached her. When Noni noticed she stopped walking mid-step. They faced off in front of the glass door.

"What are you doing here?" she asked, stunned to see him.

"I just want to be here for you, Noni. It's my baby too. We wanted this for so long. It didn't seem right to not be here," Dom said.

'Noni wanted to deny him this, but she knew that she couldn't. She didn't say a word as she turned and walked inside the building.

'Noni remembered the nights when she had prayed to give her husband a baby, but as she sat on the opposite side of the waiting room from him, now she wished she had never gotten pregnant at all. This just wasn't how she envisioned it would be. She was so terrified that she would pass HIV to her baby that she almost wanted to just go through with an abortion. It was only her Gram's voice in her head telling her to have faith that made her even make the first obstetrics appointment in the first place.

"Noni Meyer?" the nurse called. Both Dom and Noni stood. Noni was hesitant to start this journey with Dom. Everything he touched turned rotten and she didn't want the negative energy he awakened within her to sabotage this pregnancy. She was already facing enough without having him around to make things harder.

'He was already here however, and she didn't want to make a scene by turning him away. They followed the nurse to the back.

"You can change into the gown and the doctor will be in a bit," the woman said after taking her vitals.

'The silence that filled the room said more than any conversation ever could. Dom was filled with dread as he realized there was no making things right. Noni could only hate him so greatly because she had once loved him so much. Normally their interactions were so easy, but things between them lately were so strained…they were forced and Dom felt it in his heart that things would never go back to the way they used to be. Too much had happened. He had taken her for granted one too many times.

'The doctor walked into the room. "Hello, Mrs. Meyer," the doctor greeted.

"'Welch," Noni corrected. "Ms. Welch, but you can just call me Antonia." Noni held out her hand and shook the doctor's hand.

'Her correction was a blow to Dom's pride. It felt like someone had knocked the wind out of him. Her eyes met his and she looked away, focusing all of her attention on the woman in front of her.

"'Well Antonia. I'm Dr. West and I'm going to get you through the next 30 weeks. According to your primary care doctor you are already ten weeks in. Today we're going to take some blood work, run some tests, and most importantly get a look at baby. Sound good?"

'Noni nodded, but her face didn't express the enthusiasm that it should.

"'I tested HIV positive a few weeks ago. Will my baby be born with it?" she asked.

"'There is a really great chance that this baby will be born perfectly healthy if we get you started on the right medications now," the doctor informed.

'Noni breathed a sigh of relief as she nodded her head. "I'm terrified," she admitted.

"'You and every other new mother on the planet," the doctor said as she reached out and gave Noni's hand a reassuring squeeze. "I'm going to take really good care of you and your baby. Now lean back and let's take a look."

'Noni laid down as the doctor placed a cold jelly on her abdomen. She then rolled a scope over the gel and a cloudy image appeared on the screen next to the exam table.

'The room filled with the sound of a steady hum. "What is

that noise?" Dom asked, as he frowned in confusion. "Is the baby okay?"

"Just let the doctor do her job, Dom," Noni said, irritated by his presence, but she had to admit, she wanted to know too. "Well is the baby okay?" Noni asked in frustration.

"That sound is the beat of your baby's heart. It's strong and steady," the doctor said.

'Noni gasped as she looked at Dom. "Do you hear that?" she asked him. Dom moved closer to her, taking the seat directly next to the monitor as he became emotional.

"Yeah baby. I hear it. I finally get to hear it," he said.

'They had been through so many trying times together during their attempts to conceive a child. The miscarriages she had suffered before had occurred before they had ever been able to detect a heartbeat. This first time, this miraculous rhythm, was the most beautiful thing they had ever heard. For a brief moment, nothing else mattered.

"I'll print an ultrasound for the both of you and give you a moment of privacy while I put in the prescriptions you will need to keep both you and baby healthy. Congratulations," the doctor said.

'When they were alone Noni lifted her eyes to the sky. "I can't believe I'm pregnant."

"I never thought it would happen for us," Dom admitted.

"And now that it has, everything we hoped to give our child no longer exists," Noni said.

"That's my burden Noni. I fucked everything up but our kid… our kid will know love. He will know how much I love him and how much I love his mother. You may not feel the same and after everything I've put you through, I understand. Don't ever doubt what I'm about though. I'm about you and my baby, Noni. I'm an imperfect man, but losing you is humbling me. I'm going to change. I'm going to be a better man. You might not ever forgive me and you probably won't ever give me another chance, but I'm going to make you happy. I'm going to do everything that I should have been doing. I'll never leave you or this baby on stuck. I promise you that Noni."

'Noni scoffed, discounting everything that fell out of his mouth. She had heard it all so many times that it no longer moved her.

"'I will never deny you access to your child, but this doesn't change anything between you and I," Noni said.

'KNOCK! KNOCK! KNOCK!

'Maya frowned when she heard the loud banging on her front door. She slowed down the treadmill she was running on and then grabbed a towel to wipe the sweat from her brow before heading to the door. She wasn't expecting company and she had given Noni an extra copy of her key. Whoever was at the door was lucky she was even answering it at all. *I don't do the pop up thing, niggas better call first,* she thought as she snatched open the door.

"'Merci?" She couldn't hide her surprise.

"'Where is she?" he asked. Even when he wasn't trying to be cool he gave off an effortless swagger of confidence. Despite the hurt she could see reflecting in his eyes, he was still such a powerful force of a man. His dreads hung from beneath the baseball cap that hung low over his eyes.

"'She isn't here, Merci," Maya said.

'He swiped his hand over his face in frustration as he exhaled deeply. He was clearly bothered by Noni's absence in his life. He had called her on repeat until the number no longer worked. He tried to give her space. He had thought she would cool down and take a moment to think before coming back. An entire week had passed and Merci couldn't take it. He was hooked on her and he didn't care what obstacles stood in their way, he just wanted to be with her.

"Where is she?" he asked, persistently. "She's shutting me out."

'Maya shook her head. "Y'all muthafuckas and y'all drama," she mumbled as she sighed. "I don't want to be in the middle of this. She's my friend, Merci and if you hurt her, I swear to God I will murder you in your sleep. She's been through enough so if you aren't going to stick around through all of this then just keep it moving."

"Where is she?"

"What are you? A parrot?" Maya said.

'Merci chuckled at that. "Just help me out, Maya," he said.

"She's at the doctor. Off 13 mile and Gratiot," Maya revealed. "The appointment is probably almost over now though..."

'Merci turned and rushed to his car. He hit 90 mph on the expressway, rushing to get to Noni. He hoped he didn't miss her. Merci knew there was nothing suave about chasing her all over town, but he wasn't trying to play it cool. He just wanted his girl back. How Dom could have her and seek companionship elsewhere was truly a mystery to Merci. Once he had experienced Noni, he craved nothing else but more of her essence.

'He pulled into the large parking lot and luck was on his side. Noni came strolling out as beautiful as a sunny, summer day. His smile was brief. He only got to enjoy her for a moment before Dom came crashing into the frame. He watched Dom place his hand on the small of her back and lead her to the car.

He burned with anger as he watched Dom open the door for her. She was clearly emotional and Merci's heart sank when Dom tucked a stray hair behind her ear then kissed her on the cheek. He didn't need to stick around to see more. He started his car and pulled out of the lot.

Chapter 30

"What are you doing?" Noni asked. "Dom let me make myself crystal clear. I am not and will not ever be with you again. All we will ever be is parents to our child. If it wasn't for this baby, you wouldn't even know where to find me." She got inside the car and slammed the door without giving him a chance to respond. She pulled off and as she drove fear filled her. For the first time in five years she was on her own. She would have to dig deep to figure this thing out. It wasn't just about her anymore. It was about her baby and she was determined to never have to ask Dom for anything.

'Noni spent the entire night crying. She allowed herself to feel every single depressing emotion that plagued her. She went through pity, anger, sadness, hatred for twelve hours. Noni didn't stop herself from bawling. She wanted to get it all out because after this she wouldn't spend another second feeling sorry for herself. She was in a stage of regeneration. Her life didn't look like what she had envisioned, but she could repaint the picture. She had relied on Dom to make her happy for too long, when she should have been finding happiness from within. If she owned her emotions, no one else could have control over them. As she pulled herself from the bed she was exhausted. Going through five years of memories had been trying, but it was over. She was living with HIV and she was starting over from scratch. It was her reality. There was no point in avoiding it.

'Noni showered, dressed to perfection and then stood in front of the mirror. The reflection was beautiful but it was the inside that was scarred. She gripped the pills the doctor had prescribed in her hands. There were so many different types of medications. Six different bottles sat in front of her and she popped them open one by one, swallowing one of each. It would be her daily routine if she wanted to fight this. She hid the pills beneath the duvet in the bedroom, not wanting Maya to have a visual reminder that Noni was sick. Then she walked out.

'"Wow. Good morning, boo! Looks like you feel better. What are you all dressed up for?" Maya asked.

'"I'm going to General Motors today to apply for a job," Noni said.

'"That's really good Noni. I'm proud of you," Maya said.

'Noni nodded and gave a quaint smile before heading out the door.

'When she stepped outside Dom stood, parked in front of Maya's building leaning against a white BMW 6 series with a pink bow sitting on the hood. Beside it sat an identical black car with a blue bow on top.

'"What is this?" Noni asked.

'"I noticed you were driving Maya's whip. You're going to need your own transportation when this baby arrives. What they call it? A push gift? You got your pick," Dom said.

"Where did you get the money for this, Dom? All of our money is tied up. The government won't release it until the attorney proves it's legitimate," Noni said. "So how did you buy these?"

"I've got a little bit put up that the feds don't know about. That's not for you to worry about. I'm more than capable of taking care of you and our baby. You know me. You'll never want for anything," he said. "I'm a fuck up, but I've never required you to go without."

'Noni made her way to Maya's car. "I can't accept that. It's too much," Noni said.

'Dom followed her. "It's not nearly enough, Noni," he said. He grabbed her arm and she turned toward him. "Just take the car."

"I'll let you know when my next appointment is, Dom," Noni said as she hopped into Maya's car and left.

'Dom watched as she drove away from him. He knew that her love wasn't for sale. It never had been. Noni had never been easy and she couldn't be bought, but he wasn't taking the car back. He left the white BMW sitting there in the parking lot, placing the key in the visor before hopping in the other car and departing. It would take more than a new car to make up for all the things he had done to create this rift between them.

"Hi, I'm here to see Mr. Ginwald," Noni said as she stood on the top floor of the General Motors building. The secretary in front of her looked up over the top of the wire framed glasses she wore.

"'Do you have an appointment?" the lady asked.

"'No, but if you just tell him I'm here, he won't mind meeting with me," Noni said.

'It had been five years since he had offered her a job. She hadn't taken it then, but she desperately needed it now. It was the first step to regaining her independence.

"'I'm sorry, Mr. Ginwald doesn't have any breaks in his schedule," the secretary said.

'Noni grasped her resume in front of her and sighed deeply. "Well I'll just wait for him to tell me that himself," Noni said. She took a seat in the lobby, knowing that it could take hours before she got the face to face she had come for. She had become accustomed to everything coming so easy to her. Whatever she wanted, Dom had gotten it for her. He had granted every one of her materialistic wishes, it was the things money couldn't buy that he had trouble providing. It was the loyalty he had neglected to give.

'Noni shook Dom from his thoughts. She needed to stay focused. The only thing she could afford to think about right now was getting this job.

'Three hours passed before Mr. Ginwald walked from the back office.

"'Mr. Ginwald, can I have a moment of your time?" Noni asked.

'Mr. Ginwald looked up at her, surprised. "You're Dominick's..."

"'Ex-wife," Noni finished for him. "Antonia Welch."

"I'm sorry to hear that," Mr. Ginwald said. "I didn't realize…"

"I'm here to speak with you about a job," she said.

"'Well I'm on my way to my next meeting. You've got five minutes if you walk with me," Mr. Ginwald replied, never breaking step as he hurried down the hall. Noni practically had to jog in her stilettos to keep up.

"'We met five years ago at the Michigan Business Gala. I had just gotten my Master's in international business. I have a B.S. in accounting."

"'I remember offering you a job. You were fresh out of college. Your resume was promising. You turned me down," Mr. Ginwald replied. "Nobody turns me down."

'Noni chuckled. "I'm accepting now," Noni said.

'Her cell phone rang in her bag and she quickly silenced it as she stepped into the elevator with Mr. Ginwald.

"'You're five years too late, I don't need a financial officer anymore," Mr. Ginwald said.

"'Seems like I'm right on time. GM is struggling to maintain amicable relations with the foreign countries the company has outsourced tens of thousands of jobs too. A part of that reason is because your international relations liaison is incompetent. He doesn't speak the languages fluently. He's never traveled abroad so he doesn't respect the customs of the people you do business with. I can smooth out those ties and ensure that GM keeps business relations for years to come in both Asia and South America."

'Mr. Ginwald looked at Noni in complete surprise. "You do your homework, don't you Antonia?" He chuckled in amusement.

'She smiled. She surprised herself at how easily she had gotten right back on the horse. She handed him her resume. "I'm not the right person for this job," Noni said. "I'm the only person for this job. That's my resume. I have no work experience in the past five years. I was busy playing housewife. I'm ready to get back to work. I need to get back to the old me."

'Mr. Ginwald nodded. "I'll have my assistant email you the benefit and salary package. If it is pleasing to you, then you start at 9:00 a.m. sharp, Monday morning."

"'You're hiring me?" Noni asked.

"'I'm hiring you," Mr. Ginwald confirmed. The elevator doors opened and he stepped out, leaving Noni smiling from ear to ear.

"'Yes!" she shouted when the doors closed. The happy dance she did all the way to the lobby wasn't enough to display her joy. She didn't even notice the doors had opened and a group of executives were staring at her, until one of them cleared their throat.

"'Oh!" she exclaimed, slightly embarrassed. She hurried off the elevator as the group of people shuffled in.

'Noni's phone rang again and this time she answered. "Hello?"

"'Noni, it's Dom. Are you driving right now?" he asked.

'She frowned. "No, I'm at the GM building downtown, but I'm about to head back to Maya's. Why?" she asked, confused.

"'It's your Gram, Noni. I'm so sorry, baby but she passed away in her sleep last night. You're her emergency contact and the hospital just called the house," Dom informed.

'The phone fell from Noni's hand and her legs immediately folded underneath her as her knees hit the pavement.

'Noni didn't cry. She couldn't muster up the strength to shed more tears. This hurt more than any tear could ever represent. Devastation rained over her as she sat there, feeling lost. Gram was the one person who gave her guidance in the world. Without her, Noni was lost. She would have to figure out the rest of her life without the help of her cheat sheet. Noni had lost the woman who had helped make her what she was. It felt unreal and all sense of time was irrelevant as she sat there completely shell shocked. She just couldn't fathom a loss so big. She didn't know if an hour or five minutes had passed, but when she heard Dom calling her name, she was relieved to see him. He could remind her to breathe, to blink, help her to stand, because she just couldn't do it on her own.

'Noni clung to Dom as he picked her up from the ground. "It's okay, baby girl. I'm here," he said. He placed her in the passenger seat of his car and even put her seatbelt around her before climbing behind the wheel and pulling off. He headed straight to the hospital. She didn't have to ask him, he knew that she would want to see Gram and speak to the doctors herself.

'Her phone rang again. It was her doctor calling. Noni silenced the call. She couldn't deal with anything else right now. If the universe sent her any more bad news she wouldn't be able to handle it.

Chapter 31

The sound of the organ played loudly throughout the church. Noni stepped inside, completely taken aback by the amount of people in the room. Dom had taken care of every single arrangement and he had paid attention to every detail so that Noni wouldn't have to. He had done a beautiful job. Her Gram had been a member of St. Sinai Church and it seemed that the entire congregation had shown up to tell Gram goodbye.

'Noni stood, clinging to Dom as all of the guests came up to her to express their condolences. She had to admit. He had been a rock during this entire storm. He had even gone as far as to call Mr. Ginwald and have him push her starting work date back a few weeks so that she could have time to bury Gram. Through every late night and every tear she cried for the past week, Dom had been present for it. She had been staying back in their home with him and Thomas, as he made the preparations and she had to give him credit. Noni noticed a drastic change in him. It was like he had remembered how to be her friend again. He was kind, caring, accountable and available to her. She had even warmed up to Thomas again, realizing that he was the same little boy that she had always loved, regardless of how he was made. The way that Dom had been catering to her made her believe in the magic of second chances. She wasn't foolish enough to say she trusted him or even that she forgave him, but she relished in his attention. This was how it should have been all along and she couldn't help but appreciate having a few days of bliss. Feeling his hand on the small of her back as she tackled one of the hardest things she had ever done in her life, made her feel secure. She remembered that safe feeling he used to give her years ago and suddenly just like that it was back. She felt her phone vibrating inside her clutch and she opened it to take a peek at the screen. It was her doctor's office. Dom noticed as well.

"'Maybe you should call them back, Noni," he suggested as he leaned over to speak low in her ear. "They've been calling you every day, twice a day for a week. It could be important."

"'I will. I just can't take anything else. Not right now. Not today," she whispered in reply.

'They took their seats and Noni let herself lean into him as he wrapped his arm around her shoulders. It was like touching him allowed her to absorb some of his strength. If she was honest with herself she would say that she liked the attention that Dom was giving her lately. She had begged him to be this type of man for years and now he was finally obliging her. She felt guilty for still loving her husband. She knew that it made no sense. After everything he had taken her through, he shouldn't even be able to get a glimpse of her. She should have gotten ghost on him long ago, but what wife didn't want to make her marriage work? What woman could just walk away without looking back? Noni was beginning to feel like she had put in all the work to make him a better man and now she was about to walk away to let the next woman reap the benefits of her tears. Dom owed her happiness. He owed her everything. If it weren't for him, she wouldn't be living with HIV. Part of the reason why Noni was considering reconciliation was because he was the only man that would accept her status because he had caused it. No other man deserved the burden.

'Noni sat through the entire service and surprised herself by shedding very few tears. When she heard how Gram had touched the people around her, she realized that she had done what God had put her on Earth to do. Noni was comforted in the fact that her memory would live on.

'When the eulogy was delivered she stood and made her way out of the church. Her phone rang once more. Noni ignored it. She feared the worst and knew that when she finally answered, she would have an entirely new set of problems to deal with.

'She looked up and her breath caught in her throat as she saw Merci walking out. She glanced at Dom and knew that he hadn't noticed. "I'll be right back. I need to use the bathroom."

'She rushed ahead of him, pushing through the crowd to get to Merci. Her heart pounded frantically as she searched for him. She couldn't imagine how Merci felt seeing her there with Dom. It felt like she had been busted even though she knew she had nothing to explain or did she? She had pushed Merci away when he had done all the right things, only to go back to the man who had done all the wrong ones. It didn't make good sense, not even to her, but it was how the cards had played out.

'Noni panicked when she didn't find him. She placed her hand on top of her head in distress as she turned around, looking for him in every direction.

'"Everything okay?"

'Dom's presence surprised her. "Um, yeah, I'm fine," Noni stammered. He led her toward their chauffeured car as Noni looked curiously over her shoulder trying to figure out where Merci had disappeared to. A part of her wondered if she had even seen him at all. Noni left with Dom, but she couldn't help but turn around to look for Merci once more.

"'Can you take me back to Maya's?" she asked as he opened the passenger door for her.

"'You not coming home?" Dom asked.

"Not tonight," she replied. "I kind of just want to be alone. Besides, you need to get Thomas from daycare and I just need some peace and quiet tonight."

Dom wanted to protest, but he had known her long enough to know when space was required. "Okay," he said. He tucked her in the car before rounding the front and climbing into the driver's side. He hesitated before pulling off. Her temperature had suddenly changed. She was cold, her mind distant, and her mood had shifted to indifference. "Are we good, Noni?"

Noni just nodded. She didn't have the energy for a full-blown conversation. She had Merci on the brain and seeing him had only teased her about the fact that they would never be together.

Her phone rang again and she sent it straight to voicemail. "Noni…"

"I can't answer it right now," Noni said, cutting him off.

When they pulled up to Maya's apartment Noni got out the car without saying goodbye. She wasn't trying to be rude she was just so distracted by the 'what if's' of life.

She was halfway up the walkway when Dom called her name. "Noni!" he said as he got out and followed her. It was like every step she took towards Maya's apartment building was placing her further from his reach.

"Dom…I need time to think," she said as she turned toward him.

Her phone rang again and this time she answered. "What? What is it? What horrible thing is so important that you're calling me back to back on the day I bury my grandmother. What now?!"

"I'm sorry Antonia. I don't mean to bother you, but I assure you I am not calling you with bad news," Dr. West said. "Your blood panel came back and your HIV tests are negative."

"What?" Noni asked, confused as she suddenly felt like she was suffocating. She felt dizzy. *Am I dreaming? Is this real?* She thought as she reached out to hold onto Dom's forearm to stop herself from falling.

"There seemed to be a mix-up at the lab with your blood tests. You are HIV negative, Antonia. I'd like to test you again to make sure, but I have the utmost confidence in my lab technicians. I have every reason to believe that you're healthy," Dr. West informed.

"What's wrong? What is she saying?" Dom asked. He couldn't read her reaction.

Noni dropped the phone and her mouth fell into an O of pain. She gasped as she felt the familiar feeling of life leaving her. She had just received the best news she had heard in her life. She wasn't sick. She didn't have HIV. It was a horrible mistake, but her life was too complicated for good to stay good for long. In the exact same moment that she had felt relief, an excruciating pain took over her body. She knew exactly what it was. It had happened to many times before, but when the wetness seeped down her inner thigh, her lips began to tremble.

"Noni, baby, what's wrong?" Dom asked.

"I'm having a miscarriage," she whispered.

"No, no, no, no," Dom said as he picked her up and rushed her back to the car.

Maya appeared on her balcony, hearing Dom's screams all the way from inside.

"What's wrong with her?!" Maya screamed.

"Something's wrong with the baby!" Dom shouted.

"I'll meet you at the hospital!" Maya hollered.

LOVE BURN

"'Your body is rejecting the pregnancy. You can stay here and we will keep you comfortable while you miscarry. Your body knows what to do. In the rare instance that we need to go in and evacuate your uterus, we will put you to sleep so that there is no pain," the doctor informed.

'Noni didn't even respond. She lay exposed with her legs in stirrups as the doctor stuck instrument after instrument inside of her. Dom bent over and kissed her forehead.

"'It's going to be okay," he said.

"'I don't have HIV," she whispered.

"'What?" Dom asked.

"'That's why the doctor was calling. To tell me that," Noni said. She never looked Dom in the eye as she spoke. She just turned her head to the side and looked at the white wall as she lay helplessly on the cold doctor's table.

"'That's so good. That's so good baby. Thank God, Noni. We gone be okay. Everything will go back to normal. I promise you. I swear on my life, I'mma be better. I'm a new man, Noni. I learned my lesson. I value you, baby. It shouldn't have taken me this long, but I get it now. I get that you are me and I am you, so hurting you hurts me. I just want to make you happy," he said.

'The doctor removed his hands from Noni's vagina and snapped off his gloves. It was obvious he was intruding on a private moment. "I'll be back to check on you in a little while. You'll want your privacy during this time. If you have pain or have any questions…"

"'I've been through this before. I have no questions," Noni replied, still refusing to make eye contact. Her voice was sterile, cold. Noni felt so low that she couldn't evoke emotion.

"We can try again, Noni," Dom said. "We can…"

"There is no we, Dom. This is over," Noni said, finally turning her face to look him in the eye.

'Her words hit him so hard that he recoiled.

"Noni…baby…"

"Just leave Dom," she said. "The one thing that could have kept us together is spilling out of me."

'Dom had to blink away the emotion that overcame him. He wasn't a soft type of nigga, but the thought of losing the one person who had touched his soul chipped away at his armor. He couldn't come up with a response. So instead of pleading his case and manipulating her love to get her to stay, he kissed her forehead once more before walking out of the room.

'Noni savored that kiss. It was the sealing of the end. They both knew it and although it hurt, Noni was relieved that it was over. Dom had been the cocoon to keep her from spreading her wings. Noni was ready to become a butterfly, but first she had to survive this great loss once more. Losing life was the ultimate smack in the face for a woman. She couldn't create life. Her womb wasn't strong enough. She wasn't woman enough. The one thing that was supposed to make her a Goddess, didn't exist within her and that hurt. It hurt more than anything. Not only was she mourning the loss of Gram, she was mourning the end of a marriage and the loss of a baby. As a woman she was expected to carry many burdens, but all of this pain and sorrow happening around her simultaneously was a disaster. It was enough to break anyone down. Her head was spinning and her heart no longer beat the same. She had compiled hurt on top of hurt and she didn't know how to dig herself out. Sure, she was relieved that she wasn't sick, but she didn't quite know where to go from there. How did she even begin to pick up the pieces to her life? It felt impossible to go back to the way things used to be.

'Maya pushed open the door slightly. "Noni?" she called, asking for permission before entering the room.

'"Come in," Noni replied.

'"Oh, friend," Maya whispered as tears came to her eyes. She walked over to Noni and sat beside her. "What do you need me to do?"

'"There's nothing anyone can do. It's out of my control. I just have to let nature take its place," Noni whispered, shattered as her voice quivered.

'Maya reached in her handbag and pulled out an old leather bible and Noni couldn't contain her pent up tears. They spilled out of her. It was Gram's bible. Maya opened it and began reading, "Proverbs third chapter fifth verse. "Trust in the Lord with all thine heart and lean not unto thine own understanding."

'Noni was sobbing as Maya continued to read the words. She was such a broken woman. The past five years had led her to this moment. She needed to regain her strength, her trust, her focus. Noni needed to take control of her life and live in her purpose, whatever that may be. She didn't understand why so many horrible things had transpired in her life, but as Maya sat by her side, reading quietly peacefulness settled onto her soul. It wasn't for her to understand because she was walking a path that was designed for her by her creator. No matter how hard life became, she knew that he was preparing her for something greater. She would have to withstand the hard times to prove she deserved whatever God had in store for her. The bible verses were filling her up. It was like her spirit had been on E and Maya was giving her fuel to fight for the life she wanted. She reached out and grabbed Maya's free hand and closed her eyes as she took a deep breath, continuing to absorb the word of God. As her baby slowly leaked out of her, she felt something else entering her. Her faith was being restored and she knew that in the end God would magnify her. He would show her the reason for all of this turmoil, but until then she wouldn't question him. She would just have to walk in faith in hopes that one day she would understand and that one day her wishes would align with God's timing to make all her dreams come true.

Chapter 32

Noni sat behind her desk on the top floor of the GM building. Her office overlooked the entire city. It had only been two weeks since she stepped into her new position and she was beginning to adjust to her new routine. Dom had called her so many times that she had blocked his number. She wasn't moving backwards. She refused too. Noni was on a new path. She was putting herself first, something she had never done with Dom. She had dodged a serious health scare as a direct result of putting up with his bullshit. She forgave him for all the things that he had done to her, but she would never forget. There was no way she would ever go back to being the woman she was when she was with Dom. Her pride wouldn't even allow her to accept his calls. Noni had a lot of healing to do, spiritually, emotionally and physically. She knew that she wouldn't get all of him out of her system overnight. For five years he had been the sun and she the world that rotated around him. Everything had been about him and although he crossed her mind from time to time she couldn't give in. She craved his presence more out of habit than anything else and the old adage was true, bad habits are the hardest to break. So to prevent herself from sliding back to the familiar she threw herself into her work. She checked the clock that sat on her desk. It was half past

LOVE BURN

ten and her first meeting of the day would be arriving at any minute.

'Her desk phone rang and Noni answered.

'"Your 10 a.m. has just arrived," her receptionist said.

'"Thank you Lola, send him in," Noni replied.

'The door opened. There he stood. God's reason for it all. Merci. He was the reason why she had to learn what loving a bad man felt like. It was necessary so that when he came into her life she could appreciate how good of a man he was. Her heartbeat sped with the intensity of thoroughbred horses. Suddenly, she was lightheaded. His eyes burned into hers, his stare so intense that she couldn't break it if she tried.

'He stood before her clean in a dark navy, Gucci suit. The fit was so specific that she knew that it had been tailored for him personally. There were very few occasions when she had seen him in this form, but when he did it, he did it well.

'"I've never had a woman make me chase her so hard," Merci said with a charming smirk as he admired her from across the room. "I'm sorry about your Gram," he added.

'"Were you there? At her funeral?" she asked.

'He nodded. "I knew you would need somebody on that day. From the looks of it, Dom had it handled," Merci replied.

'"I don't know what to say to that," Noni replied. "I can't explain why I kept going back to him."

'"I asked myself that," Merci said. "And I thought about leaving you alone but I can't, ma. We can't help who we love and I love you. You're a part of me now."

'He crossed the room and stood directly in front of her. "I miss the shit out of you, Noni."

'"I miss you too," she replied as she leaned her head into his hand as he caressed her face. His touch was so gentle, so caring. He made her quiver in her delicate places.

'Merci placed his thumb on her lip, tracing the outline of her perfectly pouted smile as she closed her eyes.

"Marry me, Noni," he whispered. Her eyes popped open in shock.

"Merci," she whispered.

"So much has happened to me..." she sniffed away the burning sensation that filled her eyes.

"I know, ma. A little birdie named Maya told me everything," he said. "I know he hurt you. I know you're half of a woman because he broke you. I know the test results were a mistake. I know you lost your only family when Gram died. I know you lost your baby. I know everything and I don't care about none of that. The baggage, the drama...if that's what you come with, that's what I'll accept. I know you're guarded. I see you up here on the top floor on your independent shit and I respect it. I'm not trying to take that from you. I need you though ma, today. I ain't about the bells and whistles. I want to stand in front of you and promise to be your man. I want to make you my woman. We can grab a judge, jump a broom, whatever...but today is the day you'll take my last name." He pulled a ring box from his breast pocket. He opened it to reveal a flawless seven-karat stone.

' She gasped and covered her mouth as a million thoughts filled her head. Could she really say yes to this? Would rushing into something new be a mistake? Was the love she felt for Merci real?

"All you got to do is say yes, ma. I'll never hurt you. I'll never leave you. I'll body any nigga that ever disrespects you. I ain't a perfect nigga, but I'll love you perfectly, Noni. Only you could have me out here on some sucker shit," he said with a chuckle. She had to smile at that.

"I...I..." she stammered. Noni was stuck. She wasn't ready to take a risk on love again and his proposal terrified her.

"I'm so afraid to love you," she whispered.

"'I know," Merci said. "But say yes anyway."

"'I jumped into my last situation..." she stammered, searching for an excuse to turn him down.

"'I know, but tell me yes anyway. Trust me to love you, Noni."

'Noni paused as she looked at the ring. She could see her entire future dancing in the shimmer of the stone. Raw emotion clung to her eyelashes and she lifted her gaze to meet his. "Yes," Noni whispered.

'Merci's lips covered hers and she placed her soft hands on the sides of his face. She felt God all around them. It was like an energy pulsed through the room and Noni was completely swept up in it. This man was heaven sent. He was designed for her and she felt it in her soul that he was the destination on the arduous path that life had taken her down. Love had never felt so good and as she pulled back to stare in his eyes. His infatuation could be seen by a blind man. He looked at her with such admiration and respect that she knew that he would never hurt her. Noni had finally found happiness and she didn't care if she never received another blessing, Merci was enough. With him love didn't hurt, it didn't burn, it didn't deceive, or disregard. The type of love he gave her, was healing. His love renewed her, revived her, and saved her. Merci was patient and kind. She would never have to question his loyalty. Merci was everything she had ever asked for, but most importantly, he was hers. He had never made her question the value she held in his life.

'He released her and grabbed her hand to place the stunning ring on her finger. "Let your boss know you'll be out for a week and meet me downstairs," he said.

"'What? Wait. I can't just..."

"'I was dead ass when I said I want to marry you today. Just you and me, in St. Tropez," Merci said with a wink. "At the top of the fort, overlooking the harbor, as we make everything we wished for while we were there come true."

'In that moment life was perfect and Noni was no longer worried about anything that had occurred before. All the pain, the hurt, the lessons learned had been worth it if it had led her to this day…to this man. Noni knew that she would love Merci in this life as well as the next. She grabbed her handbag without hesitation and held his hand as they walked out together, headed to the place where their love story first began.

The End

Printed in Great Britain
by Amazon